CARNAL CARNIVALE

Carnal Carnivale

Sadie has received a personal invitation to a very special carnival. First stop, the House of Mirrors, where she is met by a very virile-looking roustabout—mirrors that expose worlds of erotic pleasure of which she has never dreamed. Journey with Sadie and her lusty companion on this very special ride of seductive and passionate illusion...

Previously available only in electronic format, these erotic short stories and novellas by Adrianna Dane have now been combined to create this colorful paperback collection!

Included in this anthology of delights...

Nights In White Satin
No Choice
Come Into My Parlor
Mariposa Soul
Sequestered Passion

Also included in this special paperback edition is the never-before-released bonus story, *Sadie's House of Mirrors*!

Praise For Adrianna Dane

Nights In White Satin

"…Ms. Dane not only takes readers into an incredibly well-written love story, but also journeys into the heart of the circus with descriptions of sights and sounds that put you right under the big top…"

—Laurie, *Romance Junkies*

Sequestered Passion

"5 Angels!…A Recommended Read!…*Sequestered Passion* has been expertly written and provides a wonderfully insightful look into the BDSM community…"

—Heidi, *Fallen Angel Reviews*

Come Into My Parlor

"4 1/2 Lips!…A book that will have you thinking ahead and trying to guess the ending…No matter how you think this story might end, you're wrong! Adrianna Dane is on my must-read list and has definitely outdone herself with this intriguing story that has a very film noir feeling to it. While she always guarantees a hot, exciting read, *Come Into My Parlor* was exceptional."

—Kerin, *Two Lips Reviews*

Mariposa Soul

"5 Stars!…What an amazing book! Although the sex…is beautiful and magnificent, sex itself does not lead the plot. I have read quite a few male/male romances, but this is the first one in which there is intelligent discussion of the dangers and difficulties of living a gay lifestyle…I was enthralled reading about these two men. Ms. Dane is a wonderful author and I received a great deal of pleasure from her book."

—Marcy Arbitman, *Just Erotic Romance Reviews*

ALSO BY ADRIANNA DANE

The Boy Next Door
The Diary Of Lillian Manchester, Book I: The Stranger
Eluria's Enforcer
Esmerelda's Secret
Fertility Rite
Graphic Liaisons
If You Dare...
I Want
Images Of Desire
Immortal Treasure
Kierra's Thread
Jebediah's Promise
Legend Of The Beesinger
Primal Magic: Scent
Ravager's Redemption
Realm Of The Ice God
Smooth Finish
Sylvie's Gift
Whisper

CARNAL CARNIVALE

BY

ADRIANNA DANE

AMBER QUILL PRESS, LLC
http://www.amberquill.com

CARNAL CARNIVALE
AN AMBER QUILL PRESS BOOK

Amber Quill Press, LLC
http://www.amberquill.com

Layout and Formatting provided by: ElementalAlchemy.com

PUBLISHED IN THE UNITED STATES OF AMERICA

*For all the people who support me and my muse.
From my husband, to my publisher, to the
readers, and everyone in between.*

TABLE OF CONTENTS

SADIE'S HOUSE OF MIRRORS

PART I

CARNAL CARNIVAL

SADIE'S HOUSE OF MIRRORS
PART I

"Here you go little lady," the older gentleman said as he handed her the small rectangular admittance pass in exchange for the coupon she handed him. "You enjoy yourself tonight."

She reached for the ticket and he held her hand for a long moment, staring into her eyes. "You'll find what you're looking for, missy—a once in a lifetime experience. Just take your time. There's a lot to see. It will be something you'll never forget. But I can tell"—he winked at her—"you're going to have a real good time tonight. Now hurry along, and enjoy the entertainment."

She veered toward the right entrance, but he called after her. "Not that one, missy, you take the one to the left. That's for special visitors, like you."

She looked at him curiously. "The left? Are you sure?" It looked to her as though the one to the right would take her onto the main grounds of the carnival.

"Right-o, luv. Head to the left and follow the red fence line. It will get you where you want to go all right."

She started down the path, thinking it looked rather deserted, considering all the people waiting to come in, but she followed his directions.

When she'd returned from lunch the other day, she had found the coupon and a flyer for the carnival setting on her desk. Her curiosity had been peaked when she picked up the coupon to get a closer look at it and read the words "free admittance for one special friend." Who could have placed in on her desk?

She'd set it off to the side and gone on about her day, but had kept glancing at the flyer and the coupon, unable to put them out of her mind. Finally, as six o'clock came around, she'd picked up the coupon and the flyer and left the office. Instead of heading home as she'd intended, she found herself driving to the outskirts of town where the flyer indicated the carnival was located. It was as though some unseen force had taken over and was directing her movements.

The path seemed like a never-ending trail that wound around the circumference of the main grounds, and the noise and music were becoming more muffled the farther she traveled. She looked around at the gaily painted fence marking the perimeter of the path. Suddenly, she seemed to be enclosed within a fine mist of some sort and her heart sped up just a little faster. Where was this leading? She wanted to turn around and head right back, certain she had taken the wrong path. Then she saw the outline of a building of sorts before her, and the shadow of what looked like a person standing on the step as if waiting for her.

She hurried through the now thick fog to reach him. Thank goodness for another person because the fog seemed to be getting denser by the minute. As she drew closer, she gulped in a sharp breath, not strictly of relief, but of shock and intimate arousal. Unexpected sensations threaded through her as she gaped at the stranger.

Was he one of the roustabouts for the carnival? Tall and muscular, with raven black hair confined at the nape of his neck, and eyes dark as night, his gaze roved over her, stroking her senses. His broad shoulders were encased in a black T-shirt that stretched to its limits, molded to the sculpted biceps, tapering down to a narrow, defined waist.

And then there were the black jeans that stretched across muscular thighs and tightly molded over a flat abdomen, hugging a perfect ass. Her eyes widened at the immense bulge indicating a cock worthy of her rapt attention.

Her gaze flew to his, her pussy juices already coating her thighs at the figure of primitive, seductive, raw male standing before her.

He nodded and smiled with a flash of perfectly even white teeth, a sparkle entering those dark, intense eyes, drawing her forward. "Evening, miss. We're glad you could make it. I think you'll enjoy the evening. My name is Hank and I'll be your escort for the evening. Please step up and we'll begin the tour."

How could she resist? His voice was rough, yet smooth at the same time, gliding over her like warmed malted chocolate. He held out his hand and she lifted hers. His engulfing clasp was firm and strong as he helped her up the steps.

There were two rails on the floor indicating that this was some sort of ride, then she saw the brightly colored cars in shades of royal blue, ruby red, and buttery yellow, as one of the red cars rolled silently toward them. Hank reached out, stopped it, and slid open the door.

It was the most unusual ride she had ever seen at a carnival, fashioned almost like a small, old-fashioned carriage. She stepped over to it and looked inside, surprised to find the whole interior of the car was lined with what seemed to be plush red velvet and it appeared quite spacious. For a traveling carnival, it seemed to be quite ornate. He held out a hand.

"After you, miss."

Pausing for only a moment, she accepted his hand, stepped into the car, and sat down. It certainly is comfortable, she thought as she sank into the luxurious material. And it certainly felt good after a long, hard day at work. Already she felt the stress easing from her body.

When he climbed in after her, only then did the car seem quite small. Sitting this close, he smelled awfully good—very male with the clinging scents of pink cotton candy and apples, a touch of tasty hot cinnamon and earthy evergreen. A feeling of intense heat radiated from him like the lingering glow of a fierce bonfire. A surge of electrical energy zapped through her and her pussy flooded with her juices. What she wouldn't give for a man like this in her bed—even if it was for just one night. Thank goodness he couldn't read her thoughts.

After he sat down, he reached to the side and two fluted glasses containing sparkling amber liquid appeared in his hand. He held one out to her and she accepted it. She could swear he must be some kind of magician.

He snaked an arm around her shoulders as the car began to move forward, and they entered a corridor lined with mirrors, reflecting their images back to them. Slowly, the car gathered momentum. It felt like it was moving steadily upward. He leaned close and she looked up into the most mesmerizing eyes, so very close she could almost feel the moist heat of his lips touching hers.

He held up his glass and clinked it against hers.

"To an enjoyable and entertaining visit."

She lifted her own glass and swallowed some of the champagne. "Are you sure I'm supposed to be here? This all seems very elegant, like it should be meant for someone much more important than me."

He drained his glass and then much to her surprise tossed it out of the car. Her jaw dropped at the action.

"You are quite special, miss." He drew her closer into his hard embrace. The car moved nearer to a set of ornate, mirrored double doors and he leaned down; she could feel his breath against her ear. "Are you ready for a once in a lifetime experience?"

She found herself trembling, uncertain what to expect. This was a carnival ride like no other she had ever experienced. Feeling unexpectedly daring, she downed the rest of the champagne and tossed the glass out of the car, mirroring his actions of a moment ago, then turned to look at him. "I guess I'm as ready as I'll ever be."

The doors ahead swung open as if by magical command at her words and the car passed through. She felt Hank's teeth nibbling at her ear and she shuddered with pleasure.

"Welcome to Carnal Carnivale, miss, where your every sensual fantasy is yours to experience."

NIGHTS IN WHITE SATIN

CARNAL CARNIVAL

CHAPTER 1

She hovered at the fringe. Poised. Trembling. The scents of buttered popcorn and sugary cotton candy blended with the aroma of fresh sawdust, tantalizing her. Reminding her.

The slippery white satin lining of the cape teased her naked, heated flesh. Gentle strokes gliding across her sensitive nipples heightened her awareness, and fearful anticipation edged her desire. Darkness and the ebony exterior of the cape masked her in shadows.

Her eyes were riveted to the center arena, her vision imprisoned by the magnetic personality bathed in the center spotlight. She awaited his summons, a glance would call her to him. The bleachers were packed to capacity, eager adults waiting for the sensual exhibition to begin.

At the center of the arena stood a large, black-barred circular cage. At its nucleus was an oval bed with an ornate iron headboard and baseboard on a raised dais. Luminescent, white satin sheets glowed in the murky lighting. It beckoned her from the darkness. A showcase worthy of the Grand Finale.

At the entrance to the cage stood two muscular guardians, faces painted—one in the guise of a leopard, the other a tiger. Their bronzed bodies gleamed and shimmered in the half-light, exuding primal, leashed power—controlled by the Master. Each wore tights in the pattern of the predator he represented, molded against the tight, thick muscles. Solid arms folded across their broad hairless chests. Chiseled, expressionless features.

But they weren't her focus.

She awaited their Master. The Lion-Tamer. He stood at center arena, slightly beyond the large circular cage. It was his gesture she needed. Tall. Lithe. Fluid. Clothed in black silk trousers and a flowing white satin shirt, he was the one she sought. His face was cloaked in mime white, with a single midnight teardrop painted beneath his right eye. A bullwhip curled in rest, draped from his left hand, tapping against his hard-muscled thigh. An exclamation of his control. She shuddered with pleasure at the energy radiating from him.

Anticipation coursed through her, settled and pulsed a slow, steady beat inside her. She felt her juices stir and seep to her thighs. Tension coiled and she had the greatest urge to run to him, plead for his attention. He demanded patience. And she would obey.

Her breath caught in her chest as he slowly turned his tawny head, his gold-flecked, green gaze slashed to her through the darkness, pierced its cloaking density. He raised his left hand and pointed. The summons she'd awaited. A layer of tension peeled away.

Without breaking focus, she walked to him and placed her right hand in his outstretched left. The anticipation of the audience thrummed around her, the heat of the spotlight warmed her as his grip tightened, linking her to him. His electricity zinged through her hand, along her arm, and down through her center, pooling between her thighs.

Glancing at her briefly, he turned and led her to the entrance of the cage. The single narrowed spotlight echoed their footsteps. The leopard at the entrance stepped aside and opened the door. The Lion-Tamer led her inside. They were followed by the leopard and the tiger. She heard the clank of steel as the tiger secured the door. There was no trepidation inside at her situation, only fear she wouldn't meet his standard for this performance. Excitement tingled in every pore.

The Lion-Tamer faced her and released her hand. She felt his gaze burn through her as it slid down her shrouded form, then back up to connect and hold her once again.

As he took one step away from her, with his right hand he signaled to the leopard and the tiger. They moved as one to flank her. And waited. A moment of silent anticipation. For the crowd. For her.

The Lion-Tamer nodded. Once.

They stepped forward. The tiger released the single glittering clasp at the neck of the cape. The leopard then removed it with a sweeping flourish, leaving her naked and open for all to see. He walked away to dispense of it and then returned.

She shuddered at the loss of the protecting barrier of the cape, her nipples beading tightly. The heat of the spotlight warmed her, amplified by the fire of command in the Lion-Tamer's inspection. Again, he nodded.

The tiger and the leopard each grasped one of her arms, turned her, and presented her to the audience. For a moment, emptiness consumed her at losing eye contact with the Lion-Tamer, and she felt abandoned. Panic flooded her and the muscles in her arms corded, ready to seek release, to flee. The grips of the leopard and the tiger tightened. A flicker of unease passed through her.

She felt his heat as he stepped close behind her. Scented his power and control. He hadn't abandoned her. Relief softened her.

The tiger and the leopard pulled her arms up and horizontal from her body, displaying her to the audience for their pleasure. Oddly, she felt no embarrassment at this exhibition. Only worry that she might not please the Lion-Tamer. She straightened her spine, and raised her chin in the manner she knew he expected.

Attuned to the unseen vibrations surrounding her, his approval stroked her. She felt the firm control of his hands as he cupped each of her full breasts from behind. They were warm, his fingers teased at the sensitive buds. Her eyelids fluttered, and her head dropped back in a long sigh of pleasure. She heard a loud hum of appreciation ripple through the crowd—echoing through her body.

Strong hands gripped each of her legs as the leopard and the tiger repositioned her, widening her stance. She felt the cool air caress her overheated center, exposing her more completely. She tingled with the knowledge the pale curls of her mound glistened with evidence of her arousal beneath the naked spotlight.

As one, she felt all support release her. Opening her eyes, she focused, trying to pierce the veil of darkness beyond the spotlight, unable to do so. She waited, displayed as her Lion-Tamer demanded. Awaiting his next command.

The tiger and the leopard appeared before her, each holding a glittering rhinestone clamp. The tiger bent forward, taking the right nipple into his mouth, he sucked hard and tugged lightly with his teeth, then released it and stood upright. Apparently still unsatisfied at its hard, glistening peak, he rolled it between his thumb and index finger. Her breathing quickened with answering desire. Finally satisfied, he positioned and secured the clamp, then stepped back.

Tight, centered pain quickly followed the initial pleasure, gradually receding, until the leopard stepped forward and attended in the same manner to her left nipple. Her body throbbed, each nerve exposed, demanding attention. Yet she waited, lust coiled tightly inside, poised for release.

She felt the heat of the Lion-Tamer at her back as he stepped to her. The leopard and the tiger moved aside as the Lion-Tamer's hands again rose to cup her breasts, displaying her once again to the audience. His thumb and index fingers moved over her breasts, pinching her sensitive nipples, forcing the clamps to dance and sparkle beneath the intense aura of the spotlight. She inhaled sharply and arched as the enhanced pleasure and pain arrowed through her, building the untamed need. Another hum of approval washed over her.

He removed his hands from her sensitive breasts and smoothed them along her shoulders, guiding her arms back down to her sides. Sweeping both of his hands along the length of her back and over her buttocks, he cupped and kneaded her rounded bottom. She felt a finger trace the hollow separating her two cheeks, and he stopped, poising it at her engorged, slick entrance. He teased at her lips, at her clit. Her hips undulated in answer, in need. Sensations swirled around her, dizzying light, her mind focused solely on her body's responses. His hands. His breath against her neck. She felt the pressure build as she neared the blinding summit.

He stopped, carefully balancing her at the edge. She wanted to cry out in frustration, but something inside her understood it was forbidden. She knew he waited for her to descend just enough, then he would force her upward again. He repeated it over and over, knowing just when to halt, building her fire, building the crowd's anticipation as well. A whimpering cry passed her lips, a guttural plea she was unable to suppress.

The wildness began to consume her, the need to climax driving her, aching for him to allow her to reach the summit and topple over the edge. Her skin glistened with perspiration. The scent of her arousal, the tension of the clamps, the heat of the spotlight, the touch of his hands, sent her spinning out of control. Wild with need she panted and arched, her muscles tightened. The Lion-Tamer alone controlled her every move, every response. The world spun away, her body attuned to the hands that held her, taunted her.

As she felt two fingers drive into her pulsing vagina, other hands released the clamps, sending her spinning beyond all thought, the ground beneath her giving way. Waves of pleasure and pain wound *round and round, piercing and consuming her.*

Hands held her, keeping her upright as ripple after ripple exploded over her. Dimly, she heard the thunderous applause of the crowd. Firm hands at her hips steadied her, then were removed. She was left for moments to stand alone, weaving in the spotlight.

The tiger and the leopard moved back to her, each clasping a steadying arm as they led her to the satin-covered bed. They would prepare her for the last act. The Grand Finale.

*   *   *

Celine's eyes flew open, her heart thundering, her body pulsing from yet another dream-induced, combustible orgasm. The dreams were becoming more frequent, building in intensity. More bizarre. And the more powerful the fantasies became, the worse her frustrations. It had become impossible to get through her days without being aroused by vestiges of the dreams coming back to haunt her. Guilt would swamp her.

She knew who the Lion-Tamer represented. It was Pele, her magical mime. The man she couldn't seem to forget. At least her subconscious wouldn't let her forget.

Her days with the circus were past. Finished a long time ago. She was more than satisfied with her nice, ordinary job as a C.P.A. She didn't need the glitter of the circus or the extraordinary family she'd grown up in. She'd made her decision.

So why did it insist on coming back to haunt her in this bizarre fashion now? Throwing back the covers, she vaulted from the bed. Although her profession was more sedentary than it had been as an aerial performer, she'd lost none of her agility since leaving the circus; continuing the demanding morning drills and exercises was second nature. It helped her maintain focus in the office and kept her limber. And when she repeated them at night, it would help her to sleep more soundly.

But lately, it hadn't been working. All it seemed to do was intensify the erotic nature of her dreams.

Or maybe it was because Daniel was pressing her to commit to their relationship. Of course, it wasn't fair to Daniel, but for some reason the thought of marriage, taking that final step with him, frightened her.

Daniel was a good man. *He's a safe man, good husband material.* That's what her friend Emily was always fond of saying.

Every time the word marriage came up though, it was like

something inside her rebelled. *Either end it with him or take the plunge,* she admonished herself. It wasn't fair to keep him hanging this way.

Why was it that Pele's ghost seemed to haunt her as she moved closer to committing to a relationship? Every. Single. Time. Seven years should be long enough to exorcise a memory. Shouldn't it? Didn't she deserve to have a husband and children? To be happy?

She dragged the comb through her thick blonde hair one more time. It was shorter now than it had been seven years before. When she'd been with the circus, it had touched her waist in long, shimmering waves. When she left, she'd had it cut, right up to her chin, not wanting the reminder. Not wanting to remember the one time Pele had scorched her with his kiss, winding his fingers into her long locks, bending her to him. Even now her scalp tingled with memory. Her body felt his hard, demanding heat.

She turned away from the mirror and tried to dispel her visions of the past. Her hair now brushed her shoulders, a compromise in length. Daniel likened it to cornsilk. Pele had called it whiskey satin. No. He'd called *her* whiskey satin. Smooth and warm, all the way through.

She shook her head in denial. Whenever she thought of him, she ached inside. It was better not to remember. Besides, the last time she spoke with Uncle Alberto, he'd told her Pele was no longer with the circus. She'd felt a deep void open with that knowledge as well.

No. She needed to close that chapter of her life once and for all. But, darn, she ached. For Pele. For her family. For the circus life. The ever-changing excitement and adventure.

Flipping the light switch, she spun around and left the darkened bathroom. There was no future in looking back. She'd made up her mind. Today she'd tell Daniel she'd marry him. They'd buy a nice house in the suburbs, have a couple of kids, and live a nice normal life.

She picked up the phone in the living room and dialed his number.

"Hello?" he answered, his voice still husky with sleep. *He has a nice voice,* she thought to herself. It's warm and friendly. Comforting. Yes. She was making the right decision.

"Daniel? It's Celine. Do you have plans for lunch today?"

CHAPTER 2

"There's someone here to see you." Celine's assistant, Laura, hovered in the doorway.

Celine looked up from her computer screen and the spreadsheet she couldn't seem to get to balance. "Who is it?"

Laura shrugged. "I have no idea. I've never seen him before. He's not one of your regular clients."

Releasing a sigh, Celine leaned back in her chair. She didn't have time for unexpected visitors. She was leaving to meet Daniel in half an hour. "Did he give you a name?"

"Said his name's Peter Cortland. That it was a personal family matter and rather urgent."

"Personal, huh? I don't recognize the name, so I can't imagine what he could possibly want." She combed her fingers through her hair, leaned back, and groaned. "I guess you better send him in. He's not a salesman, is he?"

"No, he doesn't talk the talk, if you know what I mean. I can usually spot them within thirty seconds of them opening their mouths."

Celine laughed. "Yes, you can. Well. We'll see if you're right this time."

It wasn't long before there was a knock at the door. It opened and Laura leaned in. "Mr. Cortland for you, Celine."

Rising from her chair, she smoothed a hand down the front of her gray wool skirt, and looked toward the door. A tall man with caramel, sun kissed hair stepped inside and Laura closed the door behind him.

"Mr. Cortland. Please sit down. How can I help you?"

His gaze rose to meet hers, and Celine's shock turned her legs to liquid. If not for the tight grasp she maintained on the edge of her oak desk, she would have fallen. Disbelief widened her eyes when she glimpsed the familiar gold-flecked green of his. She'd recognize those eyes anywhere. She'd stared into them last night—in her erotic dream.

"Pele!" she gasped, sinking into her chair.

A small half-smile curled his sensuous mouth. He stepped further into the room. "Hello, Celine. It's been a long time."

Talk about understatement. "Uncle Alberto said you left the circus. What are you doing here?"

He arched a golden brow. "Al said I left? That's odd. Are you sure?"

Celine thought back, trying to remember her conversation. "Well, he said Pele left. I never knew your real name, did I? How is it that Pele left, yet you're here now? On a personal family matter?"

"Pele hasn't performed in quite some time. Your grandfather wanted a business partner a few years back. Alberto wasn't interested. You know how he is. He likes his freedom. Sebastian offered it to me. So I now have a half ownership in the circus."

She'd known seven years ago Pele didn't have the usual air of the wanderer, that there was much more to him. It's why she'd been drawn to him. There'd been a sad aura around him. Unfortunately, she'd never been able to penetrate the wall he seemed always to hide behind. Well, that wasn't actually true. There had been the one time.

He'd arrived at the circus at a time when her family had just begun to define her role in the trapeze act. They'd had a family meeting and agreed she should focus on the aerial ballet. They wanted to add a hook, so created the duo of Pele the Mime and Celine the Silken Temptress. The subtle sparks between them had kept the audience enthralled.

She would tease and flaunt herself to him and then the crowd, pretending to flirt elsewhere, and he would draw her back to him. Then when it came time for her to mount the rope webbing, her performance glittering and dangerous, Pele was there, her watcher, steadying her as she danced in the air.

Until the night she and the rope went spiraling toward the ground.

With some sort of superhuman ability, he'd been there, his body breaking her fall before she met the unforgiving earth, cushioning her from impact. She'd suffered a dislocated shoulder, some bruising, and a bad sprain to her ankle, but it would have been far worse without his quick thinking.

They'd never discovered what actually caused the accident. Equipment was always checked and double-checked, nothing left to chance. The rigger swore he'd checked the rigging immediately before the performance as usual and everything had been good. It shouldn't have happened, but it had.

After that night, for some reason Pele had pulled away from her emotionally. The loss of Pele and the unexpected fear of returning to the air gnawed at her. Finally, she'd left the circus, unable to bear the pain of daily contact with him. It had only been amplified by the fact she'd become a disappointment to her family as well. She couldn't ascend to the trapeze, let along perform on the ropes.

And now here he was before her in the flesh. Not her beloved Pele, but someone she didn't know. Peter Cortland. Businessman. She rolled the name through her mind. A stranger. Yet, when she looked into his eyes, all she saw was Pele.

She turned away to look out the window. "I don't have long, Pel— Peter. Why are you here?"

"Sebastian is ill. He wants to see you." His voice lowered a notch. "It's time for you to come home, Celine."

She felt the pull. Admitted to herself she'd felt it for a long time, this need to return to her roots.

Swiveling back, she faced him. "How bad is he? And why didn't I know about it before?"

"He started having chest pains a week ago. The doctors kept him in the hospital and ran some tests. He may need surgery. Before surgery, he wants to see you."

It was December. The winter break. They'd be in Florida now, practicing and preparing for the new season. She remembered the routine as if it was yesterday.

It was hard to think of her grandfather as ill. He'd always been the backbone of the family. After her parents were killed in a plane crash, he'd been the rock that kept her and her sister, Nina, from falling apart. He hadn't wanted her to leave. He'd told her she'd get over her fear of the trapeze, she just needed to give it time. If only that had been her sole reason. But Pele's coldness was the real driving force for staying away, not the trapeze.

"When does he go in for surgery?" She knew there was no choice.

"They've scheduled him for the fifth of January."

His voice offered no clue how he felt about her return, his expression bland. He might as well have been wearing the painted face of the mime he'd always hid behind.

Abruptly she stood and turned back to the window. "And you? How do you feel about my return?"

She hated herself for asking, but she had to know. Tense silence filled the room, long and drawn out until it stretched her nerves to the point of breaking.

Like in her dream, she felt him behind her. Close. She focused on the reflection in the glass, watched as he raised his hands and rested them on her shoulders. The touch sent a jolt of electricity surging through her. She tensed in reaction, fighting the burgeoning desire that had begun to spiral inside.

"I want you to come home, Celine." She felt his breath against her hair. "I know I hurt you before you left. I want a chance to—"

She whirled about and quickly moved away from him. "A chance to what? It's been seven years. At any time you could have come to me. I've been here the whole time." *Waiting for you*, she stopped herself from adding. Acknowledging for the first time that was exactly what she'd been doing. "Why didn't you come before this?" She could hear the frustrated pain in her voice and wanted to scream, to rage at him. All these years she'd waited for him to come. To realize he loved her.

Then finally, when she'd at last given up, knowing it was a false hope, when she'd made up her mind to give Daniel the answer he'd been waiting for—now he strolled back into her life, turning it upside down.

"Celine, I didn't know how to come to you. It's as simple as that." He ran a hand through his hair and she heard a deep sigh escape from him. "If it's too late, I know it's my fault. But when Sebastian asked me to come to you, I knew it was my chance."

"And what if this hadn't happened? Would you ever have come?"

"I don't know." The heavy words dropped between them. "I'd like to think I would have, but...there's so much you don't know about me. Things I should have told you and didn't, reasons I ended up hurting you."

"Can there be any reason good enough to do what you did? Do you have any idea how abandoned I felt? Did you even care? God! I loved you and you turned off just like that. No reason, no explanation. I don't know that I'm able to give you another chance." She shouldn't have said it. Why had she exposed herself like that to his ridicule?

A shadow of the dream came back to haunt her. In the dream she was naked—completely vulnerable. A shiver ran along her spine as the images of her erotic fantasy tangled in her mind. She'd wanted—needed his approval.

He stalked across the room and grabbed her by the shoulders. "Is this reason enough to consider what I have to say?" he growled.

Lowering his head, she saw a flash of green, and then he dipped and seized her lips in a hot, savage claiming. His hand tangled in her hair, holding her firm. His tongue penetrated, stealing her breath, demanding her response. With the other hand, he bent her to him. She felt his hard arousal and whimpered with need.

He lifted his head and pinned her with a primal, sensual look. "Your taste is as hotly sweet as I remembered. You're like a drug. One taste and I'm hooked. Seven years ago I lived in a fog of painful memories. I came to Valentini's for the most part to stop the pain. It saved my life."

Releasing her, he stepped away. "I thought I'd healed. Until your accident. It brought it all back."

"Why didn't you talk to me then? Tell me what you were feeling, instead of shutting me out?"

"Dammit, you were only nineteen. I'd been through too much, you were so young and I was too old for you. It was too heavy a burden to lay on your shoulders."

"Old? You can't be that much older than me. What were you? Twenty-four? Twenty-five at the time?"

"Twenty-four," he confirmed. "But life made me feel like I was a lot older."

"Then tell me now. Why did you push me away?" She needed to understand. That had always been part of her problem. She'd never understood his sudden coldness.

"Come back," he urged her. "It's complicated and now's not the time or the place to go into it. Come back for your grandfather. Come back for me."

She tried to hide her trembling by clasping her hands behind her back. The fierce brand of his kiss fired her desire, reminding her how badly she still wanted him. Quenching her smoldering thoughts, she looked up. "What if there's nothing left? What if we've both changed so much there can never be anything more? What if you've left it too late?"

A look of sadness and regret flickered in his eyes. "If that's the case, if that's how you feel after we've talked, I won't bother you again. I'll go away while you spend time with Sebastian. I don't want to cause you more pain, Celine."

"I don't know if I can get used to calling you Peter." A half smile curved her lips.

His return smile was rueful. "Well, it's Peter you'll need to become acquainted with. It was Peter hiding beneath Pele's white face, his silence. The greasepaint of the mime is gone—Pele hid the man and his scars. I don't want to hide from you any longer. Do you think you can give Peter a chance?"

Celine searched his face, for what she didn't know. Did she really want to give him the opportunity to hurt her again? She turned back to her desk and her gaze connected with the clock face.

"I have to go. I'm late!" Her lunch with Daniel! She snatched her purse from the bottom desk drawer.

He grabbed her arm before she could race from the office. "Celine. You'll come?"

She nodded distractedly. "Yes, I'll come. I need a couple of days to sort things out here and to request a leave of absence." She raised her head to look at him. "I'm doing this for Grandfather, not to rekindle the ashes of something that's long dead."

Solemn acceptance flashed in his eyes. "I understand. I'll wait—"

"No. I'll finish up what I need to and fly to Orlando when I'm done. I'll call and let you know my itinerary. Now, I have to go. Daniel's waiting," and she rushed from the office.

As the taxi moved through the streets, she reviewed in her mind the meeting with Peter. That searing kiss revived all the emotions she'd locked away—ones she'd buried beneath a need for self-preservation. What was she going to say to Daniel?

With her thoughts in turmoil, there was no way she could tell him she'd marry him. And it wasn't fair to keep him waiting while she flitted off to go back to the circus. If she were truthful with herself, she'd admit the only reason she'd convinced herself that marrying Daniel was the right thing to do was because the dreams frightened her.

She now knew she didn't truly love Daniel the way he deserved to be loved. And it wouldn't be fair to him to keep him in this limbo of waiting for her to change her mind.

Instead of telling him she'd marry him, she'd be ending the relationship. Because even if she couldn't have Peter or Pele, or whoever he was, giving Daniel only half a heart wasn't fair to him either.

How had her life ever become so complicated?

CHAPTER 3

Who the hell was Daniel? He ran the name through his mind for the thousandth time since Celine had uttered it in her office.

He should have contacted her sooner. The shadows and scars from his past may very well have cost him dearly.

He paced the airport terminal as he waited for her plane to land. When he'd entered her office, seen her for the first time in seven years, it had taken all his self-control not to pull her into his arms immediately. All the feelings flooded through him. The memory of her smile, her touch, her lips. Her innocence had reached to that part of him he'd closed off. He'd started to feel like it was safe to live again. There was a reason to want to live. She'd offered him hope for a future. Until the accident.

Why hadn't he sent the letters he'd written? *Because they'd been bleeding heart letters, that's why.* Tomes written in the black pit of eternal night. That bottom dresser drawer was filled with letters to her—and to Anna. A bolt of pain struck his chest and he winced in reaction.

The loudspeaker broke into his thoughts, announcing the arrival of Celine's flight. He paced before the baggage carousel. What could he say to her? How did he begin? He'd left it far too long. But there'd been no words to describe the terror that had gripped him at the possibility of losing her to death. How close he'd come to doing that when she'd fallen. Like a man possessed, he'd reached for her and had at the very last minute cushioned her from connecting with the solid

21

ground with his own body. Coming that close so soon after Anna, was more than he could bear. Better for him to let her go. He'd teetered at the border of sanity after losing Anna, it wouldn't have taken much to drive him over the edge.

Maybe this Daniel person loved Celine the way she deserved to be loved. And maybe Celine had found someone she could love who didn't carry all the emotional baggage he did.

He'd had a very good reason for not going after her all these years. She was right. He probably would have left things if it hadn't been for Sebastian. Better that he not have to face her with a choice he wasn't prepared for. Would Anna's death always haunt him so poignantly? He couldn't come to terms with the possibility of it happening again, but would Celine understand that? Could she accept that he didn't think he could face fathering another child? He had to try to make her understand.

And why did the thought of Celine carrying his child send heat coursing through him, causing his body to tighten with desire, rather than fear? For the present he wasn't going to think about that. First things first—he had to confront her with his past. It was a burden he'd never wanted to lay on her shoulders. But seeing her again—he wanted her too fiercely not to offer her a choice.

By the number of people now converging on the escalator, Peter assumed everyone had disembarked from the plane. Studying each face intently, he recognized her slender frame, the late afternoon sunlight catching in her shining cap of gold.

Her hair had been much longer when she'd left. The shorter style fit her though. Soft curls framed her face, enhancing the slant of her sapphire eyes and the tilt of her chin, giving her almost an elfin look.

Her searching blue gaze connected with him and he saw the glint of recognition. She straightened her shoulders as if ready to meet an unpleasant confrontation head on. He regretted that she felt the need to brace herself against facing him.

She carried herself differently. He noted a sureness in her gait as she stepped from the escalator and walked toward him. Seven years ago she'd looked like a puff a wind would have whisked her away, a sharp, well-muscled frame, economical and light for the demands of her aerial performance. He'd always had the feeling she'd float away at any moment.

Now her body hinted at sensuous, womanly curves. The white linen slacks smoothed and rested lovingly at her gently rounded hips, a narrow gold chain belt glimmered and swayed seductively with her rhythm as she stepped from the escalator.

A white jacket was folded neatly over her left arm. The cotton candy pink knit tank top she wore scooped low, and clung lovingly to full, rounded breasts. The hem of her shirt flirted between honeyed skin and the waistband of her slacks as she walked. She shifted the carry-on bag to better anchor it on her shoulder, resettled the jacket, and his eyes widened as the tank top shifted higher for a brief second.

Shit! He blinked, unable to believe what he saw. *That wasn't there seven years ago.* She'd had her belly button pierced and a gold ring nestled and glimmered in the light. The sight of it almost drove him to his knees as need swamped him. Then a pang of jealousy invaded. *Had she gotten it done for Daniel?* Talk about the temptation of Eve.

He was going to have to get a grip. She couldn't be rushed. Quickly he scanned the fingers of both her hands as she moved close—and breathed a sigh of relief. No rings, no diamond. Maybe these last seven days his thoughts about her with another man had magnified without reason. Maybe the relationship wasn't as serious as he'd first thought. He hoped not.

Why had it never occurred to him she might be seriously involved with someone? Because he'd tried not to think of her at all. Every time she moved into the forefront of his brain, he ended up writing more letters in the despair of night that would never be sent.

She halted in front of him and for the life of him he couldn't open his mouth. He just stared at her, drinking in her presence. Her light floral scent drifted over him.

"Hello, Peter. Thanks for meeting me." Her smile was tentative as she looked up at him.

He reached out. "Let me take that for you."

Stepping away from him, she shook her head. "No, it's fine. I can handle it." The squeak and rumble of the carousel signaled the arrival of the baggage from the plane. "But you can probably help with the other two bags I brought with me." She readjusted the strap on her shoulder and turned toward the carousel.

He couldn't help it. His gaze was glued to that sexy little belt, watching it sway as she walked. His mouth watered. Fantasies took over as he pictured her wearing only the gold chain belt and that little ring piercing her navel.

He blinked and forced the images away, trying to even out the temperature of his body. He cleared his throat. It was like traveling on an out-of-control freight train with each minute that passed in her company.

When she bent over to grab first one floral-covered tan suitcase and then its smaller mate, his mouth watered at the well-formed derriere she presented for his inspection.

She straightened and turned toward him. Her head tilted in silent question.

Again he cleared his throat. "Is that everything?"

"Yes. Is something wrong?"

"No. Nothing. Let me take those." He needed to do something with his hands to stop him from grabbing her instead.

After relieving her of the burden of the cases, he turned toward the doors. "We'll go out this way. My car isn't too far away."

As they emerged into the parking lot, he directed her to his silver-gray Explorer. Once he'd loaded the cases in the back and they were on the interstate headed out of the city, he relaxed and tried to focus on maneuvering in traffic and ignoring the scent of the woman sitting next to him.

"How is my grandfather?"

Peter glanced at her. She wasn't looking at him, but instead appeared intently focused on the road ahead. Looking at her caused a stirring of memory. He remembered the feel of her slender form in his arms, the touch of her soft lips. *Slow down, pal,* he reminded himself.

"He's fine for now. He's at his apartment. Nina's staying with him until we get there."

"Nina? My sister's with him? I thought she and the others would be on tour? Maybe Vegas or Reno." It was normal for the more popular acts to be on tour to other parts of the country, always performing somewhere, even when the main circus was on winter hiatus.

Peter had found it odd as well when Nina had returned ostensibly because of her concern for Sebastian. Family commitment had never appeared to be at the top of her priorities. "I'll admit I was surprised when she offered to stay, but she's here. The rest of the family is still on tour. Sebastian wouldn't hear of them shortening their schedule. Nina was apparently the compromise."

"Oh, yes. I remember well. Nothing stops the Great Valentinis. They'll still be performing after they've all turned to dust," she commented wryly.

"Celine—"

She released a long breath. "I know, I know. I'm not bitter, really

I'm not. Uncle Alberto and the rest of the family have performing in the blood. I always understood that. I guess I disappointed them."

Unable to help himself, he reached out and placed a hand over hers. "Don't revisit it, Celine. They understood when you left. It was simply that they expected, the same as me I guess, that you'd eventually return."

"But I didn't."

"Why didn't you? Was it the fear of going back up that kept you away? No one would have forced you to return to the air. Or is it this Daniel who occupies your attention?"

"Daniel? What about Daniel? How did you—? Oh, yes. I mentioned him when you came to the office, didn't I?"

He nodded. "I gathered he's someone special." There. He'd said it. But did he want to know the answer?

She seemed to hesitate before answering him. "Yes, he is special."

His hands tightened on the steering wheel. Obviously, she was going to make him ask outright. "I see. Do you love him?"

"Why the twenty questions, Peter? You haven't been interested for the last seven years. Why now?"

How could he answer that? He'd cared more than he wanted to admit. He'd stayed away from her for that very reason. Was he really going to be able to put the ghosts to rest? Could he prove to her that he was worth the risk?

Finally, he answered her. "There were reasons. I want us to talk, Celine. Will you at least listen to what I have to say before making up your mind?"

It seemed like an eternity before she answered. "I'll listen, Peter. But I can't guarantee I'll understand that any reason would be good enough for you to shut me out of your life so hurtfully. And to think you can just waltz back in and pick up where we left off. How could you possibly think I could trust you after all this time?"

"I don't know, Celine. But I have to try."

*   *   *

Celine felt like her whole body was tied into knots as she stepped from the SUV once it came to a halt before the apartment complex. The close quarters on the drive to her grandfather's home was an exercise in self-control.

The man exuded potent magnetism. At ease in his own environment, Peter moved with fluid masculine grace. He didn't carry the build of a weightlifter, he moved with a flexible animal silence, confident in his own skin. Skin tanned caramel by the southern sun, resilient. How was she ever going to maintain distance, remember her promise to herself not to become involved with him again?

Her dreams hovered at the fringes of her mind and she yearned so badly for him to touch her. To kiss her again, like he'd done seven years before. And seven days ago when he'd come to her office, it had seared her just as badly.

They stopped before an apartment on the ground floor and Peter rang the bell. It was Nina who opened the door. Her sister, whom she hadn't seen or heard from in the last seven years.

Taller than Celine by a head, she maintained the taut, slender frame of a dedicated trapeze artist. Her ebony hair fell like a thick, shimmering curtain down her back, caught at the nape by a silver barrette. Everyone had always commented that the two sisters were two sides of a coin. Where Celine was the light, Nina was the dark.

"Celine!" Nina greeted her. Celine had the feeling the smile she offered was a façade. It didn't quite reach her eyes. She leaned forward and hugged her, the sophisticated perfume she wore permeated the air around her. Celine had a strong urge to break free, but fought it. "Thank God you were able to come. He's been waiting." Anchoring a slim arm around Celine's waist, she led her inside. "It's been so long. We'll have to make time to catch up while you're here."

Nina guided her into a spacious living room decorated in earth tones. Sebastian sat on a brown leather couch. He'd changed since the last time she'd seen him. He looked smaller, older, more frail. She pulled away from Nina, and hurried to him, kneeling on the floor before him.

"Grandfather," her voice was husky with unshed tears. He held out his arms and gathered her to him.

"Celine, my child, finally, you've come home."

"Yes, I'm here." His scent reminded her of her childhood and happy times with the circus. The scent was fresh cut wood mingled with the aroma of his favorite pipe tobacco. He'd always been there, supporting her, comforting her. It was only right she should be with him now.

She tipped her head back and looked up to study his weathered features. "How are you feeling?"

He smiled and patted her back. "I'm fine. It's nothing serious."

"What do you mean, nothing serious? Your health is a very serious matter."

"It's only a little valve they need to do some work on. Don't worry so." He leaned back and looked her over. Her grandfather always had the uncanny ability to size people up. "You look good, granddaughter, but you've been away too long."

"Grandfather?" They turned in unison to look at Nina. She had a set of car keys in her hand, a slight pout on her red lips. "I'm leaving now so you can visit with Celine. I'm sure you have a lot to discuss."

"You didn't need to stay, Nina. I'm fine. I don't need a babysitter." Celine was surprised to hear a bit of an edge in his voice.

"I know that," Nina responded coolly. "But I wanted to see my sister as well. Now that I have, I'll be on my way. I'm headed over to the grounds to check on how the set-up is going. I'll be there if you need me. Celine, Grandfather knows the number to my cell phone, it's on his speed dial if you should need me. We'll talk later."

She swung around regally, with the grace of a ballet dancer. Peter stepped back from the doorway. She stopped in front of him.

"I assume you'll stop by later?" she purred softly.

Stop by later? What was that supposed to mean? Celine wondered, as an unexpected stab of jealousy shot through her. Of her sister? Celine realized she'd been away a long time. Things changed. Was there something personal between Peter and Nina?

Peter nodded. "I'll talk with you at the office. I appreciate your help with the programs for the show."

Nina reached up and stroked the side of his face. "Any time, Boss." Peter jerked back, but Nina had already turned away and was out the door like an exotic breeze.

Celine saw her grandfather scowl. "Your sister is quite a handful. She will get herself in trouble one of these days. She's only here now because she had a run in with Alberto. Al told her to take some time off. And she's not very happy about it."

Nina had never been easy. She'd always been the flamboyant one, demanding attention. And her dark beauty always ate up the limelight.

Peter pulled his keys from his pocket. "I have to be going as well, Sebastian. I'll be late if I don't get a move on. I'll check in with you when I'm done."

Sebastian nodded. "Bring by the program and schedule. We'll go over it."

"You know what the doctor said. You're not to overdo," Peter reminded him.

Sebastian raised his hand in a gesture of dismissal. "Forget him. I know my body. I'm not going to the office, right? What harm can it do if I promise to stay here and take it easy? I'll just be visiting with my granddaughter."

"All right. Celine, don't let him get out of hand. He tends to be stubborn."

Celine smiled. "I'll take care of him. We have a lot to talk about."

She watched Peter as he turned and walked out the door. It was like a light had gone out...some essential energy gone. It left her feeling lost.

"He's a good man, Celine."

She turned back to her grandfather. "Yes, he is." That had never been the problem. She just didn't know if she could trust her heart to him again.

"Since he found his calling, he's changed. I think for a long time there at the beginning, he was lost."

Celine turned a quizzical gaze on her grandfather. "What calling are you talking about?"

"He volunteers time in the children's wards. Wherever we are, he always makes time for the children. It's the only time he wears the mime face any more."

She was curious. What had brought this about? "When did he start doing that? And why?"

"After you left, we talked a lot. It's his way of remembering his daughter."

She couldn't have been more shocked if he'd told her Peter was an escaped criminal. "His daughter? Peter has a daughter?" Was he married as well?

Sebastian turned sad eyes in her direction. "Yes, his daughter, Anna, died from cancer when she was four years old. That's when Peter came to us. Has he never told you about his life?"

She turned her head to stare at the door Peter had just passed through, her eyes wide with shock. Why had he never told her?

"What about his wife?" She licked her lips. "Where is she?"

He patted her hand. "I think you need to talk to Peter. There's obviously a great deal he hasn't shared with you. And much you need to know."

All of a sudden her world shifted. It was like standing in the House of Mirrors with miles of distortions staring back at her. What secrets had Pele hidden behind the face of the mime? In her mind, the black teardrop took on new, painful meaning. How could she not have known?

CHAPTER 4

Celine stood to the side of the doorway of the large, sunny room. It was the children's ward of the hospital. This particular room was specially designed for therapeutic recreation. Shelves filled with books, dolls, and games lined the gaily painted walls. Aides and volunteers were in various locations around the room quietly helping children with projects or reading to them.

Celine's attention was glued to the mime at the center of the room, his tall frame hunched down before a young girl in a wheelchair. He appeared to be demonstrating to her how to juggle two balls, one yellow and one red. The little girl giggled when she tried. She dropped the balls and Peter dove to recover them. Several other children had gathered round to watch, and a lump formed in her throat.

A nurse dressed in blue scrubs stopped to watch the entertainment. "He's great with the kids," she said in a quiet voice. "He has such patience with them. And they all love him. There's a special quality, a gentleness, that seems to draw them. Sometimes the parents need to meet with the doctors and Pele keeps the kids so occupied, the time flies for them. It helps them to forget just for a little while, why they're here." She offered a bittersweet smile to Celine and then continued on her way.

Celine's grandfather had seen her restlessness and finally encouraged her to take his car and find Peter. He'd given her directions to his apartment and to the hospital and told her where she was most likely to find him.

Her stomach clenched. It wasn't her plan to confront him here—she just needed to try to understand. He'd hidden this from her. Why?

Finally he stood and with gestures indicated to the children that it was time for him to leave. She had to smile at their combined roar of protest.

Stepping away from the door before he could see her, she turned and quietly left the ward, deep in thought. As she exited the hospital, blinking at the bright sunlight, the late afternoon heat rose from the pavement to stifle her. Slowly, she made her way to the navy blue Volkswagen, thoughts jumbling in her head.

Unlocking the car, she climbed inside, started it, and cranked up the air conditioning. He'd had a child—a daughter. And she'd died from cancer. That's all her grandfather would share with her. He told her she needed to talk with Peter.

But Peter hadn't exactly been forthcoming with her about his past. What made her think he would do so now?

At the office, he'd told her there were things he needed to tell her. Was he ready to open up to her at last? As she glanced up, she saw a man dressed in white emerge from the hospital. It was Peter. He stopped to chat with the guard and then made his way to his car. He probably would be headed home to remove his makeup and costume.

She made up her mind. The only thing to do was confront him before he had a chance to think about it and come up with excuses to delay their much needed discussion. Damn him for not confiding in her seven years ago! Things could have all been so different for them. It wasn't fair that she was now being forced to take matters into her own hands. He'd hidden so much from her—things that now made sense of some of his actions.

Pulling into the parking lot outside the duplex apartment complex, she noticed her hands were trembling. Nervous anticipation sliced through her. Before she could change her mind, she got out of the car and walked with determined steps to his apartment and rang the bell.

The door opened and he stood before her still cloaked in the garb of Pele.

"I think you owe me that explanation." She waited expectantly for him to invite her inside.

After a moment's hesitation, he stepped back, allowing her to enter. "How did you get here?"

"Grandfather let me borrow his car and told me where to find you." She stopped in the middle of the living room and rounded on him. "I saw you at the hospital. Why didn't you ever tell me you had a child?" There was a catch of hurt in her voice that she was unable to suppress and she turned away again. Why hadn't he ever told her such an important thing as that?

"Celine, I'm sorry if I've hurt you yet again. I should have told you."

She felt his hands at her shoulders. She shrugged them off and moved away from him. Turning back, she raised her chin and faced him from across the room.

"How much more have you hidden from me, Peter? Do you also have a wife tucked away somewhere?" She wanted to stay calm, but the longer she thought about it, the more agitated she became.

"Let me get this makeup off and change, then we can talk."

"Fine. I won't be put off this time."

"I know that. I planned to tell you. Would you like something to drink while you wait?"

"No."

Turning, he walked with a stiff gait toward another doorway, probably his bedroom, without saying anything else.

Celine turned back to survey the room around her. The walls were light beige, the furniture looked comfortable in varying shades of dark green. She noticed several framed photographs on a small side table and walked over to study them more closely. There was one of a much younger Peter holding a toddler in his arms. They were both smiling into the lens of the camera. Celine surmised it was a photograph of his daughter. A wave of unexpected jealous pain arrowed through her at the knowledge it had probably been his wife who took the picture. She carefully set the photo back down on the oak table and turned away.

An urgent need washed over her to touch Peter. Pivoting away from the table, she walked to the doorway she'd seen him pass through. He sat before a dressing table staring at his reflection.

"Peter."

She saw his shoulders stiffen at the sound of her voice. He reached to pick up a towel and a jar of cleansing cream. He looked away from her reflected image. "I'll be out in a minute."

Taking her courage in hand, she stepped farther into the room and walked to him. She knelt before him and looked up into his face. How did she begin to tell him what was in her heart? She bit at her lower lip.

"Peter, I—"

"Don't," he stopped her with a shake of his head, the look in his

31

eyes solemn. "I don't want your pity, Celine."

"It's not pity I'm offering." She took the towel from his hand and began to clean the white makeup from his face, stopping at the painted black teardrop. For the first time she thought she understood all that it represented in his life.

She stared at it for a long time, feeling the black void it represented, the suffering and loss inside him. Leaning up she pressed her lips to its center. Closing her eyes, she opened her heart, tasted the terrible pain and loneliness that was encompassed by that lonely, sad symbol.

He stilled beneath her touch. She placed a hand against the front of his white satin shirt, felt the erratic beating of his heart. "I've missed you so much," she whispered against his skin, the scent of greasepaints and man teasing her senses.

Peter's arms wrapped around her and he lifted her, settling her on his lap. "God, Celine, you're more temptation than a man can stand," and he tilted his head to capture her lips.

They coaxed her response, his tongue traced the crease, urged her to open to him, which she did. Willingly. His tongue dueled with hers. She felt the heat, the need, and she surrendered.

With her hands she pulled at the fastenings at the front of his shirt and pushed it down his shoulders. She needed to touch him, to feel his warm skin beneath her fingers. Wanted to feel him inside her.

It all came back to her, the dreams, the aching need building and consuming her.

Peter raised his head to look at her, searching, questioning. "If this is pity you're offering me—"

"It was never pity," she responded, her voice husky with desire. "I need you, Peter, now. I need to be a part of you."

"What about Daniel?"

She shook her head in denial. "There's nothing between Daniel and me. He wanted to marry me, but I couldn't. Not once I saw you again." Then she asked the question she dreaded an answer to. "What about you? Are you married?"

He sighed and gently helped her to stand. "No. Not anymore. But before we go any further, I think we need to talk about the past. To clear up what I haven't told you."

With a supreme effort at control, she pulled away from him. "I understand." But she didn't. She needed him to make love to her and he wasn't going to do that. A fist clenched around her heart. Did he still love his ex-wife?

He must have seen something in her face because he pulled her back to him and cupped her face. His green gaze connected and chained her movements. "I want you so much I can't think straight. But there are things you need to know before I make you mine, before I claim what I should have long ago. Do you understand?" His lips when they sought hers again, promised her everything she'd ever wanted. Then he leaned his forehead against hers. "Do you have any idea how much I want to make love to you right now?"

"Yes," she answered as she gulped large amounts of air and tried to catch her breath. "Because I ache with the need to have you inside me."

"Damn, don't say that." He carefully set her away from him. "Wait in the other room, Celine. I can't think with you near me like this. And I need to have a clear head when we talk."

"All right." She turned away on unsteady legs. As she left the room she tried not to glance at the bed; tried not to envision them tangled and naked. And it was a big bed, covered in a forest-patterned quilt. It wasn't covered in white satin like her erotic dreams, but it was definitely a bed they could get lost in for a long time. The blood in her veins heated, the liquid at her center ran hot and thick with her desire.

She'd better get out of this room fast, before she stripped off the pants and shirt that constricted her breathing and said to hell with the explanations.

*   *   *

Peter wiped at the greasepaint, his mind otherwise engaged as he tried to get his raging cock to settle down. He throbbed with the need to make her his. Finally. She had to be made aware of his reasons first. She needed to know he hadn't turned from her because he didn't love her. In fact, he'd loved her too much, right from the beginning.

But he was not, he assured himself, making love to Celine until she knew everything. She had to know what a coward he was seven years ago.

What if it happened again? What if he was faced with the same choices? What if Celine should become ill—was he strong enough to stand by her and see her slowly disintegrate, the same way Anna had? Could he go through that again?

He'd failed Celine once. How could he be certain he wouldn't do it again?

This time would be different, he tried to convince himself. Last time it had been too soon after Anna's loss. Did he love Celine enough to

33

face his inner demons? He couldn't bear it if he hurt her again. Could he control the fears that fought to consume him?

If it hadn't been for Sebastian, he knew he probably wouldn't have gone after her, no matter how much he tried to convince himself otherwise. He'd shut himself off for a reason. Could he now re-open that path to his emotions all over again?

One thing he knew was that he'd been offered a second chance and he didn't want to squander it this time. He'd been a shell of a man ever since Anna's death. It was only with Celine he'd started to feel again. He was honest enough with himself to admit that had scared him shitless. Enough so that he'd pulled away from her with a vengeance. Then he'd stayed numb for seven years. Safe. No entanglements that might shake the brick wall he'd built to retain his sanity.

Then he'd walked into her office seven days ago and it was all there for him once again. That solid wall had exploded into rubble. Colors of the world were vibrant once again. The scent of life permeated him. And he didn't want to go back to what he'd been. He didn't want to lose her and he'd come damn close to doing just that.

He rose from the dressing table and shedding clothes as he went, walked into the bathroom and turned on the shower.

One thing was certain. He'd lay it all out for her and if she walked away after knowing the complete truth, well, at least he would have tried. He would have faced his past. It was a heavy burden to lay on someone else's shoulders. He'd only wanted to protect her from it.

Who was he trying to kid? He was trying to protect himself. His sanity had hung by a loose thread, ready to unravel at any second. It almost had when Celine fell from the ropes. And he'd run scared because of it.

Funny thing was, no one knew it all, not even Sebastian. But he was going to lay his soul bare with Celine. If they did have a future, it couldn't be based on pretense. She had to see him in the honest light of day.

CHAPTER 5

Celine busied herself with making dinner in the small walk-in kitchen. Rummaging through the cupboards, she discovered several boxes of spaghetti and a jar of prepared sauce and decided it would make a quick and filling meal. She had a feeling Peter didn't often cook for himself by the looks of the contents in the cupboard.

As the sauce simmered and the spaghetti cooked, she looked around for the telephone. Her grandfather would worry if he didn't hear from her. She didn't like leaving him alone, but she needed to settle things with Peter. And her grandfather had encouraged her to do so.

Speaking with him on the phone, he eased her concerns by informing her that his next-door neighbor was keeping him occupied with a rousing game of checkers. He berated her for trying to treat him like a helpless old man, informed her he was just fine, and would visit with her later.

Sebastian had always liked Peter, right from the start. He'd been pleased when it looked like Celine and Peter would come together offstage as well as on. When Celine told him she was leaving the circus, he'd told her he felt she was making a mistake. But she hadn't listened to his arguments, hadn't wanted to hear what he had to say. And she hadn't been able to get away fast enough.

Just as she replaced the phone on the base, she sensed Peter's presence behind her. She looked up and saw his reflection in the sliding glass doors.

She devoured him with her eyes. This wasn't the whimsical unisex facade of the mime clown, one who lyrically floated through the crowds, mimicking and spreading laughter and magical delight to children and adults alike.

Nor was it the intensely dominating creature of her dreams. The one who molded and awakened her naked body like sensual putty in his hands. Who revealed every dark passionate facet of her inner secret fantasies.

No, the image reflected back to her was definitely all male. Broad shoulders and a solid chest were enhanced by the close fit of a white T-shirt. Blue jeans enhanced narrow hips and well-muscled thighs. He stood quietly behind her, studying her with a searing intensity she found unnerving. His sandy, sun-kissed hair was still damp and looked darker in the dim light of the room. The late afternoon had also darkened his jaw with a five o-clock shadow, giving him a brooding, rugged definition she found enticing. Her gaze drifted downward, noting his feet were bare, and the casual ease with which he stood storming her hard-fought attempt at control.

Sucking in a great gulp of air, it seemed to lodge painfully in her chest. The sight of him was so heady it caused her head to spin and her stomach tumbled in response. Her hands balled into fists at her sides as she fought to retain control and she turned away from the reflection and faced the real thing.

For long moments he consumed her with his eyes like a man starving and unable to believe he'd found sustenance. A statue carved from granite, he seemed incapable of looking away, unable to move. Desire hovered in the air, was a tangible thing as it arced across the room like an invisible umbilical cord feeding her heightened awareness, her need.

Finally, Peter broke the connection as he looked away toward the kitchen, tilted his head and sniffed the air. "Is that dinner I smell burning?"

Celine blinked, as if awaking from a trance, whirled about and raced to the kitchen. "Oh God! I've burned the sauce."

Peter followed her into the kitchen and peered over her shoulder as she turned off the stove and removed the saucepan from the burner. "It looks salvageable to me. Just a little tinge of smoky flavor."

Celine let out a stuttering laugh. "Flavor? Is that what you call it?"

"Sure. It's sort of a mainstay in my diet."

She stepped toward the sink with the pot of sauce. "I'll have to remember that. You like burnt flavoring."

"Well, I'm not sure like is a word I'd use to describe it. But I've learned to tolerate the taste over the years. If I threw out everything that I scorched, I'd go hungry or broke. Probably both."

She grinned up at him over her shoulder. "I kind of thought that might be the case. Your cupboards look pretty sparse. Not much of a chef, are you?"

She was caught by the sparkling glint of humor in his gold-flecked, moss-colored eyes. Her attention then riveted to his mouth and her laughter died away. She remembered the feel of those sculptured, firm lips. It was a mouth she wanted to taste again. As she watched, almost like he'd read her thoughts, his head dropped closer. Her lips instinctively parted. Without looking away, he reached out and removed the saucepan from her unresisting hand and set it on the counter. Lowering his head, he seared her with his kiss.

Turning her toward him, a hand brushed against her shirt, grazing a sensitive nipple and his lips caught her gasp of desire. Again, he brushed his thumb lightly across her breast and she felt the desire zing through her, settling a fireball in her stomach to flare and simmer.

Pulling back, he gazed down at her, his pupils dilated, a banked fire smoldering. "Forget the pasta," he ground out. "I'll call for pizza delivery." He released her, moved to the stove and turned off the remaining burner beneath the overcooked spaghetti. He turned back to her. "We need to talk. Now."

He cupped her elbow and pointedly directed her to the living room. She let him lead her to the sofa. Once she was settled, he walked back to the side table, picked up the phone and efficiently ordered a pizza. Once he replaced the phone, he turned to look at her.

Celine raised a brow and a hint of a smile curved her lips. "You have pizza delivery on speed dial?" Anything to relieve the tension that clung to the room.

Grinning, he shrugged. "And a Chinese takeout. I know my priorities."

The grin faded from his face as he stared at her for a long, solitary moment. Celine didn't know how to help him. A faraway look entered his eyes and she assumed he was revisiting the past. A look of bleak sadness flitted across his face. It hurt her to see it there.

"Peter, maybe this should wait. I don't want to cause you more pain."

He refocused on her. The left corner of his mouth rose in a regretful smile. "No. It can't wait. It's a conversation seven years past due, don't you think?"

He turned and gazed out the sliding glass door and was silent for a long time. "Cindy and I were high school sweethearts. It's certainly not a new story."

"Cindy was your wife?" she asked him quietly.

"Yes. Toward the end of our senior year she wound up pregnant so we were married. When you're young you think you can beat all the odds. And we did fine for a while. I worked days and attended college classes at night."

He turned back to Celine. "It's one of the reasons I didn't want to lay my problems on your shoulders. You were so young, about the same age we were when Anna was born."

"Anna was your daughter."

"Yes." He glanced down at the photograph Celine had picked up earlier. "A beautiful little girl with large dark eyes and long black hair. She looked a lot like Cindy."

"How old was she when she was diagnosed with cancer?"

He inhaled deeply, the expression on his faced still, as though he was bracing himself. "She was two when they diagnosed it as leukemia. Just a baby." He paused, staring out through the glass, lost deep in his memories.

She couldn't stand the thought of him having to relive the tragedy of losing his daughter. "Peter, don't. It's too painful."

He shook his head. "For two years she fought it as it spread through her. And she was a fighter. We did everything we could. But in the end it wasn't enough." His voice had lowered to a tight whisper. He cleared his throat.

"After she died, I threw myself into work—two jobs and I finished up my classes. Paying the medical bills was the only thing I had left that I could do for her. It was my total focus and it drove a wedge between Cindy and me."

He whirled around and she cried out at the terrible pain she saw contained in his eyes. They'd gone from emerald to a deep green, almost black—smoky dark mirrors, hiding so much. The expression on his face, intent and chiseled as though he physically tried to contain the depths hidden inside.

"Peter—" she begged. She wanted to go to him, but there was a look of remote determination that stopped her. She shouldn't have asked this of him.

But he forged on. It was as though once the floodgates had been released all the pain spilled out, needing to be purged. "Anna was almost four when she died. Cindy and I were only twenty-two. I felt about a hundred and twenty-two."

He released a humorless laugh. "I thought I was the strong one, shouldering the responsibility. I didn't think I needed any help. I could handle work and school because I didn't have to feel. I didn't know how to cope emotionally and I locked myself off." He shrugged tiredly. "Cindy needed someone to be there for her who could feel and hold her when she cried. I wasn't doing the job. She found someone who could." He sighed. "I didn't blame her when she left me, and it only fueled my determination to keep all those feelings locked away. Every time I wrote a check for the doctor or the hospital, it was like Anna was right there with me. And it was okay. That's all I needed to survive. Or so I thought."

Unchecked tears streamed down Celine's face. All she could see in her mind was how alone he'd been, how driven and desperate. "What happened?" her voice was barely above a whisper.

"Eventually the bills were paid off and there was nothing left for me to do for Anna. Once the last check was written, it was like I'd lost my connection with her. I panicked. I looked around me and there was nothing. It was like this black tunnel waiting to swallow me up and I teetered right at the brink."

"What did you do?"

"I wandered the streets one night and then I heard the music. Early on when Cindy and I first got married, I fell on a part-time job working as a clown. I even had Pele's face registered with the clown registry. I found when Anna was so sick in the hospital, the only thing I could do to bring a smile to her face was to dress up like Pele. Behind the makeup was Peter who hurt when she hurt, but Pele could make her smile. It kind of stuck with me. The music came from the civic center. The Valentini Circus was doing a performance and it drew me. It acted like the one beacon in the darkness, a connection I could still have with Anna. Your grandfather hired me and it was the only thing that kept me from falling off the edge of the world."

He turned back to her and his vivid green gaze met hers. "And that's where I found you. You were a breath of sunshine and energy. You drew the goodness out of everyone around you. You became the light and the warmth for me."

"Until I fell."

He nodded. "Until you fell. I panicked. It wasn't until that moment that I realized how much I'd come to care for you and it scared me half to death. I'd only just begun to pull away from the edge of that black tunnel. Only just started to hope for something beyond merely existing. But the fact I almost lost you, that you almost died, sent me running again. And I pushed you away. I hurt you because I was a coward. In the end I wasn't there for Cindy and I wasn't there for you. And I couldn't save Anna."

"Oh, Peter, no. Don't say that. I just wish I'd known what you'd been through."

The doorbell sounded, diverting their attention and halting the conversation, slicing at the tension and sadness filling the room. Peter strode to the door. Celine had forgotten about the pizza he'd ordered.

She sat back and waited while he paid for it and spoke conversationally for a moment with the delivery person. Piecing everything together in her mind, she wondered how Peter had managed to maintain sanity after everything that had happened to him. He'd actually been younger than she was right now, yet the weight he'd shouldered was that of someone much older. Could she have survived the loss of a child? Their child?

Unconsciously, she placed a hand against her abdomen. It had to have been devastating. No wonder he'd closed himself off from her. Would she really have done any differently given the same set of circumstances? Unlikely.

She looked up as he walked back into the room carrying the box containing the pizza.

"Are you hungry?"

She shook her head. The thought of food right now turned her stomach. "Not really."

His look was one of sympathy. "I'm sorry. I didn't mean to upset you. I'll put this in the kitchen for now."

"You can go ahead and eat if you're hungry."

"I'm not. Maybe later."

He returned to the living room. "Well, now you know the whole story. All the grizzly details, including my feet of clay."

She looked up at him, horrified he would think such a thing. "How can you say that? You survived a terrible tragedy. You're right, I was too young to understand. If I'd been older, more worldly, I would have seen beneath the surface. I could have helped you."

It pained her to think if she'd been different, more mature, she could have soothed him, offered him some comfort. Instead, she'd only been concerned for herself. Her own pain at his rejection of her. She hadn't looked deeper for the answers. And she'd done her own share of running away. How could she blame him, when she'd done exactly the same thing?

He strode across the room and knelt in front of her. He took her tightly clenched fists into his hands and brought them to his lips. "Don't do this. I didn't tell you all of this for you to blame yourself for any of it."

She looked up at him, fighting the tears threatening to fall. "When you walked into my office seven days ago, I think we both stopped running."

She unclenched her fists and cupped his face. Such a strong face— handsome and sensitive. The memory of him was the reason she'd never been able to make a permanent commitment to any of her relationships. Daniel had been the closest she'd come. And the closer she came to telling him yes, the more vivid her dreams of Peter became. They'd literally demanded her attention.

If Peter hadn't walked into her office that day, she probably would have made the biggest mistake of her life. And she would have done it simply because she was scared of facing her own set of truths.

But he had. And she wasn't nineteen any longer. She needed to show him exactly how much she loved him and to heal the pain contained inside both of them.

She leaned forward and placed a kiss on each of his eyelids. "No more running, Peter. I need you to make love to me. I hurt with wanting you. Now. Please. It's you I hunger for. I've stopped running. Have you?"

CHAPTER 6

He couldn't believe the precious gift she was offering him. After everything he'd told her, she still wanted him. After knowing what a coward he was.

Pulling away from her, he leaned back on his heels. "I wouldn't have come to you if it hadn't been for Sebastian," he admitted. He needed her to know all his weaknesses.

"I know that. And I wouldn't have come back to the circus. We both would have been stuck on the fringes, in the shadows. We have Grandfather to thank for allowing us a second chance." She leaned toward him. "Let's not waste it this time." She moved to her knees, and wrapped her arms around his neck and drew his head down toward her. She felt him stiffen and she looked up questioningly.

He pulled away from her. She had to know all of it. "I don't know where this is going, but there's more I need you to know."

"What is it?"

"I don't want there to be another child. Do you understand what I'm saying? I can't go through that again."

He watched her closely, trying to gauge her reaction. He felt the loss when she pulled back.

"I understand how you must feel, but…" she trailed off.

He nodded, knowing she would leave him now. Seeing his cowardice for what it was.

She licked her lips. "I'm scared of saying the wrong thing," she began, then was silent for long moments.

He waited, giving her time.

"I want you, Peter. And one day I want to bear your children. I'd be lying if I said otherwise, and I want to be honest with you as well." Again, she leaned forward to cup his face, her eyes searching. "Are you dead set on this?"

"I want you to be happy, Celine. But I don't know that I can handle the possibility of losing another child."

Her fingers stroked the side of his face. He reached for her hand and brought it to his lips. Would he lose her now?

"I love you, Peter. I know your fears. It would be foolish for me to say I understand what you went through, because I haven't lost a child. This isn't something we need to decide today. I want to be with you. If that means no children, then it does. It's you I want; you I need. But I've tried to go on for seven years without you, and I don't want to do it any longer."

"I know, because. I feel the same. But before we go any further I wanted you to understand. You can still walk away."

"I do understand. That's everything. Right? No more secrets?"

"No more secrets," he confirmed.

"I'm not going anywhere. Living without you has been hell and I won't wait another second. No more words," she whispered as she drew him close again, her lips claiming his. They were soft and her taste was sweet and silky. He pulled her flat against him, felt her feminine curves surrender to him. His cock throbbed, his need to fill her, feeling velvet heat surround him sent him surging to his feet. He lifted her and she wound herself around him.

No fantasy, no dream, this was the real thing. Celine was in his arms, here in his home. And he had to have her in his bed.

"I need you, Celine," he growled, and he felt her cling tighter to him as he strode toward the bedroom.

Gently, he set her on the bed. She lay back and he knew his eyes held all the frustrated hunger of seven long years.

"I need to see you," he rasped out.

She sat up and moved her hands down to clasp the edges of her pink shirt. He stopped her, needed to peel away the wrappings himself. To discover all the secrets she had for him.

Lowering her arms she leaned back, her beautiful cornflower blue gaze locked with his. Waiting. He lifted the pink shirt up and over her head, revealing the flimsy transparent lace bra beneath. Her breasts were still enticingly hidden from his vision.

He tossed the shirt to the floor. Leaning forward, he captured a lace-covered nipple in his mouth, sucked at the hardened nub, teased with his tongue, his teeth, and Celine arched closer and gasped. He reached with his hand to knead her other sensitive nipple, then attended to it with his mouth. She tasted of sultry summer nights, her skin soft and supple beneath his questing mouth.

"Peter—" Her voice was low and husky.

Raising his head, he studied her flushed cheeks, her heavy-lidded bedroom gaze. Again he lowered his head, branding kisses along her midriff, his hand reaching to unclasp the gold chain belt and then unbuttoning and sliding the zipper of her pants open.

His cock pushed painfully against the front of his jeans as he lowered his mouth to capture and tongue the little gold ring at her belly. He raised his head. "When I saw you at the airport, this little ring almost drove me crazy, do you know that?"

He felt her chuckle. "I felt rather wicked when I had it done."

"What possessed you to have your belly pierced? It's damn sexy." Although he wasn't sure he wanted the answer, he needed to ask the question.

"It was a birthday dare from a friend."

He lifted his head to pierce her with a look. "A friend?" His hands gripped her waist, a possessive surge rising through him.

"A *girl*friend, Peter."

He felt the tension ease from his shoulders. Blowing lightly across the center of her stomach, he pushed her white trousers down her legs and dropped them to the floor.

"Damn, you smell sweet. Like a field of wildflowers, clean and pure." He shifted her farther onto the bed. He was ravenous to taste her. Her arousal permeated his senses and was evidenced by the wet texture of her white bikini panties. He slid them down her legs and tossed them behind him.

"Peter, I need to touch you, to see you as well." Her voice was breathy, holding an aching desire at the fringes. One he wanted to fan into full blown flame.

"You will, sweetheart. Soon." But first things first. He spread her thighs, found the moist lips of her center. The pale curls of her mound glistened, her lips slick with her dewy nectar.

Had he ever seen such a beautiful sight? Her desire was for him. An overwhelming urgency surged through him. How many times had he dreamed about this moment? He lowered his head and with his tongue traced the line of her tender slit. He felt her moan hum against his lips. Her pelvis jerked upward and he sank his tongue deep into her liquid velvet core. With his thumb he teased at her clit, feeling it swell and harden beneath his ministrations. She was so damn responsive to him.

Lifting one of her legs, he placed her foot flat on the bed, then did the same with the other one. He opened her further, admiring her deep pink clit, hard with arousal, her labia engorged with her passion. He knew she was at the edge, ready to soar, but he didn't want her to fall quite yet.

He leaned back and gazed up at her. His balls tightened and his cock throbbed with the need to feel her velvet heat surrounding him. But he'd waited too long and he was going to savor every succulent inch of her, knowing the minute his cock entered her, he wouldn't last long.

Her head was thrown back against the pillows, her lacy-covered breasts rose and fell with each panting breath. The little gold ring at her navel teased him, had him burning. He'd never get enough of her.

"You're a vision for a drowning man," he rasped out, then moved back. He dipped to her thighs, placing kisses along her inner sensitive flesh, forcing her higher. Running his tongue along the crease, he then turned his attention to her other leg.

He slid one finger into her vagina, and her heat almost singed him. Another finger joined the first. "You're so hot and ready for me, baby." Slowly, in long strokes, he fucked her with his fingers as he feasted at her thighs. Her creamy passion scented the air around him, filling his world. A fine sheen covered her body, her cries of need echoing in the room.

Her hips arched and rotated, responding to every touch of his tongue, his fingers, his lips. Finally, he clamped his mouth over her clit and drove his fingers deep as her climax pulsed through her. Her screams of release filled all his senses. Her pleasure wrapped around him and his dick responded, pressing hard for release.

He moved up the bed and pulled her into his arms, petting and stroking her as she shuddered and slowly returned from the summit of emotion.

He looked down at her as she lay within his arms. She was everything that encompassed his dreams—his fantasies of the woman to share his life. He shuddered at the thought of losing her again and his arms tightened around her.

She tilted her head back and looked up at him through slitted eyes, a small contented smile on her lips. Raising a hand, she stroked the side of his face. "Now that you've got me warmed up, I think you need to shed some clothes, mister. We're not done."

He grinned down at her. "Hell no, baby. We've got a lot of time to make up for. I've just started."

*　　*　　*

Through eyes heavy-lidded with need, Celine watched him rise from the bed like a sleek panther. The pleasurable strains of the mind-boggling climax he'd given her still held her in its grasp.

But she needed him filling her, leaving no room for the loneliness they'd both experienced over the last years. She needed his warmth and passion like she'd never experienced before.

Quickly, he shed his clothes and she experienced a driving stab of lust and heat overwhelming her. Her gaze fell to the hard, thick shaft springing free as he pushed his jeans down his legs and stepped out of them.

She rose to her knees, his naked body calling to hers and moved to the edge of the bed. Reaching out, she surrounded his hard flesh with her hand. He inhaled sharply. "You're beautiful," she breathed. Slowly, she traced her fingers along the soft ridge. Velvet steel spasmed beneath her touch. A hint of pre-cum glimmered on the head and with her index finger she spread the creamy liquid over the circumference and along the slit, then brought her finger to her lips and sucked. It tasted musky and exotic.

Her gaze rose to Peter's face and she noted his expression was filled with heavy lust, his green eyes dark and needy. Her gaze held his. "I've never tasted a man's cum before."

His nostrils flared. "Never?" he asked, his voice low and gritty.

"No. I've never wanted to."

"What about now?" He fisted the root of his heavy penis with one hand and shifted his pelvis forward. "Your sweet lips wrapped around my cock would feel like pure heaven about now."

She looked down at the purple head he presented to her. It glistened along the slit as more pre-cum oozed. Again reaching out, she clasped one hand over his, with the other she curled her fingers around his balls, then lowered her head and took him into her mouth. His groan of pleasure wrapped around her.

He was so big, so thick. She swirled her tongue beneath the ridge, along the slit. Tasted him, kneaded his sacs, felt him wind his fingers in her hair, pulling her closer. Heat rose and spiraled through her. As she sucked and took him deeper, the fire in her belly seared through her. His taste was hot and male, pulling her farther into the vortex of passion.

"Goddamn, yes," he groaned. "Take me, sweetheart. Suck it. Deeper." He thrust his hips forward. She moved her hands and clasped the cheeks of his ass, felt him tighten, then he quickly moved back, pulling his shaft free from her mouth. "No more."

His heavy gaze moved over her as she sat before him on the bed. "Take off your bra," he ground out.

Celine reached behind her and unsnapped the clasp. She drew the straps down along her arms and tossed it aside. Peter's hot gaze slid over her.

He reached out a hand and teased a firm nipple and she gasped at the sensation. With his other hand he forced her thighs apart and tested her readiness. "You're ready for me. And I'm more than ready to take you."

Turning from her he opened the nightstand drawer and reached inside to remove a small packet.

Celine leaned over, stopping him. He looked up at her questioningly. "No. It's okay. I'm protected. I want to feel you inside me. Only you. Please."

A sigh of relief left her when he nodded, slowly replaced the packet and closed the drawer. He trusted her and she would never betray that trust, no matter how much she wanted his child. With any other man she wouldn't have suggested it, but with Peter it was different. She couldn't stand the thought of any barrier separating them. Turning back to her, with gentle hands, he lay her down and spread her legs. Centering himself above her, he claimed her lips. She surrendered herself willingly to his coaxing tongue.

His hard shaft separated and pierced her channel. With slow, steady pressure he entered her. His tongue wooed her lips, circling, spearing, thrusting. His cock teased her vagina, penetrated and retreated, a little more each time, until finally he was lodged fully inside her. He claimed her all the way to her soul. What she felt was too overpowering for mere words.

"God," he whispered. "You feel so good. Like sliding through warm, liquid silk." He licked her lips, tracing the rims. "Whiskey satin," he murmured, before thrusting his tongue deep inside.

He captured her moans of pleasure, her sobs of joy. His shaft tunneled deep, separating her, filling her. Hot, liquid heat pumped through her veins. She arched toward him. He pulled back and surged forward, moving into a steady rhythm. As his cock moved out, his tongue thrust in. His hands tugged and kneaded her sensitive nipples. There was no part of her body not responding to the pleasure of his possession.

He built a steady rhythm, thrust and retreat, plunge and tease, until her world was swept away and the only thing left was for her body to respond to his touch, his thrusts, his demands.

He swept her up, up until she couldn't breathe, all she could do was beg for release.

"Please, oh, God, please," she begged him. Her own hips arching to meet him, fire for fire. And then she screamed and shattered as sensations built and released. She felt him plunge once more, and lodge deeply inside her and she held him close as he followed her into the purity of their shared culmination of bliss.

She murmured a protest as he retreated from inside her, feeling empty. He pulled her into his arms and stroked her hair. "I can't let you go."

Celine snuggled closer. "Nobody asked you to. I don't want to be anywhere else but here, with you."

"Are you sure?"

She nodded against his chest. "Yes, I'm sure. You're the only man who's filled my dreams for the last seven years. There wasn't room for anyone else."

"Dreams, huh? What kind of dreams?" His hands stroking her body were fueling her passion again. How could she need him so soon after that last explosive climax?

She reached down and stroked his semi-erect penis. Obviously, he wasn't unaffected either. "Just dreams." There was no way she could tell him the exact nature of those fantasies.

He captured her lips, stroked with his tongue. His other hand moved to her mound. "You want me again." Two fingers entered her and she opened her thighs, sighing with pleasure. "What kind of dreams?"

She gasped as his fingers began to slowly tunnel into her sensitive channel, spiraling her upward yet again. "I can't tell you," she gasped, her hips arching against his fingers, wanting him deeper.

He moved above her, his thick shaft poised at her slick entrance. One thrust and he sank fully inside her, grinding his hips against her. She shuddered with need. He stopped. She arched toward him. He halted the movement with a hand to each side of her hips.

Lowering his head, he nuzzled at her neck. "What kind of dreams?" He nibbled her ear, a stab of desire arrowed through her. His breath sent tingles shimmering along her body.

She whimpered. "Peter, this isn't fair."

He pulled back and speared deep. Once. Ground against her clit. Once.

"All right," she moaned. As she haltingly relayed her most erotic fantasy, he moved in and out in slow rhythm with her words, drawing out her pleasure, grinding against her, heating and stoking her passion. And as she finally gasped the last words, he plunged deep. She screamed as he sent her falling over the precipice and again into the waiting arms of delirious, heavenly oblivion.

*   *   *

Celine turned and stretched like a cat after a delicious nap. She blinked rapidly at the morning sunlight as it struck her full in the face. Turning away and pulling the blanket up over her, she needed a moment to become fully awake. Maybe several moments to remember and savor the memory of making love with Peter. Last night was no dream. Her lips curved upward in a very satisfied smile.

She felt heat rise in her cheeks at the thought of revealing her erotic dreams to him. "Oh, God, I can't believe I did that," she mumbled to herself and slunk farther down under the covers.

If he hadn't incited such a haze of lust in her, wild horses wouldn't have drawn that information out of her. But he had. Swear to God, his hands were secret weapons. Her lips curved up yet again and she rubbed her face against the pillow remembering how those magic hands of his had played her body so well. She inhaled his scent from the pillow.

As erotic and exciting as her dream-lover Pele had been, the sensual reality of Peter was so much more. His kisses, his steely length filling her—no, the dream would never be competition for his presence in her bed. In her life.

She heard a sound coming from the adjoining bathroom. It was humming. Pushing the covers back, she slipped from the bed. Grabbing the top sheet, she wrapped it around her sarong fashion. In the light of day she felt a little self-conscious about walking around naked.

Scanning the room, she noticed her clothes strewn around the floor. Since she didn't have her luggage with her, she decided to hunt for a pair of his jogging pants and a T-shirt she could borrow, because she didn't relish the same wrinkled clothes she'd traveled in yesterday.

The sound of his voice drew her toward the bathroom. She stood in the doorway observing him. Darn, but she felt her body responding already to his presence. He'd obviously recently taken a shower and stood before the sink. Blue jeans hung low on his hips, hugging his delicious ass. He was shirtless, and his golden muscles rippled as he moved the electric shaver smoothly over his firm jaw and down his throat.

She clutched at the sheet wound around her. How would he feel this morning? Would he be sorry he'd made love to her?

He set the shaver down and turned toward her, leaning negligently against the ridge of the sink. She fidgeted with the edge of the sheet, looked downward at the black and white tiled floor. He moved toward her, and her gaze was caught by the dark hairs along his lower abdomen arrowing down beneath the waistband of the jeans. A wave of heat swamped over her, knowing what those soft blue jeans hid.

Putting his hand beneath her chin, he forced her to look at him. "Having second thoughts?"

Her eyes widened in surprise. "No, of course not. But I thought you might be."

He lowered his head and kissed her. The scent of his aftershave and soap swamped through her. The kiss didn't carry the same carnal heat of the night before, but teased and seduced. Promised. She tasted peppermint toothpaste and realized she was sorely in need of a long shower and clean teeth.

Lifting his head, he looked into her eyes. "No second thoughts here. But damn, if I stand here much longer, I'm going to have you back in bed before breakfast. You're much too sexy wrapped up in my sheet."

She pulled back and walked around him. "I'm thinking a shower is definitely in order first. Then breakfast. Do you by chance have an extra toothbrush?"

He pointed to the medicine cabinet over the sink. "There should be an unopened one in there."

She started to drop the sheet, then looked over at him expectantly. "Well?"

He looked back innocently. "Well what?"

With one hand she motioned for him to leave. "Out. Go fix coffee or something."

The grin that spread across his face had a bit of the devil in it. "But

I wanted to watch."

"What? Are you a voyeur or something?" The thought of him watching send a shaft of desire racing through her. At this rate, they'd never get past the bedroom. Years of pent up desire were taking their toll.

He leered at her. "Only with you, sweetheart." She threw a towel at him and he quickly turned and ducked. Leaving the bathroom, she could hear him chuckling from the other room.

She laughed and shook her head as she turned the shower on. A shaft of fear raced through her by the fact it all felt too right to be here with him. To have wanted this for so long and finally be here was overwhelming.

Dropping the sheet, she stepped into the shower. She was a tad sore and the soothing rain of warm heat felt good. She'd take it one day at a time.

Feeling human again and with a clean towel wrapped around her, she walked into the bedroom. She could smell bacon and her stomach rumbled at the thought of food.

At the dresser she pulled open the top drawer looking for something to borrow to wear. She found a soft gray T-shirt imprinted with the Valentini Circus logo. She dropped the towel and pulled the shirt over her head. It engulfed her and its hem fell to just above her knees. Now for some jogging pants or shorts with a tie maybe. Just something she could wear until she'd had a chance to wash her own clothes.

None of the top drawers offered what she was looking for. She knelt and opened the bottom drawer. Her eyes widened in surprise at what she found. The drawer was filled with neatly stacked letters. Feeling like an intruder, she quickly moved to shut the drawer, but her eyes fell on the inscription on the top envelope closest to her. It was her name.

She sank to a cross-legged sitting position and with trembling fingers, pulled the envelope out of the drawer. She looked back in the drawer and saw another pile of envelopes, but these were addressed to Anna. Icy fingers crawled along her arms. Again, she looked back at the envelope in her hand and bit her lip. It wasn't sealed and it was addressed to her. Slowly, she lifted the flap.

CHAPTER 7

Dear Celine,

Another sleepless night without you. Will my memories of you forever haunt me? I can't forget you, no matter how much I try. Are you happy? Have you found someone to love you the way you deserve to be loved?

I look into the bitter emptiness that's become my life and I ache for your warmth. I want to come to you, but I know you merit more than what I'm able to offer. I know I could never make you happy.

I'm surrounded by the bleak night and the echoes of the silent, bleeding cries of loneliness are my only company.

Have you found happiness, sweetheart? I'll never know for certain, will I? My heart is a coward, unable to reach out to you other than in the dead of night.

Tears falling, Celine folded the letter and carefully placed it back into the envelope. With shaking fingers she lifted another from the stack and opened it.

Dearest Celine,
Another night of agony without you. Without Anna. I told you about my daughter, remember?

"What are you doing?"
She dropped the letter and whirled around to look up at Peter who

was standing in the doorway, a shuttered, shadowed expression on his face. His eyes were narrowed, pinpoints of hard, glittering emerald chips, lips drawn tight. An expression so terribly still, yet fierce, it might have been carved from rock.

He leaned down and picked up the letters, with deliberate intent, tossing them haphazardly back into the drawer and slamming it closed.

"I-I was looking for something clean to wear. I thought there might be some jogging pants."

Pivoting sharply, he turned away from her. "You should have asked." He strode to a tall dresser on the other side of the room. With short, jerky movements he opened a drawer, and tossed a pair of navy blue jogging pants onto the bed. Then he slammed the drawer shut, the dresser shuddering in protest.

"Try those," he bit out. His hands were clenched around the brass handles of the drawer and he wouldn't turn around to look at her. She felt his anger reach out to claw at her.

Celine unfolded her legs, rose from the floor, and walked to the bed. With shaking hands, she hastily wiped at the traces of tears that covered her cheeks from reading each word of the letters. The tense silence in the room clung to her, heavy and thick like a dense New England fog.

Swiftly, she pulled on the pants and tightened the belt. They were much too large for her slender frame, but at least the rope belt would keep them in place. She wanted to say something, to ease the tension, but she didn't know how to start.

"Peter, why didn't you send the letters?" she asked quietly.

"You were never meant to see them. They weren't letters to be sent."

She walked up behind him, some sense of self-preservation telling her if she didn't connect with him now, everything she'd gained would be lost. The distance he'd placed between them was growing with each minute, and she was frantic with the need to close the gap. As she raised a hand to his shoulder, he must have sensed it because he swiftly turned and moved across the room, away from her.

He was doing it again. Trying to distance himself from her. Reseal the wall he was so fond of hiding behind.

"I won't let you do it," she said determinedly. She walked toward him with steady steps. "You aren't going to put this gulf between us again."

He glanced up at her as though in shock. "What?"

She reached him, tilted her head back and with a look, demanded his attention. "You're trying to do what you did seven years ago." She reached for his hand and brought his fingers to her lips, kissing each finger. "It's too late," she whispered.

His breathing stuttered when she uncurled his index finger and took it into her mouth and sucked. She heard the whoosh as he inhaled sharply. He brought his other hand up to tangle in her hair, his eyes darkening.

"You have no idea what you're letting yourself in for." Pulling his finger from her mouth, he forced her head back and punctuated with a hard, demanding kiss. He cupped her head, holding her in place and in that kiss she felt all the need and loneliness he'd held inside like a greedy beggar, erupt and wash over her.

Leaning into him, she opened to him, taking his pain inside her, letting him know he'd never be alone again. She transmitted her commitment to him the only way she knew how.

When he pulled back she murmured a protest, but he halted her with the emerald hard determination in his gaze.

"I won't be easy to live with, but I want us to try. There are nights when the fears strangle me and they could hurt you, without me wanting them to."

She reached up to touch the side of his face and smiled. "Who said I'd be easy to live with? It seems to me we both have a tad too much stubborn. But I'm willing to try if you are. At least now I know what I'm fighting. Before, I didn't have a clue. You had so many secrets." She placed a hand over his heart. "So much you kept locked away."

"Okay then." He stepped away from her and reached for her hand. "First, some breakfast, then we'll go to your grandfather's. We'll see how he's doing and pick up your luggage."

She halted just inside the living room. "Seems you have the day planned already. I don't remember you being this organized before."

He turned back to her and grinned. "It comes from being half-owner in Valentini's, I guess. Unfortunately, I didn't get much accomplished yesterday, so it's double time today. With your grandfather ill and heading for surgery, it's up to me to handle the brunt of the office work. He was handling most of the administrative stuff before, but since the diagnosis and doctor's orders, he's out of commission for a while. We have a benefit performance coming up for the Children's Hospital in a few weeks and a lot to do before then."

"I can help with that," she offered.

"Planning on getting back in shape to do some high flying?"

The smile left her face. At the thought of getting back up on the trapeze, she shuddered.

"No, I— I can't. I was thinking of the office work." In that moment she knew somehow she was letting him down.

Strong, warm fingers lifted her chin. "Hey. It's all right. I was just teasing. I don't particularly want to see you up there anyway."

Shrugging, she offered a shaky smile. "I'm sorry. I guess I have a few of my own devils still lurking."

"You'll face them when the time is right. And, yes, I can use your expertise in the office. Nina's been helping with the program layout in her spare time."

Celine remembered back to the day before when Nina had touched Peter in what she'd interpreted as more than friendly affection.

She looked at Peter uncertainly. "About Nina. Is there...has there been anything between you two?"

Peter laughed. "Nina and me? You're kidding, right? Nina and I are like oil and water. No offense, honey, but she's a predatory feline disguised as a woman. She requires a handler, not a lover."

She felt heat rise into her cheeks as she remembered telling him about her dream. "I wonder what that makes me?" she mumbled.

Peter pulled her toward him, his hands gripping her buttocks and squeezing. He nuzzled her neck. "You, my love, are like one of those sleek, Egyptian exotic beauties. Elegant and silky." He grazed her ear lightly with his teeth and she made a small sound deep in her throat.

"Peter," she gasped as heat flooded through her.

He stopped her by capturing her lips, and thrusting his tongue into her mouth, claiming her. Releasing her lips, he raised his head, and gave what she could only interpret as a possessive, satisfied smile.

"That little sound you made. That was a purr. If I pet you just right, can I hear it again?"

Celine burst out laughing and hit his shoulder. He released her.

"As I said, Nina's a predator. And you? You're all pleasure. Mine."

Celine felt a weight lift. She inwardly breathed a sigh of relief. Her relationship with Nina was strained enough without adding another sin to her supposed many as far as Nina was concerned. Ever since Celine had been given top billing above her name, Nina's attitude had cooled toward her.

She hoped that since she no longer performed, maybe she could mend fences with their relationship. She'd never wanted top billing over Nina. Would have gladly given it up, but Uncle Alberto wouldn't hear of it. He'd said she had a gift and her performance would draw a good crowd. Nevertheless, it hadn't set well with her, and had caused a rift with Nina.

"I had to ask. It just seemed yesterday that you might have been more involved than just friends."

"You mean that little display of hers at your grandfather's?" His intent stare had her shifting uneasily. "She's always known how I felt about you. My guess is she was trying to get to you. You and Nina are as different as night and day. I've never had an interest in pursuing a relationship with her. Come on, let's get some breakfast."

She followed him into the kitchen, helped set the table as he finished preparing breakfast. It felt good and right to be here beside him.

As they sat drinking coffee, she decided to broach the subject of the letters once more—she wanted to know why he'd written them. Why he hadn't wanted her to see or read what they contained.

"Peter?"

He looked up from perusing the daily newspaper. "Yes?"

"I want you to tell me about the letters. I don't need to read what you wrote," she added hastily, "but I want to know about them. Why didn't you send them?"

Sighing, he carefully folded the paper and set it aside. "You can't let it go, can you? You were never meant to see them or know they existed."

"Then why did you write them?"

"They were my connection with sanity. The middle of the night is the worst time to wake up alone. Especially from dreams...or nightmares. Writing to you and to Anna helped me to keep my feet planted. It started out in desperation, but eventually it became a balm. Like meditating to release stress."

He leaned back in his chair and looked at her. "I'd envision you, curled up in the chair, listening to me. When I wrote to you, I could feel you there with me and the panic I always woke up with would ease. Once I'd poured it all out on paper, I was able to sleep."

He shifted in his chair, turned and gazed out the window. "I started writing to Anna and I think it was sort of a way for me to get through grieving for her. I'd never taken the time to do that before." He shrugged. "Writing the letters made my days bearable. Eventually, it got easier and easier. I finally was able to go into the hospital without it tearing me apart with memories. Spending time with the children there has helped a lot. The letters were never meant to be mailed."

"They were how you healed yourself in a way." Those letters apparently represented a way for him to release all the pain he'd bottled up inside, sort of an emergency valve to relieve the pressure. "I think I understand. I'm sorry I intruded by reading them."

"Don't. It just took me by surprise to see you sitting there. I'd envisioned you so many times. But there was also the fact that watching you read, seeing your tears, was like ripping my chest open again and exposing my shredded insides. I didn't want you to read the letters because I don't want you to ever feel that kind of pain."

She got up and walked around the table to sit in his lap. She wound her arms around his neck and leaned against his shoulder, inhaling his scent. This was where she was always meant to be.

"No more hiding," she said as she placed a hand over his chest, and felt the strong, steady rhythm. "You're going to have to push awfully hard to get rid of me now. I've got your number, mister."

He wrapped his arms around her and pulled her tight against him. "Remind me to thank Sebastian."

She laughed. "Something tells me he already knows. I've got the feeling he did it on purpose."

"I doubt very much he tried to give himself a heart attack on purpose."

She raised her head and looked up at him. "Think not? Well, maybe. But that old man is certainly one to use it to his advantage. I must say, I'm glad he did this time."

"He talks about you all the time. He's missed you, Celine. So you're probably right. He used it this time as leverage to get you back."

"And used you as the carrot to make it happen. Definitely, a sly old dog."

*   *   *

Luckily Celine's clothes were the wash and wear kind. After running them through Peter's washing machine and dryer, she once again was ready to go. She couldn't show up at her grandfather's dressed in Peter's T-shirt and jogging pants.

Just before they left the apartment, Celine had called her grandfather to check on him. He'd assured her he was just fine and to take her time because Nina had stopped over.

Nina. Things had all happened in such a flurry, she hadn't had time to think about much other than resolving her relationship with Peter.

Now that they'd found each other again, her thoughts turned to the tumultuous relationship with her sister.

She loved her sister, but she didn't understand her. They should have been closer, having lost their parents so young. But she'd always felt there was something dark beneath Nina's exterior. She'd tried so hard to understand and to close the rift.

When Celine had fallen, Nina had stayed by her side as she'd recovered from the minor injuries, expressing heartfelt concern. It had been the first time she'd felt they could mend whatever had caused the breach. But once Celine left, in seven years she hadn't heard a word from Nina. What information she did glean had come from Uncle Alberto.

It didn't set well with Celine. She loved her family and had regular contact with Uncle Alberto and her grandfather. They'd kept her apprised of what the family was doing, and often encouraged her to return to the circus, her home, and her extended family. They assured her everyone was always asking after her.

But it had taken Sebastian's life-threatening situation to make her finally return home.

She hoped it wasn't too late to find a way to reach Nina. It hurt every time she thought about her. But there was something in her manner that had always kept her at arm's length.

Now was the time to mend fences. And she was determined to discover the reason behind Nina's attitude. And to assure her, she didn't want her limelight.

"You look pensive. What are you thinking about?" Peter asked her as they walked toward the parking lot outside his apartment.

She glanced up at him. "I was just wondering how Nina will take the news that I'm staying here."

CHAPTER 8

The last two weeks had practically flown by. Although Celine had spent a considerable part of that time with her grandfather, she'd also settled into a routine helping with the workload at the office on the circus grounds. Sebastian's surgery was scheduled for the next day and Celine wanted to make sure all the paperwork was cleared up so she could be with him at the hospital.

Even in the off season, there were so many little details to be taken care of. She didn't know how Peter thought he could do it by himself. Of course, she knew he could get help from one of the temporary agencies in town, and several of the performers were often more than willing to help out on occasion. It wasn't the same though as having someone experienced, and who knew the intricacies of what needed to be done behind the scenes for the performance to run smoothly.

There were choreographers, trainers, costume designers, publicity people, drivers, mechanics, and a sundry of other employees at all levels of performance. Even though Valentini's was considered a smaller circus by far than one like Ringling's, it certainly had its share of organizational needs to be coordinated.

In the winter season, the Valentini Circus settled in the small town of Crispin on the outskirts of the larger metropolis of Orlando. Many of the employees maintained apartments, some lived in motor homes, or rented rooms at the local motels. Some of the acts, like The Flying Valentinis had other commitments during the winter months and often were on the road doing smaller performances throughout the country.

Others were stationary and practiced and worked on new acts. All the performers were required to stay at peak performance condition.

Though considered for all intents and purposes to be on hiatus, it was still a busy atmosphere with people exercising animals, practicing routines, and repairing equipment. Each day the gates were opened to the public in the afternoon, an admission was charged, and visitors could attend practices and watch the daily routine of performers, both human and animals.

It had always felt like an extended family to Celine. Some of the acts were transient—held contracts for short-term performances—other faces it seemed she'd known all her life. It was certainly never boring, and everyone always worked hard.

Sebastian ran everything with an iron grip. He allowed no disrespect among the performers. At the least hint of a problem, the offender was gone. He was the first one to try to give someone a break who was down on their luck, but get caught stealing, lying, or drinking on the job just once and he had little tolerance.

As he often told her, this was his family, and nothing would jeopardize their safety, he didn't care how good the person was at their job.

It was like a small village, a melting pot of nationalities where everyone knew everyone else and lent a helping hand when it was needed. Nowhere else had Celine ever felt that sense of camaraderie and family. She now realized how much she'd missed it.

Having Peter's love only enhanced her pleasure and contentment in returning to the circus and her family. It had been a long time since she'd felt she actually belonged someplace.

It was quiet now, the end of day nearing. Peter had left to meet with Sebastian to bring him up to date on the latest developments. Like Sebastian, Peter also managed everything closely, ran a tight ship, and Celine admired how well he fit the role. She sensed the respect everyone had for him when they came to meet with him, or when she'd observe him out and around the grounds, never hesitating to lend an extra hand when it was needed.

When Helga's husband had run off for what was apparently the third time this year, Peter had quietly met with her to offer her assistance for her and the baby until Jorge returned. He'd promised to talk with Jorge one more time, tried to soothe her fears about being turned out with no way to feed her son. Celine had been so proud of him and how he'd handled such a delicate situation.

She rose from her chair and stretched. Walking over to the open door, she stepped out and stood on the top step, surveying the grounds. A few handlers walked the horses, feeders were at several of the animal cages, but the day was winding down. The security guards had already closed and locked the main gates.

There would be one evening performance, with all the glitter and pomp of a high-profile exhibition, to be held at the beginning of February. The proceeds would benefit the Children's Hospital—this was apparently one of Peter's special projects. She was looking forward to it and would have the chance to participate in the Grand Finale parade.

It still bothered her that she couldn't bring herself to face the trapeze. Not even the lower riggings set for exercise. Celine wondered if she'd ever get over her fear of heights and be able to fly again. Would she ever feel like she could trust the equipment? Consciously, she knew it wasn't anyone's fault, but still…

She turned to walk back inside the office. Maybe someday, but right now it was paperwork that filled her time, not the adrenalin of flying through the air.

"Celine!"

She turned as Nina hurried up to her. Her voice was tinged with a sense of urgency.

"What is it Nina? Is there a problem?"

Nina was out of breath as she reached the steps of the office. "I need your help. Please. Come with me, before it's too late."

Celine pulled the office door closed and locked it. "I'm coming. What's happened?"

"No time," Nina called as she raced ahead of her. Celine hurried after her without hesitation. Nina disappeared inside the Big Top tent.

She followed at a slightly slower pace. As she pulled back the flap and entered the dim interior, she was met by silence. She peered through the dusky expanse, but there didn't seem to be anyone inside. What could the emergency be?

"Nina?" she called out to her sister, her voice echoing back.

"I'm here," her answer came from the shadows, followed by a click and the spotlight flickered on. Then she appeared from the far side.

A trickle of fear raced up Celine's spine at the glittering intensity in the expression on Nina's face. "What's the emergency?"

"I thought it was time we had a private chat." Slowly, Nina walked toward her.

"Why here?"

"The circus is our life. Well, at least it's my life. You shouldn't have come back."

Celine instinctively retreated. Something wasn't right.

"This," Nina gestured in a wide circle, "is mine. I thought it was made clear to you seven years ago there was no place for you here. You don't belong." She raised her hand that had been hidden behind her back.

Celine gasped, her eyes widening in shock at the small deadly black revolver gripped tightly in Nina's hand.

"What are you doing? You're my sister. Put that thing away."

Nina shook her head. "First you took all of Sebastian's affection. Then you took the spotlight. You always had to have the attention focused on you." Her laughter was hard and held a bitter twist to it. "But I found a way to stop you. Unfortunately, you were supposed to die and didn't. That was disappointing."

Celine kept her attention focused on the gun held firmly in Nina's hand. "Why? I never wanted top billing. I tried to tell you that. You could have had it, all of it. Grandfather loves both of us. How can you say he doesn't love you?"

"You fool! Did you know a representative of Ringling's approached him seven years ago? They wanted to sign you. I overheard them talking, working out details. They were going to talk to you that night, after your performance. I couldn't let that happen."

Celine thought her heart would break as unwelcome knowledge swamped her. "You loosened the rigging? You tried to kill me?"

"After the last inspection I climbed up and loosened the bolts just enough—or so I thought. Your performance lasted longer than I expected. If it hadn't been for Peter, you probably would have been killed."

Yes, somehow Peter had been there to cushion her from connecting with the hard ground. She'd already been making her way down the rope when it released. They'd both sustained bruises, but it could have been far worse.

"Why this?" She indicated the gun. "You got what you wanted in any event. I'm no threat to you now. I can't even tolerate the thought of climbing up the ladder let alone performing."

"Maybe not, but I know you're planning to marry Peter."

"What should that have to do with anything? You'll still be in the spotlight. It will still all be yours. My marrying Peter won't change that."

"Did you know that Sebastian has left his share of the circus to us—you and me? Uncle Alberto wants no part of it." Her hand tightened on the gun. "But apparently he still doesn't trust me, because he's made you trustee of my share. I found a copy of the Will at his apartment. After everything I've done, he's had the nerve to think I would tolerate you policing me."

Celine cringed inwardly at the hate she saw emanating from her sister's eyes. "Nina, I never knew. Let me talk to him. We'll go together, get him to change it."

"It's too late. When you marry Peter you'll be in control of the other half as well. I can't tolerate it. Do you understand? My younger sister in control of me. Nobody controls me!"

So much rage poured out of Nina, like toxic dredge, it spilled over and sought to drown Celine in its poison. This absolute hate was what Nina had kept hidden all these years.

How could she not have known?

Nina took a deep breath. "Walk to the ladder."

Celine hesitated. She couldn't be planning what she thought. "Nina, let's talk this out. Please don't do this."

"Now!" Nina's loud command, punctuated by her raising the gun, caused Celine to flinch and begin walking.

If she could only gain some time, maybe someone would walk in. She stopped at the ladder, looked up, and shuddered.

"Start climbing." Nina nudged her with the gun at the small of her back.

Celine felt like she was in the center of a nightmare with no way to awaken. She kicked off her shoes and lifted one foot to the first rung. "Nina, please," she begged, her voice trembling with fear.

Again, she felt the hard nose of the gun jabbed against her back. "Climb and don't stop until you reach the platform. Remember, I'll be right behind you."

As slowly as she could, Celine climbed, one rung at a time, afraid to look down, afraid to let go. It ran through her mind that if Nina followed close enough behind her, she might be able to kick the gun from her hand. Unfortunately, she stayed just far enough out of reach.

She prayed that someone, anyone, would walk in and see them. She had to find a way to stop her sister before it was too late. For both of them.

Finally, she reached the platform and stepped onto the small claustrophobic space. Nina followed right behind her.

"What now, Nina? You're my sister, for God's sake. You can't mean to shoot me." Tears flooded her eyes at the knowledge of how much her sister must despise her to do this.

"This is my world, my domain, do you understand?"

"Yes, I do. It's always been yours, I never wanted to take it from you."

"But you did. Look down, Celine."

"No."

"Look down! That's where you belong. Do you see the net?"

A tight fist of panic grabbing her, Celine lowered her gaze to the ground far below. It seemed to call to her and she weaved, a sense of dizziness overcoming her as she felt the lightheaded effects of falling crawl through her. She reached out and clutched at a pole to help ground and steady her.

"Yes," she gasped, "I see the net."

"Good. I'm not going to shoot you. I won't have to. I loosened the lines on the net. It will look like an accident."

With determination she focused on Nina and raised her chin defiantly. "I won't jump. You'll have to shoot me."

Nina smiled coldly. "No, I won't have to shoot you. You'll jump. But the net won't hold. This time I made absolutely certain. It will look like an accident. Like you were trying to overcome your fear of heights and...well...."

Menacingly, she moved toward Celine. As she reached out and was about to push her, Celine twisted and grabbed for the gun. They struggled, as Celine tried to gain control and push Nina away. Nina clamped down on Celine's hand, straining to pry her loose.

With a superhuman effort, Celina yanked free and pushed. Nina fell back, grabbed at Celine's leg, managing to catch at the fabric of Celine's trousers, pulling her off the edge of the platform with her. Celine kicked out in an instinctive gesture of self-preservation as she was pulled over the side of the platform, clawing for purchase, her nails digging in desperately.

She heard Nina gasp and cry out as Celine's other foot connected with her chin. Suddenly she was free of Nina's weight. As she clutched the edge of the platform, she heard Nina's screams echoed throughout the huge tent as she plunged to the ground.

Gasping for breath, her arm muscles bunched with the pain of gripping to life, legs dangling, Celine glanced down at the ground.

Nina lay sprawled, her head tilted at an odd angle, blood oozing beneath her to spread across the ground She'd totally missed the altered safety net and impacted with the hard earth full force.

Celine frantically looked around her, needing some way to regain safe footing. Her fingertip stranglehold on the platform wouldn't hold forever. Then her gaze connected with the performance rope dangling several feet away. It had failed her once; did she dare make the attempt to reach for it?

It would require her to release the platform, twist, and still have enough strength left to catch and grip the rope. God, she didn't know if she could do it.

Again, she looked down at the ground from the dizzying height. If she missed the rope, she'd be killed for certain. This wasn't the way she'd planned to face her fear of heights.

There was no one to help; she was going to have to do it on her own. Sweat clung to her and her hands shifted; her tenuous grip on the platform wouldn't last much longer. Inhaling deeply, she visualized Peter in her mind. The need to live for him and for herself and their life together. Taking determination in hand, she released her hold on the ledge, twisted sharply, and reached across the expanse of air, imbued with a fierce lust to live.

CHAPTER 9

Sitting on the lowest bench of the aluminum bleacher seats, Celine tried to wrap the blanket more closely around her. Unfortunately, she was trembling so hard her fingers wouldn't work. It didn't help that her hands were now wrapped in gauze. Each of her palms contained fiery red rope burns. The EMTs had seen to her injuries, spreading a numbing antiseptic and wrapping them in bandages. They'd wanted her to go to the hospital, but she'd refused. Although she still felt the uncomfortable throbbing, at least she was alive to feel the pain. A dreadful lost feeling overwhelmed her.

Nina's lifeless body had been taken away, but she couldn't tear her eyes from the dark patch remaining that marked the spot where she'd fallen to her death. Inhaling on a sob, Celine closed her eyes as tears seeped beneath the lids and down her cheeks. She felt the bench shift as someone sat next to her and a pair of strong arms wrapped around her and pulled her close.

"Sweetheart, I'm so sorry." Peter pulled her against him.

Celine allowed his warmth to penetrate her. She felt cold, like she was sitting in the middle of a freezer. She couldn't stop her teeth from chattering. She wanted so badly to feel warm again, but knew there was no chance of it happening anytime soon. Nina had sucked all the heat away.

Peter pulled the blanket closer around her. "I shouldn't have left you here alone. There were so many indications that Nina was unbalanced and we ignored them."

Celine looked up at him through a blur of tears. "It wasn't your fault," she sniffed. "I knew something wasn't right between us, but I never thought her hatred went so deep."

His arms tightened. One of the uniformed policemen walked over and offered her a plastic container. She smelled warm coffee. Peter reached out and took the cup.

"If you try to hold this, you'll burn yourself." He blew on the liquid, took a small sip, and held it to her lips. "Try to drink a little. It will help warm you up."

She nodded and allowed a couple of small sips to pass between her lips. She felt the hot liquid travel all the way down, but it didn't really help. Her memories kept her in the bleak caress of winter chills. She shivered.

"How did you know we were in here?"

After a painfully slow hand over hand descent, and just as she had reached the bottom of the rope, several people had raced in and Peter's arms had caught her before she fell to the ground because her legs couldn't seem to stop trembling long enough to hold her weight.

"I happened to see the reflection of the spotlight and was asking one of the roustabouts why it was on. We heard Nina's scream."

A huge shudder passed through her at the memory of that torturous sound. "I thought I was going to die, Peter. It's a good thing I've kept in shape all these years or I probably wouldn't have been able to hold on or make the descent."

He pulled her off the bench and into his lap. "I know, honey. You can't know what thoughts went through my head when I heard that scream. Thank God for your determination. I don't know what I would have done if she'd succeeded and it had been you I found on the ground instead."

Another small shudder rippled through her. "It almost was. When I looked down at the ground from that platform, I thought I saw my own death coming up to meet me." She looked up at him. "Then I thought of you. It was you that kept me fighting. There was no way I was letting you crawl behind that brick wall again." She studied his face anxiously. "You won't try will you? I've had to fight enough for one day."

He cupped her face and offered her a pale attempt at a grin. "No more hiding. You've got me now, you can't throw me back." He leaned forward and kissed her. She wrapped her arms around his neck.

Someone clearing his throat yanked her back to the present and she looked up. Another policeman stood before them.

"If you don't mind, ma'am, the investigator would like to ask you some questions now. That is, if you feel up to it?"

Celine inhaled deeply, then stood. She wobbled. Peter rose and put an arm around her to steady her and wrapped the blanket closer.

"Is it necessary for her to do this now? Can't you see she's about done in?"

The policeman looked apologetic. "I'm sorry, Mr. Cortland, but if at all possible we need to get Ms. Valentini's story of what happened now. While it's still fresh. We'll try to make it as painless as possible."

Celine laid a bandaged hand on Peter's arm before he could protest further. "It's okay. I want to get it over with." She turned back to the policeman and nodded. "I'm ready."

Within the space of a few weeks she, and Peter as well, had been forced to face all the fears that had served to keep them apart, and they'd come out the other side. The rest should be a cinch.

*   *   *

Peter watched as Celine paced the hospital corridor. The last few days had been difficult for her. Not only was Nina dead, but her grandfather was now facing a life and death situation as well.

Nina's funeral had been hard. That, together with the headlines in the paper had served to cause her recurring nightmares. He'd held her in his arms, but he couldn't remove the memories of her last moments with Nina. She'd had little sleep since she'd arrived in Florida, everything happening so fast.

He knew she avoided going into the main tent as much as possible. If she needed him, she often sent one of the young boys, who were happy to feel useful and run errands.

The circus had once been her home, but now he had a feeling it had become her nightmare. If he planned a future with her as a part of it, he had to find a way to help her get past those memories. Though she tried to ignore it, the circus was in her blood. In his as well, and as intertwined as they both were, he had to try to find a solution for them.

His footsteps echoed in the silent hallway as he made his way to her side. He'd stepped across the street to the delicatessen for some sandwiches hoping to tempt her appetite. As elusive as sleep had been for her, her appetite was worse. He hoped to encourage her to eat with something besides hospital food.

There was a time when he would have walked away from all of this. A time when he would have been afraid of opening himself up to more pain. No longer. Celine was worth taking the chance. He'd known it when he'd let her go before and he wasn't going to throw away this chance to have her be a part of his life now.

Somehow he'd find a way past her pain. He didn't think she was aware of how she had distanced herself from him over the last few days. He understood it because he'd done it himself.

Peter now had an inkling of how she'd felt when he'd locked himself away. In knowing that, he wasn't about to let her do the same thing.

*   *   *

Celine paced outside the waiting room trying to walk off the worrying energy that filled her. Sebastian had postponed his surgery after learning of Nina's death. He'd taken it hard and blamed himself for not understanding and dealing with her problems sooner.

Celine had finally put her foot down and made him reschedule the surgery. She wasn't about to lose another family member. It had been hours now since her grandfather had gone into the operating room.

Peter walked up to her and clasping her lightly bandaged hand, pulled her into the waiting room, forcing her to sit. He sat beside her and opened the white paper bag he'd carried in. Pulling out a wrapped sandwich, he handed it to her.

"No—" She wasn't hungry and knew she wouldn't be able to eat.

He forced her to take it. "You're going to eat. As it is, you haven't been able to sleep well since Nina's death. You have to keep up your strength somehow."

Reluctantly, she took the sandwich and set it in her lap. He was right, she hadn't been sleeping well. Nightmares replayed over and over again of the moment when Nina had gone plunging to her death. Nina's screams reverberating in her head, on and on.

Every time she awoke, Peter had been there to soothe her. But her mind was still heavy with the knowledge that if she hadn't come back, Nina would still be alive.

"Eat the sandwich," he coaxed her.

Her hands were healing. The red slashes, reminders of her desperate grasp to live, would soon fade away. If only her memories could do the same.

She forced herself to pick up half the tuna sandwich and take a bite. It was like chewing cardboard. But she forced herself to swallow.

"Are you satisfied?" she asked him. It felt like a lead ball residing in her stomach.

"Not nearly," he responded. "Eat the entire half and maybe then I will be."

She looked up at him grudgingly. "I never realized what a bully you are." With a sigh, she again lifted the sandwich to her mouth.

He put an arm around her and handed her a bottle of orange juice from the bag. "Here. This might help."

Something to drink she could handle. She twisted the cap off, tilted the bottle, and swallowed. It helped to wash down the sandwich. Finally the half was gone. "Satisfied now?"

He nodded. "For the moment."

He leaned back and finished his own sandwich and drink.

"You have to stop blaming yourself for Nina's death," he said into the silence.

Celine rose and turned away to look out the window at the cloudy afternoon sky. "I can't help it. If I hadn't returned, she'd still be alive."

"You don't know that. She's been on a path to self-destruction for quite some time."

"I just wish I could have reasoned with her. I still don't understand what I did to make her hate me so much she wanted me dead."

He walked up to her and wrapped his arms around her. "You'll never have all the answers. Nina was the type of person who didn't like to share. She wanted it all. And she was prepared to do anything to have it. It may be that she was projecting on you her own set of petty jealousies and desires. But you aren't like her. You never were."

She leaned into him. "She was my sister. I still can't believe she wanted me dead. Can't believe she was the one to loosen the rigging seven years ago in order to be rid of me."

"I'm sorry. Life doesn't make sense. But we have to move on. People don't always respond the way we'd like." He turned her to face him and tilted her chin upward. "I love you, Celine. I'd do anything for you, but I can't bring her back. You can't bring her back—anymore than I could Anna. We both need to move on. We won't forget them, but we have to look to the future."

"I know," she whispered as she leaned her head against his chest. "I love you, too. I'll try."

She heard footsteps and turned as the surgeon walked into the waiting room. Celine felt a pain begin to tighten in her chest.

"Ms. Valentini?"

"Yes," she gulped, afraid of what he was going to tell her.

He smiled and the pain loosened. "Your grandfather is doing just fine. He's in recovery now. The valve repair went well, and you should be able to see him shortly."

Celine smiled, feeling like at least part of the weight resting on her shoulders had been removed. She felt lightheaded.

"Thank you, doctor. Thank you so much." She reached out and shook his hand.

"You'll need to keep reminding him that he needs to take it easy for a while. I've a feeling he's not very good at doing that. We'll give both of you some instructions before he leaves."

She nodded. "I understand. He'll take it easy if I have to sit on him to make him listen."

The surgeon chuckled. "Looking at you, I'm not sure your weight will be much of a deterrent, but you can sure try."

Celine smiled back in gratitude. Maybe everything would be okay after all.

CHAPTER 10

The circus performance to benefit the Children's Hospital was a huge success. It had all gone smoothly, like clockwork. Even Jorge had returned, making his wife very happy.

Celine had ridden one of the beautiful white Arabian mares in the Finale parade dressed in the rhinestone and satin of an aerial performer. At the start she'd felt like a bit of a fake, but everyone welcomed her participation and pooh-poohed her protests about participation. After all, she had survived a death-defying feat, even though there'd been no audience to witness it.

Sebastian was still recovering and unfortunately wasn't allowed to attend the performance because his doctor felt it would be too stressful. He'd been left under the watchful eye of his neighbor in a solid championship game of checkers.

Everyone was gone now and Celine sat before the dressing table mirror staring with unseeing eyes at her reflection. There were a few stragglers, but for the most part everyone had hurried off for a grand celebration party to be held off grounds at a local restaurant. She hadn't felt much like partying herself.

Her mind was elsewhere as memories flooded through her with people and past performances. Ones where Nina had been alive and well and performing. Would she ever be able to get beyond the pain and remember the happy times?

Like the time she'd taken Nina's place in her bed so Nina could sneak out with one of the young animal handlers. Or the Christmas they'd been performing in Las Vegas and Nina had surprised her with the gift of a silver bracelet Celine had been dreaming about owning but never had the money to buy. Nina laughing, performing, teaching Celine the different ways to fall into the net without being hurt. How had it all gone so wrong?

Celine sighed, dashed away several tears gathering in her eyes, and reached for the face cream. She was about to remove her makeup when suddenly the lights went out.

"Hey," she called out. "I'm not done in here yet." Her heart thumped in her chest. Who was still around? Who would have done that? Was there someone still there who shouldn't be?

A hand fastened on her shoulder and she screamed and attempted to rise.

"Don't."

Thank God. It was a voice she recognized and she relaxed beneath his warm fingers.

"You scared me half to death. What are you doing?"

"It's a surprise." She felt his warm breath against her neck. "Do you trust me?"

She tried to turn and look at him, but it wouldn't have done any good anyway. It was so dark in the tent. She couldn't even see her hand in front of her face.

"What are you up to?" she asked suspiciously.

"I told you. A surprise. Do you trust me?" He was close and she could smell greasepaint, meaning for some reason he was in costume. She could vaguely make him out in the mirror because his face was painted white. Though ghostly, it would never be a sight she would fear.

"Yes, I trust you."

"Then from this moment you won't say another word. Not until I tell you. Tonight I want you to feel and to focus on my touch. Okay? Just nod if you agree."

She opened her mouth to answer. She felt a finger against her lips, so closed them and nodded instead, curious as to what he was up to.

"Good." He lifted his hand from her shoulder. She felt material brush against her face and then something soft and silky was placed across her eyes and fastened behind her head.

"I want you to concentrate only on me. On us. No moment beyond this. After tonight there will only be good memories left. For both of us."

She turned her head and tilted it in silent question.

"In time," he responded, a hint of a smile flavoring his words.

She had to admit, he had her intrigued. She felt a trill of excitement zing through her.

He helped her to stand. She felt a moist kiss at the tip of her shoulder. He unzipped her costume and a hand slid the strap down one arm. He repeated it on her other side. The kiss, then the hand releasing the strap.

Turning her to face him, slowly he peeled the costume down her body, lifted her legs one at a time and removed it completely. What in the world was he up to?

The only things she was left wearing when he was done were her sandals and the blindfold. She felt the chill of the night air and her nipples beaded tightly. The problem was, she wasn't sure if her body's responses came from the night or from arousal. His hands touching her as he removed her clothing had been warm and intoxicating.

She felt his mouth clamp onto one nipple and suck. She gasped and arched, nerve-endings spiraling to life. She felt a hand clasp her other nipple, teasing and tugging and she inhaled sharply at the sensations. Without sight, her other senses were fully attuned to each touch.

Celine felt the loss of his heat as he moved away from her. Then she felt something heavy settled about her shoulders. It must have been a cloak as she felt the slippery lining glide against her skin. She heard the snap of a clasp at the front. Then he turned her and guided her outside. The moist air caressed her face and she could feel the dew-kissed grass brush against her naked legs. Every touch, not just from him and his nearness, but from the night—everything—felt sensual and erotic.

Where was he taking her? All of a sudden a thought flashed through her mind. She gasped as she remembered telling him about her erotic dream. He wouldn't...would he? At the memory of that dream her stomach began to burn, and she felt a dampness begin to pool at her center.

A stillness in the air surrounded her again and it felt like they'd entered another enclosed space. Their footsteps crunched on loose gravel. Then soft, loose earth flattened beneath her feet. He halted her and she heard the squeak of a door echo. The lion cage? He encouraged her to again walk forward a few steps then halted her again.

It felt like she was in an enclosed space, noises outside muffled, the whinny of a horse, the howl of a dog, muted and distant. She could smell sawdust and damp air. The air shifted as he moved in front of her.

The clasp of the cloak was released and cool air struck her as it was lifted from her shoulders, leaving her feeling exposed. The rustle of material and her own stuttered breaths were the only sounds in the night.

Anticipation aroused her as she waited. What next? How far would he actually go?

She felt his hands at the back of her head and the blindfold was released. Celine blinked and looked around her. With his hands on her shoulders, Peter stood behind her and slowly moved her in a full circle so she could view her surroundings.

It was her dream, but not her dream. They were definitely inside the main tent. She was naked and standing in the middle of a cage. But the cage was completely draped in white satin, hiding them from view of an unsuspecting or unexpected audience.

To her left was a bed, not round like her dream, large cushions spread out on the ground, reminding her of a harem setting. They were covered in yards more of white satin. When had he done this? She warmed in embarrassment at the thought someone must have helped him and wondered who else knew.

She had to smile when she noticed the large stuffed tiger and leopard propped on a couple of the display stands at the other end of the cage. It was just fine with her, she admitted, that he wasn't going to share her with a real audience or real assistants. Some things were meant for fantasy alone.

She tried to face him, but he stopped her. He brought his hands up beneath her arms and cupped her firm breasts. She leaned back against him. *Oh God, it feels so good.*

He teased her erect nipples, sending shafts of pleasure spearing downward through her center. His lips drifted along the curve of her neck.

The heat of the single spotlight magnified the fire building inside her. He'd done all this for her and she was going to enjoy it.

His hands roamed across her ribcage, sliding down over the curve of her hips, one hand cupped her mound, the other smoothed across her buttocks. It seemed he was everywhere, calling all manner of response from her body. Pulling the heat from her every pore.

God, she wanted to turn to him, have him buried inside her, deep and forever.

He whipped her around, captured her mouth, and sank his tongue deep inside her moist recesses. She closed her eyes, allowing the feelings to engulf her, letting him lead her far, far away from reality.

He lifted her and pulled her close, and she wrapped her legs around him, felt his rigid cock hard against her hot entrance through the thin fabric of his pants. She wound her arms around him, needing him closer. Not getting close enough.

She felt him move, walk forward, and she felt the slippery cool satin beneath her as he knelt and placed her on the decadent bed.

Releasing her lips he moved down her body, nibbled at her breasts, continued downward until his mouth was at her core. His tongue entered her swift and sure, delving deeply, driving her upward. She arched her hips, wanted more, needed…so much.

He moved away from her, then quickly back and she felt his naked, hard shaft at her moist entrance.

All she could hear was her own pant of need, a moan escaping as he pierced her and slid fully inside, filling her completely. She screamed with the peak of pleasure as it found her. He pulled back and thrust forward. Again and again.

Then she felt it as wave after wave crashed over her, her body convulsing around him.

She was cleansed by his passion, by his love, freed to open her heart and to allow him to possess all of her. As the pulsing desire consumed her, she opened her eyes and saw her lover for the first time that evening.

She widened her eyes in shock. A sob of immense joy filled her as she realized fully all that he was offering her. Lying completely sheathed inside her, his own body pulsing in release, his gaze locked with hers.

The black teardrop, which had always been there, was gone. It had been replaced with two intertwined hearts, one green and the other blue—the exact blue of Celine's eyes.

They didn't need words. What they shared was more, beyond words. She understood and wept, overcome with the profound depth of their moment of bliss. She knew why he'd made his declaration here in the Big Top.

He was her Knight in White Satin—had proven it in so many ways, had always been so and would always be. The circus was in their blood, a part of who they were. And her memories of this place would forever more be branded and intertwined with him and the heart he had finally opened to bring her home.

NO CHOICE

CARNAL CARNIVAL

NO CHOICE

Dammit! It just wasn't right. She'd managed to avoid the repair shop for a lot of years, so why the hell did her car have to break down on this night, on this street? At five minutes to ten on a hot summer Friday night, she'd be damned lucky to get anyone to come out to help her with the car. Let alone try to beg for help from someone she'd turned her back on seven years ago.

She released the latch, and the hood of the old 1972 blue Mustang creaked upward. She should have replaced the car years ago, but couldn't seem to make herself trade it in for a newer model. She hated making choices like that. The old Mustang held a whole lot of memories. Like the night of the Senior Harvest Dance with Derek Cory in the backseat and the windows all steamed over. He'd hooked one of her legs over the back of the front seat and pushed the other up so her thigh lay against the outer softness of her breast. He'd buried his huge cock so deep in her that night she saw stars and climaxed at least three times—one after the other. Her lips curved upward in fond remembrance of that night.

Another memory surfaced. The night of the Senior Prom with Mason Jennings. It's a wonder the car hadn't melted around them that spring night. It had been unseasonably hot and all the windows were rolled down. He'd pulled her onto her knees, facing the open passenger window, forced her legs as wide as they'd go considering the circumstances, and pushed into her from the back. Oh, man, had she felt him fucking her—every thick inch.

Just as they both spasmed simultaneously in orgasm, her hand must have clenched the handle because the door had burst open, sending them tumbling to the damp grass next to the car. But, damn, she had to give him credit, he never pulled free of her and instead had cupped her breasts, rolled to the side, and kept pumping, thrusting and retreating, sending her into another searing climax. She'd tried to bite back the scream, but it had come out muffled and her lip had bled for trying to force it back. When it was over and he'd slid from inside her and they'd both come out of the haze of lust, they'd erupted into peals of laughter, unable to stop, with tears rolling down their faces. But it hadn't ended there, because he'd pulled out a fresh condom, pushed her onto her back, and right there, beneath the full moon brought her to two more orgasms before they left the secluded cove. Now that was most definitely a night to remember.

It had always felt as though each wanted to outdo the other that year. Her whole world had revolved around the two of them. But at the end of summer, after her graduation, she'd felt them waiting, looking for her to make that final choice. Something she simply couldn't do.

Just thinking back over that last year, her pussy was sopping wet. She'd missed them so much—both of them. But she couldn't face them—face the questions, the demands, the need to choose between them. She guessed in a way she had made a choice back then. It was the choice not to choose between them—not to hurt one of them. She'd known all along if she had chosen one, she would always have longed for the other as well. It just would have hurt too damn much. Pretty stupid when you stopped to think about it.

She looked up at the sign over the repair shop door and frowned. That whole senior year had been made up of choices. First Derek, then Mason. She'd wanted them both. They'd both wanted her. She'd ended up with neither. She'd turned her back on both of them because she couldn't decide. And she'd had fantasies about having them both. At the same time. She'd been certain at the time that they would have thought less of her for even voicing such an outrageous idea. So she'd smothered the thought. It just wasn't meant to be.

Even now—seven years later—she kept her distance from them, living in a town several hours away, knowing she still couldn't decide between them. She still wanted them both just as much as she ever had, and the two of them were still as close as they had been back then.

Living and working two hours away hadn't helped with the memories. Particularly on nights like this, when she had to drive all the way here to meet a potential client, and the urge to stop in to see them was overwhelming.

She peered under the hood of the Mustang, unable to see anything. What the hell did she know about repairing cars anyway? She had no idea what she was looking for. She knew about investing money and she had an ingrained instinct for knowing what stocks to trade when. She had a knack for convincing clients to hand over their portfolios for her to manage and doing a damn good job of it. But nothing about cars. Yet she knew of a couple of guys who did. And she trusted them like no one else. She could not think of one person over the span of the last seven years she trusted as much as Derek and Mason.

Tonight she'd been out to dinner with a client and was finally heading for home and a weekend of peace and quiet when it stopped dead. Right here. The damn engine wouldn't even turn over. Again, she glanced up at the repair shop, noting a light seemed to be on in an upstairs window. It appeared someone was still up.

Giving up the fight, she stalked over to the door and banged hard with her fist. *Ouch, that hurt.* Would whomever was inside hear her? She waited. The steam bath of summer clung to her skin, and she swiped at the back of her neck. The white linen suit she wore felt damp and sticky against her skin. And no one came to the door.

She lifted her hand and banged again.

"Hello? Is anyone in there? I need some help out here," she yelled.

As she waited, she unbuttoned her jacket and peeled it off. The thin silky short-sleeved blouse she wore underneath clung to her like a second skin.

This just couldn't be happening. It wasn't really the best part of town, let alone the best time of night to try walking any distance. She was in a section where her cell phone didn't seem to have any coverage. *Make a note—look into changing companies because this isn't the first time it's happened at an inconvenient moment.* She supposed she could walk until it kicked back in and then make a call, but damn, she was right here and there was a light on.

Just as she prepared to again pound her aching fist against the door, it swung open and she stumbled into a stone wall.

"What the hell!" a male voice barked.

She remembered his smell—earthy, hard, and masculine—and knew exactly who was holding her. It felt damn good being in his arms again, but she carefully released herself from his steadying grip and stepped back, looking up, way up. That was a lot of years ago, and things change, even though her response to him hadn't. Well, yes it had, it was magnified.

"Hello, Derek, it's been a long time." Could anyone be in a more uncomfortable situation than this?

"Ginnie Thomas?" His eyes widened and his expression had turned to one of shock rather than annoyance.

Derek had been the captain of the football team—broad, rugged, and tall. Every girl in school had wanted to date Derek, but he had singled out Ginnie. And, boy, did Derek know how to show a girl a good time and make her feel all female. He'd done that and more. And he sure as hell knew how to use his rugged body and sensual silver tongue. Even though she'd given in to her feelings for him on that very first date, he hadn't been the kind to tell stories. Had she ever been a pushover. Ginnie remembered going to school the next day expecting to hear her name whispered about, but it never happened. And Derek had asked her out again and again. Even when he and Mason had gone on to continue their education at a local college, he'd continued dating her.

Two years older than her, she'd thought for sure he wouldn't want to continue to see her any more what with all the new friends he'd be meeting, but she'd been wrong.

"Yes, it's me. I'm sorry to bother you, but my car broke down. I saw the light on and hoped someone might be here to help me out."

Derek squinted past her to the dark shape of a lone car parked on the side of the street in front of the shop. Then his expression altered to one of surprise. "You're still running around in that old beat-up Mustang? I can't believe it."

He stepped back from the door and motioned her inside. Brushing back a damp lock of errant hair, she stepped inside the darkened room. Looking around, she realized she was standing in the front office of the garage. She could smell gasoline and oil, but doubted it was as strong as in the six-bay garage extending toward the left, beyond the office door separating them.

But Derek led her off in another direction, behind the counter, through another door and up a flight of stairs. He turned to look at her over his shoulder.

"The apartment upstairs is air-conditioned—I think you'll be more comfortable there. Besides, Mason is up there watching television. I'm sure he'd want to see you. I still can't believe it. Ginnie Thomas."

He stopped on the landing and she almost bumped into his hard abdomen as he turned toward her. She found herself staring directly at his belt, and just beneath that the evidence of a very hard erection bulging against the zipper of his jeans. She remembered the feel of that thick shaft—she remembered it very well.

Only self-control stopped her from licking her lips and reaching up to feel the cock that had given her so much enjoyment in the past. He turned her on now no less than he had seven years ago, and, in fact, it seemed more so, as she had ideas of ripping his clothes off right here on the landing and asking him to fuck her.

She couldn't do that, of course. She was a mature businesswoman, not a teenager any longer. Back then, the minute he parked the car out at Overlook Cliffs she was all over him like hot chocolate sauce on vanilla ice cream.

"I—uhhhh—can't wait to see him," she managed to mumble. He stepped back to allow her room to ascend to the landing beside him. Stepping up, she joined him, her body responding with all the passion of remembered teenage trysts running rampant through her mind—and her body.

They stood there staring at each other for moments that seemed to stretch on and on. "We missed you after you left for college. We thought sure you'd come back, but you never did." He reached up to stroke the side of her face. "You're just as pretty as you ever were. More so. The years look good on you, Gin. Real good."

"I-I meant to come back, but things came up. You know how it is when you're a teenager." She was stalling, not wanting to tell him the real reason she hadn't returned.

He lifted her left hand and stared at her bare fingers, then his gaze again rose to hers, questioning. "No rings? We thought for sure you'd be married by now."

"No. No marriage, no engagement, no steady." She lifted his hand and smiled. "And you?"

He grinned. "Nope, free as a bird. Mason, too. Guess we never found the right woman. Nobody who could measure up to you."

He was silent for a long moment as he looked past her, as though seeing into the past. "We were going to come see you at the beginning of your sophomore year in college. But then we thought it might not be a good idea. You'd have come home if you'd wanted to be with us."

Us. She knew he meant him and Mason. Oh, she'd wanted to see them all right, but they would have wanted something from her she couldn't give them. They'd have wanted her to make a choice, and she just couldn't do it. She hadn't wanted to give up either of them.

Mason was Derek's best friend, almost a brother—had been since the time they'd entered kindergarten. They were both on the football team. Derek had sable hair with lighter, caramel highlights and Mason had the summer-streaked blond. Mason looked more like he belonged on a surfboard, and Derek—well, he belonged on a windswept mountaintop. They both loved the outdoors and shared a passion for working on old cars. The last time she saw them, they were in their own sophomore year at college, and sharing an apartment. They had always been inseparable so it was no surprise when she heard they'd gone into business together. Mason's dad had decided to retire and had sold the station to the two of them. She really shouldn't have been surprised.

It wasn't how she remembered. They'd expanded from three car bays to six and whenever she passed by there always seemed to be a steady stream of customers. They'd whitewashed the building and apparently had renovated the warehouse above the shop and turned it into an apartment, at least over the offices.

Theirs had always been an odd relationship. She'd gone out with Mason because, during their freshman year in college, Derek had asked her to. He'd said Mason felt at ease with her and needed a female friend right now, and he was on the rebound and needed some cheering up. Would she mind?

Hell, she'd always been just as attracted to Mason as she had been to Derek and she'd hated the thought he might be sad. How could she refuse a request like that? How many boyfriends would ask their girl to help out their best buddy in a time of need and not be jealous when it turned into something more than they'd all expected? It had turned into something deeper, more complicated than she ever could have anticipated. She'd been honest with Derek from the start and had expected him to be angry with her when she told him how she felt about Mason.

But he hadn't been. What surprised her even more, was that neither of them ever seemed to be jealous when she went out with the other one, and, in fact, always encouraged her to have fun and enjoy herself. It was definitely an odd situation, but somehow she just couldn't say no to either one of them.

She'd never understood their relationship, but she loved them both so much. Sometimes she'd been envious of the closeness they seemed to share, had wanted to be a part of it. She guessed it was just a guy thing—they'd always seemed more like brothers than best friends. But would brothers even have been willing to share a girlfriend? Somehow she doubted it. Back then she hadn't wanted to reason the acceptance of their strange situation. The worst part was that she'd thought if she chose one of them everything they had would break apart, and she couldn't bear hurting either one of them, or losing what they had.

She'd opted for the coward's way out and hightailed it out of town. At least they would have their friendship intact, even if it did mean she would be alone. But the span of time had possibly changed things—and none of them were attached right now.

Without preamble, Derek dropped forward and claimed her lips. His arms came out to steady her as his tongue pressed between her lips. He tasted hard and male with a tinge of beer at the edges, the saltiness of peanuts, and a swirling heat began to invade her pussy.

She remembered one particular night when he'd brought along a six-pack after their high school team had won a particularly difficult game and he wanted to celebrate. But not the way one would have expected.

He'd taken one of the cold cans, popped it open and slowly poured it over her breasts. Her nipples had tightened as the cold liquid struck them and then he'd licked every bit off her body with his tongue and mouth. The remainder of the beer had gone unopened. But she remembered the scent in the air that night—his, hers, and the beer.

Before she really had a chance to respond to the kiss in the way she wanted, he pulled back. She looked up at him and saw a smile lingering at the corner of his lips.

"I wanted to see if you tasted as good as I remembered."

"And?" she breathed, her heart thumping in her chest.

"Well, you look all business-like in that sexy white suit, but underneath you're the same hot babe I remember." Chuckling and with that devilish twinkle in his eyes she remembered so well, he pivoted around and opened the door to the apartment, stepping inside. "Hey, Mason, we've got a visitor."

She should be angry. He'd stolen a kiss and called her a hot babe, all in the same breath—and left her wanting more. But it wasn't anger she was feeling as she slowly followed him and entered the apartment. She was at a slow simmer of need.

As she stepped inside, she breathed a sigh of relief as the cool air swamped her. She halted just inside the door and surveyed the room. It wasn't what she would have expected from two bachelors living over a repair shop. She could smell the recent remodeling in the hint of fresh paint, and saw it was actually very spacious, with modern, comfortable furniture, and surprisingly neat.

She couldn't quite say the same about Mason Jennings. In low-slung, torn, faded blue jeans and a white, ripped T-shirt, bits of his tanned flesh teasingly peeking out, barefoot and exuding animal magnetism from every pore, he looked endearingly tousled. His blond hair was just as she remembered, except right now it was in disarray and a lock had fallen forward. His blue eyes had a sleepy, bedroom sort of expression, like he'd just woken up, or was ready to hop into bed—and not for sleeping.

What the hell was wrong with her mind tonight? This wasn't like her—not at all. Right now she was having a difficult time calling on all her self-control not to proposition both of them right here and now.

She had the urge to reach forward and push the errant lock back and see if it felt as silky as she remembered. She saw his gaze widen when he spotted her. He quickly raised a hand to brush his hair out of his face. She wanted to tell him not to bother, that he was fine just the way he was.

"Ginnie Thomas?"

He even sounded the same, but with a hint of shocked surprise. Rough and smooth all at the same time, reminding her of turbulent waves breaking against the shore, beautiful and wild. A flash of the last time they'd made love at Darwin's Point raced through her mind. It had been August, just before she planned to leave for college. A lot had occurred that last summer.

That was their place—Darwin's Point, a pretty, deserted section of beach. Her gaze turned to Derek. Funny, the things that came into your mind. Derek had always liked parking at Overlook Cliffs. The cliffs were just above Darwin's Point and actually if you walked down a path, it took you to a level spot just above Darwin's Point, with a full view of where Mason liked to make love to her on the beach. She'd never thought about that odd coincidence before.

She pulled her thoughts back and turned to look at Mason, nodding her head. "One and the same. I've had a little car problem."

"Well, have a seat. It's been a long time. It's good to see you." His quick glance shifted to Derek and then back to her. "We've missed you."

She felt the heat rising into her cheeks. "It's good to see you as well. I'm sorry I haven't come by before this, but you know how it gets."

He studied her for a long moment then shrugged. "Yeah, I know what you mean. Well, have a seat."

"I'll get you a glass of iced tea," Derek interjected. "It sure must be hot as hell out there tonight. I know it was like standing in an oven earlier today."

She walked toward the sofa and sat down. "Is it ever. A glass of tea would be great, thank you."

Mason sat down across from her, apparently unable to take his eyes off her. "So you've got car problems," he finally said after a long pause. "What kind of car are you driving now?"

"She's still driving that old beat up Mustang. You remember the one," Derek said as he walked back into the room and handed a glass to Ginnie and another to Mason. Then he leaned back again the doorframe and crossed his legs, watching them both.

Mason looked up at Derek and they exchanged a look Ginnie couldn't quite interpret. They'd always had that way of seeming to communicate with each other without saying anything. Watching them, she couldn't quite believe she was sitting here across from the both of them. She'd thought about them a lot over the years and this was so unexpected.

And she was uneasy. What if they asked her the question she didn't want to answer? Couldn't answer.

Derek finally levered away from the wall. "Mason, let's go take a look at that li'l Mustang of Ginnie's. We'll push it into the garage, get it on a lift, and give it a thorough going over first thing tomorrow. We're closed tomorrow, so we can give it all the time it needs. Too late tonight to do anything." He turned to Ginnie. "I heard you worked over in Millerton. Do you live over there as well? That's a good two-hour drive. We've got a spare bedroom, Ginnie, care to spend the night? We can reminisce over old times tomorrow while we fix your car. We'll get you into a spare coverall and you can find out all about what's under the hood."

It probably wasn't the best idea to stay here so close to both of them, but she found she really didn't want to go search for a hotel, nor did she want to put them out by asking them to drive her all the way home.

"I don't have anything to change into. I didn't exactly come out with anything extra to wear."

"I'm sure we can scrounge up a pair of shorts and a T-shirt for you to sleep in if that's you're problem. How 'bout it? For old time's sake. We've got an extra room if that's what's worrying you."

Again she felt the color seep into her face. What would he say if he knew what she was thinking. "No-no that's not it." She smiled, trying to appear at ease, attempting not to show that what she really wanted was to be made love to—by both of them. What would they think of her if she voiced her thoughts? "If you're sure. I'd love to find out what the two of you have been up to over the last few years."

When could she ever resist either of these guys? When did she ever want to? And she kind of liked the idea of getting down and dirty with the both of them. That intrigued her more than anything else.

"I hate to put you out, but if it's not any trouble. I have missed you both. I'd like to catch up with you. I'm sorry I haven't stopped by before this." It was dangerous and she certainly didn't want to come between them, but she found she couldn't resist spending more time with them. Both of them. Did she dare—? No she couldn't ask them. She'd fantasized about it that last year in high school, but she didn't have the nerve to ask them what she was thinking right now.

But thinking about it was making her real hot. The thought of being naked and sandwiched between the two of them. It was a very tempting idea.

Derek and Mason both smiled. Mason reached over and grabbed his socks and boots.

"Let's go get that car into a bay."

Ginnie stood up. "Can I help?"

Derek looked at her and grinned. "In a white suit and high heels? I don't think so. You stay here and we'll be right back. Then I'll get you something to sleep in. Where are the keys? We'll take this nice and slow—we want to get it right."

She reached into her purse, pulled out her key ring, and handed it to him. She had to wonder about that last part—what he was talking about, as he seemed to pass a meaningful look to Mason. Could they possibly be thinking the same thing she was? Had she wasted a lot of years because she'd been afraid of presenting them with what she could only term as an unusual turn to their relationship?

It seemed there might be some very interesting developments this weekend. She might actually get something she'd only ever dreamed of. Suddenly she was glad she hadn't made any other appointments for the weekend.

*   *   *

Ginnie turned over and opened her eyes. Thinking about Mason and Derek, knowing they were just down the hall in their own rooms, made it hard to sleep, and being in a strange room didn't help. It was pitch black, but after finally drifting into an uneasy sleep, she'd been awakened by some sort of odd sound, other than the air switching on and off. It sounded almost like a groan.

The shorts and T-shirt they'd found for her to wear were old cast-offs of Mason's from way back in high school with the school mascot emblazoned across them. They were too large for her, but they were workable in a pinch. They'd really had to dig for something usable. The spare room she slept in was definitely that, filled with cardboard boxes of odds and ends and a sofa couch that pulled out into a bed. She was so tired it hadn't really mattered to her. If only she'd been able to sleep without being visited by her hot, unconsummated dreams of her two former lovers.

But for some reason right now she was wide awake. There was that sound again. She threw back the covers and slid out of bed. Was someone hurt?

Opening her door, she stepped out into the hall. She looked toward the living room, but then heard the sound again, but it was coming from the other direction. She turned in that direction and began to make her way down the hallway. She had gone on to bed before Derek and Mason, so wasn't sure who slept in which room. There were several doors, all of them closed, except for one that was only partially opened. That was where the sound came from.

She tiptoed down the hallway toward the door, knowing she probably shouldn't be doing this, but she'd always been the inquisitive type and couldn't let well enough alone when something, in her opinion, required investigation. She hadn't scouted around earlier while Derek and Mason were downstairs looking at her car, because her mind had been on other things, and frankly, she'd been exhausted.

With fingers pressed lightly against the door, she pushed. It was dark in the room, but the moonlight made the room seem brighter. Peering around, she saw exactly where the groans were coming from. And it wasn't because someone was hurt.

She should have been shocked by what she discovered. Instead, it felt like a light had finally come on inside her head and everything snapped into place. Talk about being naïve. How could she not have known? Mason and Derek weren't just best friends—they were lovers, and probably had been so for a very long time.

The moonlight offered her a very clear view of the tableau on the bed. The erotic scene filled her with hot lust as she watched Mason fucking Derek in long, powerful strokes. It was Derek making the passionate sounds. His legs were splayed and raised. There didn't seem to be any real urgency to the thrusts and Mason's cock glistened in the moonlight as he powered in and out of Derek's ass.

Her pussy began to cream at the sensual sight of them making love. Mason's hand was stroking Derek's cock as they moved together in the strong rhythm of undulating copulation.

"Yeah, deeper. Fuck me harder," Derek gasped in between each long, drawn out groan of pleasure. "God, your hands feel good, keep stroking me."

Ginnie couldn't believe how hot she was getting, standing there watching them. She reached down inside the shorts, past her panties, to her wet, slick slit, sliding a finger through her juices as she watched the sizzling tableau before her.

Her pussy grasped at her fingers, eager for her attention. As she watched, Mason's thrusts became more powerful. Derek arched upward to meet the demand. Her own fingers began to move faster, as she pushed deeper, adding another finger, circling and brushing over her clit. How well she remembered the feel of both those cocks tunneling deep inside her body.

Watching the two men she wanted most, naked and hot, giving each other pleasure was almost too much. Nothing could be better except her sandwiched between them. And, boy, did she wish she could be there. She closed her eyes and leaned back against the wall, feeling her orgasm build. She should have told them long ago what she wanted.

"Ginnie, come here."

Her eyes shot open and she saw both of them looking at her as they continued to fuck. It was Derek who'd called to her.

"Shed those fucking clothes and come here. We want you with us when we come," Mason said as he slowed his movements, waiting for her to join them. "It was you, thinking about you; we couldn't wait, but we wanted to give you time to get to know us again. "

She didn't need to be asked twice. She pulled her hand from her sopping pussy and quickly pushed down the shorts and panties and yanked off the T-shirt.

She stopped as she reached the bed, unable to take her eyes off these two fucking hot men that she'd yearned to be with for years.

"Where do you want me?" she whispered. She noted that Derek's cock was sheathed with a condom. She couldn't quite make out Mason's, because it was buried deep inside Derek.

"The condom's flavored. Hop on and start sucking, baby. We both know how much you like to suck cock. Give him your pussy and we'll all come together. Something we should have done a long time ago. "

She couldn't agree more. So many years missed because of being afraid to voice her own needs. Not another minute was going to be lost. With as much dexterity as she could manage, she straddled across Derek, felt the heat of his moist breath against her pussy, then lowered her head to take his rigid shaft into her hungry mouth.

It was strawberry flavored, a particular favorite fruit of hers. She licked up and down and then she almost hit the roof when Derek's tongue stabbed into her. Oh, God, how she'd missed them! Her groans joined his as Mason began thrusting inside Derek again. Mason's hands threaded through her hair.

Oh, God, this was hot. Both of these men with their hands on her, *at the same time.* She consumed Derek's cock, raised both hands and cupped Mason's tight ass. There were no sounds in the room except the pleasurable groans, the slapping and slurping of bodies coming together as they should have so long ago.

She heard Derek's groan first, felt him spasm as he began to come, then Mason's shout of completion, and finally, as Derek stabbed his tongue deep inside, she came in the most powerful orgasm she'd had in quite some time, attempting to scream her completion around the cock thrusting deep inside to the entrance of her throat. As she felt Mason stiffen, she buried a finger inside his ass, heard his indrawn gasp of pleasurable acceptance, wanting her presence there, and his hands fisted tighter in her hair.

Stars shattered before her eyes as she continued to suck, wanting to wring as much pleasure from Derek as she could. Her finger sank deeper into Mason and slowly she began to thrust as he continued to work his body back and forth between Derek's body and her finger.

He finally withdrew from Derek and she pulled her finger free. He forced her head up and branded her with a kiss, deep and long. She shimmied along Derek's body until her pussy felt the presence of Derek's cock, and Mason's. Oh, God, she needed one of them to fuck her.

She rested above Derek on her knees, trying not to place too much of her weight there. Mason's mouth demanded her attention. She lifted and Derek eased out from under them, and then she felt his heat at her back as he knelt behind her and rubbed his body against her.

This was heaven. She felt him reach up and cup her breasts, kneading and tweaking the nipples. Now she felt his cock at her back and Mason's grinding against her pussy lips, yet not seeking penetration. She rotated her hips, pressing herself alternately between the both of them.

Derek's lips were pressed against her neck, then her shoulder, his hands still palming her breasts as Mason ate at her mouth, forcing his tongue deeper. She couldn't get enough of them, either of them, wanting to blend herself inside them, and them inside her, fusing them as one being.

Mason finally released her mouth and looked down at her, then he looked at Derek behind her. Reaching past her, he pulled Derek to him and kissed him passionately, in the same manner. When he released him, Ginnie leaned back and pulled Derek to her, kissing him deeply, letting him know without doubt she wanted to feel his lips no less than Mason's. She wanted them both. Just like this. Forever.

She felt both their arms around her, supporting her, loving her, making her a part of them. And for the first time she really did feel a part of their world and more complete than she had ever been.

Mason was the first to lift away and she felt a loss when he did so. She reached for him, feeling a part of herself leaving.

He smiled at her. "I'm not going anywhere. It's time for a shower. Come on, both of you." He looked over at Derek. "And then we need to fuck, Ginnie. It's been way too long."

Eagerly, Ginnie followed him into the bathroom, which was very spacious, more so than she would have expected from an apartment this size. Derek flicked on a light, and Ginnie looked down, a little embarrassed, now that the first rush of passion had passed.

Derek reached out and lifted her head as Mason turned on the shower, which appeared to be a walk-in size, allowing more than enough room for the three of them.

"Don't be shy, Ginnie. We should have done this a long time ago. Maybe if Mason and I hadn't been worried about what you'd think of our relationship, we wouldn't have wasted so many years. It wasn't until we started college that we finally realized the kind of relationship we wanted with each other—and you. Derek thought if you could date us both separately, get to know me—and want both of us, you would understand the kind of relationship we wanted. But when the time came, we were too cowardly to tell you what we really wanted...for you to be a part of both of us. And instead, we lost you. There's always been a part of us missing."

She looked up at him. "I loved you both. It's the reason I couldn't come back, don't you see? I couldn't make a choice between you. I wanted you—like this—the three of us—but I was too scared of what you'd think of me if I told you that."

Mason had discarded his condom and turned back to face her. "We never wanted you to make a choice. We tried to make it so you wouldn't have to, but instead we scared you away. We thought if you dated both of us—got used to us separately—eventually you'd come to accept both of us. We just weren't sure you could accept that we loved each other just as much—and in the same way—that we loved you. We wanted to give you time, but the fear got the better of us."

"All of us, I think. I was afraid of what you'd think of me if I told you what I really wanted. To have you both, like this. I wanted you both. And just now," she admitted softly, "I found it so arousing watching you make love to each other. The only thing I wanted more was to be with you instead of just watching you."

Mason stepped inside the shower, reached for her hand and pulled her inside. Derek turned away to discard his condom, then quickly joined them.

Derek reached for a cloth, soaped it, then handed it to Ginnie. "Wash us, and then we'll make sure you're all nice and squeaky clean as well."

She eagerly accepted the cloth and began working it across Derek's broad chest, her hand going to his slick cock, stroking it with her soapy hand as she washed him.

She felt Mason come behind her and begin to palm her breasts with his soapy hands, her nipples tightening quickly beneath his ministrations. She felt him rub against her back and was finding it hard to concentrate on getting Derek nice and clean.

She felt Mason kneel behind her, then his mouth was on her cheeks, his hands separating the firm globes and then his tongue was lapping at her pussy. She sucked in air at the exquisite feel of his mouth.

She set aside the cloth and braced herself against Derek's chest, widening her stance to allow Mason deeper penetration with his tongue. Oh, yes, that was so wonderful, so wonderful.

Then she felt one of Derek's hands at her clit, circling and rubbing. Another orgasm started to build inside, she felt it rising higher and higher. Derek lifted her chin and claimed her mouth as she climaxed around Mason's tongue, a growl deep in her chest rising, yet stifled by Derek's deeply probing tongue.

Both of their tongues were now thrusting and retreating, almost in counter rhythm, like two small penises, and she couldn't seem to come back to earth. Neither would let her land, as time and again, between them, she climaxed, until she reached a point she could no longer stand on her own, her legs shaky and weak. Her mind was fuzzy with echoes of pleasure, hardly aware when one of them turned off the water as the other lifted her in his arms.

As Mason held her, Derek toweled her dry. He then dried Mason and finally himself. She cuddled against Mason's chest as they walked back into the bedroom and he laid her gently on the bed. Again, their cocks were already hard, and she watched lazily as they each sheathed the other and then lay beside her.

Derek ate at her breasts, suckling and tonguing, as Mason's fingers opened her lips and prepared her, testing her. Then Derek levered himself above her and she felt his cock at her hot entrance. She lifted her hips and he pierced her, her passage widening to accept him, eager for his penetration. He felt wonderful.

Mason straddled her and she willingly accepted his cock between her lips, stroking and tasting, pleasuring him, savoring the flavor, until she felt him spasm with his orgasm, coming quickly with her lips wrapped around him, sucking at him. Derek thrust inside her in long, slow strokes, building her slowly, not rushing, taking his time.

Mason withdrew from her mouth, lifted her shoulders, and settled behind her, bracing her as Derek continued fucking her. Heat built inside her quickly. Mason's hand's encircled her breasts, warm and firm, claiming her as Derek continued stroking inside her, driving her higher and higher.

Derek lifted her legs and Mason reached out to anchor them up to either side of her breasts, opening her more fully to Derek's cock, lifting her hips as Derek sank to tease at the entrance of her womb, and she screamed at the deep, exquisite penetration. He ground against her clit. Mason pulled her head back and claimed her mouth, sinking his tongue deeply inside.

Oh, God, she felt them both right down to her soul. They touched at her center and she broke apart in shattering waves of pleasure as she came and came and came. Her scream of rapture was captured by Mason's mouth. And then, when she felt Derek burst free, she came again, and finally collapsed bonelessly into Mason's arms.

This was how it was meant to be. It always had been the way it should be. If only they hadn't been afraid to voice their wants to each other.

Mason lowered her legs gently as Derek pulled his softening cock from her vagina. Derek climbed from the bed and headed to the bathroom. Mason held Ginnie in his arms, stroking her body.

She felt serene and calm, floating on a pleasurable high. She snuggled against him, her head against his heart, hearing the steady beating lulled her into a half-world between sleeping and waking.

Another body came from behind to spoon around her. Then Mason slid from the bed, and Ginnie turned to Derek—her wonderful mountain man. She felt his tightly beaded nipple beneath her cheek and turned to suckle at it. Oh, he tasted so good.

When Mason returned, he spooned around her. He lifted one of her legs and nestled his own thigh between them, then sank one finger between her opened and engorged lips.

Derek anchored a hand at her hip, kneading her skin.

"You're so beautiful, Ginnie. We've missed you a lot."

Mason's finger began to slowly thrust inside her, a hard, yet slight, lingering presence.

"We're glad you came home, Ginnie. Without you, it hasn't been right. Not since the day you left. A part of us needing to be filled and only you could do it."

She arched against Mason's questing finger. "You had each other," she whispered. "But all these years, I've been without both of you. I thought I had to make a choice and I couldn't do it. So I was left with nothing but the memories."

Derek stroked her hip, down her thigh, back up to feather across her breast. "There was no choice to make, honey. We're a family just as we are—a triad rather than a duet."

She turned onto her back and arched up against Mason's questing, undemanding hand, enjoying his touch. Their scents surrounded her, mingling with her own. And it was so right.

Theirs was a special relationship a lot of people could never understand. She hadn't herself, not until tonight.

She ran her investment consulting business from her house for the most part and could change location with ease—much easier than they could move their business. When the time came, she would be the one to change locations and be happy to do so.

As Derek had said earlier, they'd have to take it slow, make sure it was what they all really wanted, the way they wanted it. For right now, this was right. And she had to thank her old broken down Mustang for the opportunity to find out she really hadn't had to make a choice at all. Not about the car, and not between her men.

Derek's mouth pulled her thoughts back to the here and now as his tongue drove deep into her mouth. Mason added a second finger to the first and all she could think about was the pleasure of being at the heart of the two people she loved most, and the only choice she had to make was between rapture and bliss.

COME INTO MY PARLOR

CARNAL CARNIVAL

COME INTO MY PARLOR

Fucking bad move. His partner, Hank, was down with the flu and sick as a dog, so Alex made the visit to Mulberry Court solo. Not the best decision he'd ever made. It most likely fit in somewhere just behind that chase down on River Street last year when Hank hightailed after him, shoving him into the water, and ended up taking a bullet in the shoulder that had been meant for him. Alex still owed him big time for that one.

His partner always kept warning him about letting his emotions ride roughshod over his actions, that they were going to land him in a mess of hot water he couldn't swim out of one of these days. Sometimes he listened—or at least tried to. There were more times he didn't. Like now. He'd heard things about the seductive widow who resided alone in the massive Mulberry Court mansion. Lots of things. But had she killed her most recent paramour? That was a question yet to be answered.

The years as a detective had jaded him, and his gut said she was as guilty as they came. The evidence pointed directly to her being the one holding the gun.

Problem was, there wasn't enough solid evidence to arrest her. And besides, she had a damn good attorney who did his lawyering well. Something told him he might just get the answers he was looking for if he caught her unaware. Like making an unannounced visit.

He turned his beat-up Chevy into the circular drive and pulled up in front of the gothic-styled revival, peering up at the morose, rain-bloated clouds. Today the sky reminded him of the scarred surface of the revolver he always kept handy. Not his service revolver, but the one in the glove compartment—the one that had been his father's. The one he'd killed himself with ten years ago when Alex's mother walked out and never looked back. Thank God, he hadn't been tempted to do the same when his own wife left him. But then again, their marriage had been over a long time before she'd walked out the door.

The murky day magnified memories he thought he'd buried in a six-foot hole long ago. Alex would have preferred a brighter day to visit this gargoylesque monstrosity. One that didn't magnify his murky thoughts. Days like this weren't the best time for him to confront a woman who had a reputation for spending ninety-nine percent of her time glued to a man—in one position or another. He felt the lonely ripple of storm clouds pass across his soul. No, this probably wasn't the best idea he'd had in recent months. What the hell, he couldn't remember the last time he'd had a good idea.

From the gossip around the station, she'd been the one on top with this vic. He reached inside the pocket of his raincoat and pulled out the crumpled and curled notepad, squinting down at his scrawled notes, trying to decipher what he'd written.

Marco Korvanti. Age twenty-six. Professional gigolo by all accounts. High-priced gigolo. Personal escort, at least for the time being, of one Pandora Edwina Willmington, widow of industrial magnate, Alfred Price Willmington. Make that very rich, *young* widow of Alfred Willmington. And Marco Korvanti made two dead men who'd had the same lover within the space of two years.

Black Widow? He'd bet money on it. Procedurally, it was yet to be determined. He had a reputation for not going by the book and this was going to be another of those times when he followed his gut instincts. Even if it landed him in a heap of trouble as it usually did.

Again, he glanced up at the sky, rumbling with dark promise.

Marco Korvanti had been found naked and handcuffed to a bed at the Dark Temptations Inn. Now there was a place holding a lot of dark secrets and a shadowy reputation for hot sex and secret assignations. Not a place one would expect to find a respectable widow. But then again, who said Pandora Willmington was respectable?

He hadn't been on duty when they'd brought her in for questioning, but he'd read the report, heard the stories. Of course, she'd talked her way out of it. From the gossip, they'd all been hypnotized by the image of pure sex that had come strolling into the station yesterday. They'd hung on her every sensual word, practically begged to bring her coffee or tea, anything to get a whiff of her female fragrance and a glance at her bare, wet pussy. And when her attorney walked it, it was no wonder she'd sauntered out of there like a queen who'd won the war hands down, the world cringing at her feet. He wished he'd been there to see it.

Her statement was that she'd left earlier that evening after a "satisfying encounter" with the victim. He could only guess at what she considered a "satisfying encounter." Said he'd been in rutting good health when she'd left him to prepare for a charity event sponsored by one of the foundations she supported. Rather, her husband's money supported.

According to the coroner's report, Korvanti had died at approximately the same time Mrs. Willmington was witnessed giving a passionate appeal for donations at said event. But his gut said there was more to Madame Pandora's story than she was telling. And the function wasn't all that far from the scene of the crime.

Opening the door of his car, he leaned out, dropped the spent cigarette butt on the pristine drive, crushing it with his heel before he unfolded out into the damp, clinging air. Again, he looked up at the sky. Yup, it was definitely going to rain.

As he closed the door, he turned to look at the imposing stone architecture. It surprised him that she remained in the house—it didn't look her style. He would have expected her to be surrounded by a lush atmosphere, somewhere hot and moist, that complemented her reputation for pleasure—certainly something more modern than this ancient mausoleum.

He mounted the steps and rang the bell. As he waited for someone to answer the door, he turned around to survey the well-manicured grounds. Neatly trimmed shrubs bordered the circular drive. The fountain at the heart of the lush green lawn with the naked statue of Pan spouted a steady stream of clear, bubbling liquid. It was peaceful, serene even, but Alex sensed something about the place—an undercurrent of some sort. A click sounded behind him and he swiveled back toward the entrance.

He hid his surprise as the door was opened by a young, dusky-skinned man neatly dressed in tight black pants, black silk shirt, and shining leather boots. He was a head shorter than Alex's six-foot frame and his dark eyes surveyed Alex with curiosity.

"Can I help you?" he asked with a hint of Latin shrouding the edges of his question.

Alex whipped out his badge and displayed it to him. While he waited patiently for the man to study it, he attempted to size him up, figure out his position in the household. He didn't look like the typical butler for a place like this. A creature from an old monster movie would have fit in here perfectly. This guy, no. He belonged on a movie set, or maybe in a bull ring down in Spain. But he sure didn't belong in this setting.

But then neither did Pandora Willmington, by his estimation, from all he'd heard about her.

The man handed the badge back to Alex and stepped away from the door.

"Was Mrs. Willmington expecting you?" he asked as Alex stepped past him into the marble-floored foyer.

Damn, talk about opulent. He shifted around to face the young man, who looked about half his age—maybe nineteen or twenty. "No, she's not expecting me, but I have a few questions I'd like to ask her if she has time." He whipped out his notebook and a pen. "By the way, what's your name and your position here?"

"His name is Arturo and he's my personal assistant, Detective," a husky, sensual voice that reeked fuck-me, its effect floating downward, landing somewhere in the vicinity of his groin, informed him.

If he'd been anyone else he probably would have swallowed his tongue and someone would have had to call for emergency assistance when he turned to look at the owner of that voice. He should have been prepared. He felt like he'd slammed into a brick wall, and his cock rose hard and fast to attention. Nothing could have prepared him for this hot number. Nothing on this planet.

She had to be the infamous Pandora Willmington. He smoothed his expression, attempted to gain control of his misplaced lust. *Mine.* It was something that shouldn't have crossed through his mind. He might want her, more than he'd ever wanted anything in his life—but he couldn't have her. Too bad if he could taste the want, the need to feel his cock burrowing deep into her cunt. He was here to do a job.

He couldn't help stroking her with his eyes, and his thoughts. Blonde hair clung to the silk of a satin black robe with oriental markings that draped open, revealing pale flesh only superficially hidden beneath a black lace camisole. Long legs, bare, creamy, and smooth, culminated in shapely feet encased in black satin four-inch stilettos. Crimson lips, wet, pouty, sensual, kissable, a half smile of invitation, and bedroom eyes the color of expensive whiskey. Way out of his league. He licked his lips, anticipating the taste of her on his tongue.

One slender hand rested at the curve of the banister where she hovered about mid-way up the sloping staircase. Once she was sure she had his full attention, she floated down the remaining steps. Arturo hurried to the foot of the stairs and waited. He clasped her hand when she reached the last few steps and gallantly guided her down to the main floor. She stopped next to him, and Alex could see the nipples of her upthrust breasts vividly outlined, pressing against the silk. His cock throbbed painfully at the front of his pants.

She turned to Arturo and brushed against his side like a female cat in heat. One of her hands drifted around to curl possessively over the hard curve of his ass and Alex saw the muscles tighten beneath the thin black material. Arturo's eyes smoldered, and Alex could almost smell the smoke rising between the two of them. He felt like a voyeur witnessing the lustful exchange—and wanted to join in. Arturo raised her hand to his lips and placed a passionate kiss on her palm. Evidence of his arousal was more than prominently displayed against the front of his tight trousers.

Pandora raised a hand to stroke the side of his face. "Thank you, Arturo. You're superb," she purred. She turned to gaze at Alex through slitted eyes. "I'll handle our guest from here."

Alex was certain he saw a flicker of something in the young man's eyes as he released her hand. "As you wish, Mrs. Willmington. If you need me, just ring." He pivoted around, piercing Alex with a burning, poisonous look before he strode from the room.

Alex struggled to remember what he was here for and turned back to study the lethal woman who dripped sex. It was a surprise to him after all this time that his previously benumbed senses allowed him to respond so strongly. His ex-wife had done a down and dirty number on him, and he'd had a hard time evincing the least glimmer of interest in pursuing another relationship. Until today.

What role did Arturo really play in her life? Had he possibly resented the appearance of Korvanti? Had he been the one to kill him in a jealous rage? That young man harbored a lot of intense emotion below the surface. Or had he followed an order from the mistress of the house by disposing of a problem she wanted gone?

Something to think about. He filed it away.

"So, Detective, I thought I'd answered everything already when I visited your police station. What more would you like to know?"

She drifted silently across the marble foyer toward him, and he had the urge to retreat from the siren's lure. Too close and he'd be lost. The woman was definitely lethal, and the closer she got to him, the more alert his body became to the danger, to the need.

She was now near enough for him to smell the exotic scent of her expensive perfume. It swirled around him, blurring his vision, his purpose in being there.

He yanked his mind back to the task at hand. Distancing himself from this woman's allure became of prime importance.

"Detective Alex Johnson, ma'am. Exactly what role does your assistant hold here, Mrs. Willmington? Do you have a more personal relationship than strictly employer-employee?"

She was close, real close, too close. Her breasts rose and fell beneath the ebony silk bound tightly across them, prominently displayed, begging to be touched, to be molded by his hands, testing their weight as he fucked her hard. Primitive desire spiraled inside him to do just that. Visions of fucking her on that damn round mahogany table blotted out anything else. Tossing the contents of the table—the expensive vase, the embroidered tablecloth, the picture frames, all to the floor, spreading her wide and sinking deep inside blurred his vision. Duty faded like a foggy morning into the background.

As hard as he fought it, he felt the clinging net of passion descend to reel him in close, tightening all around him, cinching particularly close to his cock and balls.

"Are you asking if he's my lover, Alex?" Her question teased across his nerves, and he found it difficult to breath. Her gaze rose slowly to meet his; the molten bronze, lustful glitter penetrated through him.

"Is he?"

A delicate hand rose to finger the lapel of his tan raincoat, making him wish she was stroking something a little lower. "Are you married, Detective?"

He attempted to step away from her, to break free of the sexual haze, but she drifted after him. He began to feel like a cornered elk being stalked by a predator. "I'm here to ask the questions, Mrs. Willmington."

Her lush lips curved into a satisfied smile. She dropped her hand to clasp his left hand and raise it, sliding her gaze down to study it, then lifted her eyes back to his. Her hand was small and delicate, warm and soft. His cock hardened more painfully as he thought of it encircling and stroking his shaft. He was certain she'd know exactly how to use that hand to offer him maximum pleasure. It was a major accomplishment that he managed to stifle the needy groan building inside him.

"No ring, Alex. But there was one at one time, wasn't there? Are you divorced?" A dangerous predator, searching for any sign of weakness. She apparently saw the answer in his eyes—the fact that his divorce had become final one short month before—the indentation of his ring—the one he'd worn for ten years—still visible.

Suddenly, she dropped his hand and stepped away from him, and it was like he'd just been drenched with freezing rain. He inhaled deeply and then blinked, feeling he'd just walked out of a fog, its effects still clinging to him.

He tried to focus, but his body fought hard to maintain the sexual momentum. She turned away from him and sauntered toward a door as she lifted a hand, motioning for him to follow her. "Come with me," she called over her shoulder. She halted in the doorway and turned to glance back at him over her shoulder, a come-hither look in her eyes. "Maybe I'll even answer your questions."

Juicy bait—and he took it hook, line, and sinker. It was Lorelei who beckoned him, and, like a sailor at sea, he had no choice but to do her bidding. Was she a Black Widow wooing him into her web of lustful destruction? Hank wasn't here to save him this time, to encourage him to alter his course, and he had a feeling this was going to be one of those times when he just might need his steadying influence.

*   *   *

Walking through the doorway and over to another set of doors that opened onto a patio, she paused at a set of stone steps leading to the expansive gardens below at the back of the house. He reached her side as she stood there surveying the view.

"Do you really think I would have killed a man like Korvanti and taken the chance on losing all this—freedom? I could never be locked away and lose everything I've worked so hard to get. Korvanti was good, but not *that* good. Or maybe I should say he was bad, but certainly not worth killing. Not by me."

"That's what we're going to find out, Mrs. Willimington. Someone killed Mr. Korvanti and we're going to find out who it was. You were the last one with him. At the very least he might have said something, or you might have seen something you've forgotten."

She whirled around to face him and ran a finger along the lapel of his coat. "And you think you can inspire my memory, Detective?"

Lots of smiles had passed through his life. But never one that dripped sex the way hers did. Full, red, perfectly sculpted lips that he wanted to own, to taste, to see wrapped around his prick, sucking him deep. It was more like the contented cat who'd licked the bowl clean of cream and wanted more. A woman with a voracious appetite for sex. Her scent clung to him, seeming to insulate him from the real world. Is that what happened to all the men she took to her bed? She spun them round and round until they didn't know which end was up and which was down. The problem was, he wasn't sure he really wanted to break free of her sexy spinning. He attempted to fight the desire, to remain noncommittal—to focus on the job he was here to do.

"That's what I'm here to find out, ma'am."

"Call me Pandora. I hate being so formal, don't you?" She turned away and floated down the steps, her dressing gown caressing the stone, whispering behind her.

His hands fisted tightly at his sides as he fought the waves of arousal trying to take control.

She stopped and turned back to look at him. "Come on, Alex. I need some fresh air. I always need to feel the earth beneath my feet and the wind against my skin after a satisfying interlude of hot sex." Her gaze glittered hotly. "And I have been well-fucked, in case you were wondering." A fire raged through him at her words. Her look was one of anticipatory invitation; it peeled away the layers of his self-control and dug deep for his sex—and found it. It was a look that definitely belonged in the bedroom. "Does that answer your question about Arturo, Alex?"

She flitted down the path and he raced after her, like a champion stud dog on the scent of his bitch, meaning to bring her to ground. As he was about to catch up with her, she suddenly turned right and dashed toward a large tree in the distance. When she reached it, she whirled around, waiting for him to reach her, her breasts visibly heaving beneath the flimsy silk.

The wind whipped at her robe, revealing more of her delectable body to him. The visual image of her surrounded by the elements of a building storm was more than he could turn down. As he watched, she let the silky covering sidle to the ground.

"Are you trying to seduce me, Mrs. Willington?" he asked as he reached her beneath the umbrella of the tree.

"Pandora," she corrected. "Call me Pandora. It's going to storm any second, Alex, and I love fucking in a storm, surrounded by the elements of nature. I like getting down and dirty."

She reached up to push off his raincoat, then she reached for his belt as she rose up to claim his lips.

He felt her there, knew he should stop her, but it seemed his will was sapped from him. He wanted this vixen, wanted to feel her cunt milking his cock. It had been a long time since he'd been with a woman—not since his wife had left more than six months ago. He hadn't had the urge to scratch that particular itch. At least not until today.

Is that why he'd come here without his partner? Hoping to get laid, knowing her reputation? His pants were loosening as she undid the button and pulled down the zipper. Her cool, silky hand reached inside, and he thought he'd died and gone to heaven when her fingers surrounded him. He'd known she would feel like this.

She lifted her lips from his and gazed up at him. "Feels like you're more than ready for me, Alex. Do you want to fuck me? Is that why you came here?"

She surmised more than she should have. Is that how she managed to prowl at will through the throng of men in her life? From what he'd heard, there'd been quite a few since her husband's death.

Her hand expertly stroked his length, fingered the tip, delved into his slit. He couldn't find the voice to answer her question. Had he come here to be fucked by this siren? Hoped it would happen? She was a possible murderer, she was a suspect, and this shouldn't be happening. If Hank were here, it wouldn't.

But Hank wasn't here. And her knowledgeable hand was making him forget he even had a job.

She reached up and sucked at his lips, thrust her velvety tongue inside his mouth. He couldn't stand it anymore. He reached out and gripped her slender shoulders and pulled her closer, his tongue warring with hers, her body soft against his, her smell surrounding him.

And her heat. He felt the vibration of a deep, sexy laugh against his lips. Dammit, he needed the searing fire she built inside him. He'd felt cold and numb for far too long. He pulled away and looked down at her.

"You want a fucking, Pandora, I'm just the man to give it to you."

She threw back her head and laughed. "I knew it when I saw you waiting in the entryway. I knew you'd be good. I've never been with a policeman, can you believe it? I want to find out how you taste."

She sank to her knees, still caressing his rigid cock. His peripheral vision caught a glint of movement, and he turned his head just as her mouth consumed the tip of his prick and he shuddered with pleasure. Her hand and mouth began a steady gut-clenching rhythm. Another hint of activity, and finally he turned his head and attempted to focus on what he'd seen.

"Who the hell is that?" he managed to bark out.

For a moment his cock was free of her warm, silky attentions, then he heard her throaty laugh. "He's my gardener. There's nothing to be concerned about. He watches to make sure everything grows that should, and anything that should be pruned disappears. He's always very attentive to my garden. I like his close observation and vigilant attention to duty." Her mouth sucked him in again, and he closed his eyes, forgetting everything but the forbidden paradise she was drawing him into.

Her other hand cupped his heavy balls, kneading and stroking them. He felt the fire begin to center in his gut, spearing outward, fast and hard as he reached for his climax. Suddenly, her mouth freed him and she rose to her feet.

He couldn't catch his breath, couldn't think beyond the need to orgasm inside her one way or the other.

"You taste lovely, Alex. But I think it's time for something more. She pulled him farther beneath the tree until her back was against the rough bark. "My husband was a good teacher. He taught me how to please a man. And I was an excellent pupil. He taught me how to dress—and to undress. How to talk. And when not to. How to give and receive pleasure. Do you like what he's taught me? I can do and be anything you want. What do you want, Alex? Tell me, and it's yours."

Red haze encompassed him. He needed to form the words. "I want to fuck you," he finally ground out, pushing her against the tree.

She lifted a leg and wrapped it around his waist, opening herself to him. He no longer felt like a man, but an animal needing to mate and do it fast before the female tried to escape or disappeared into the mist. He ripped at the camisole, baring her breasts.

God, they were beautiful, upthrust, milky white with tight, deep pink nipples begging for his mouth. He lifted her and then dropped his head to consume her. Swirling his tongue over and around her pouty nipple, he sucked it into his mouth. He heard her purr of satisfaction as she arched toward him.

"Harder, Alex. Show me you want me."

He sucked hard, nipped with his teeth, and heard her hiss, driving him on, stoking the fire.

Murderer or not, he had to have her. It was as though nothing else mattered but being inside her, tasting her, consuming her.

"Yes, Alex, just like that."

He heard her whispered words and his other hand lifted to cup her other heavy breast, giving it the attention it deserved. Firm and round, her natural beauty called for his touch and he wanted to consume every inch of her.

He could smell the rain. He could smell her.

Raindrops pelted down on his head and the storm that had threatened now broke free. He saw the raindrops fall onto her skin, and rubbed the moisture over her, stroking her heated flesh. It was as though steam rose between them.

The wind whipped and howled around them, fierce and strong, reflecting the emotions swirling between them. His hands pulled at the flimsy camisole and ripped it from her body, exposing her to both the elements and himself.

"Yes, Alex, fuck me now. Right now. Do it hard and fast. Slide it in me deep."

He reached down and felt the heat of her core. Wet and hot, he slid his fingers through the searing silk of her vagina, past her engorged lips. So ready to take him. But he wanted something more first. He lowered her leg and sank to his knees.

"Spread your legs," he commanded.

"Oh, yes, anything you say. I want to feel your mouth, your tongue, sucking me." She widened her stance. He held her lips apart with his fingers as he delved inside with his tongue, stabbing as deep as possible to lap at her juices. She thrust into him, demanding he go deeper still.

He tasted her sweet, exotic cream, relished and licked at her. Exiting, he swirled his tongue over her engorged, stiff clit, gripped and teased with his teeth, felt her respond. She was so ready for him, so hot, so tight—tighter than he would have expected from a woman like her. But she was, and he knew when he sheathed himself inside her it was going to feel like exquisite heaven.

He drove his fingers inside her as he continued to circle her stiffened clit with his tongue and raze it with his teeth.

"Yes, oh, God, yes," she yelled as she thrust her hips.

He felt her release pulse all around him as he removed his fingers and sucked at her climax. Pure, honeyed cream, rich and thick. All his.

"Now, Alex, come to me now," she demanded as her fingers threaded through his hair and forced him up. Heavy, deep pants emitted from between her luscious lips.

He yanked her leg up and anchored it back around his waist, opening her to him. Centering his cock, he thrust deep into her well-lubricated pussy. It felt like heaven as she separated and conformed to him, accepting him completely.

When she had fully consumed him, she climbed onto him like a well-trained athlete, both legs circling him, the muscles in her thighs tight and hard as she began to undulate against him. His arms held her to him and her hands gripped his ass, kneading and demanding.

He began to thrust, slow and steady, penetrating deeply. He wasn't sure how long he could hold out, but he was damn sure going to try to keep this level of consuming ecstasy for as long as possible. Pure sexual heat seemed to steam in the air all around them. He breathed in, allowing it to cloak him completely.

The rain now fell in sheets, drenching them, shielding them. He felt the slick wetness on her skin as he pummeled into her. The wind and the rain and the environment pelted at their bodies as he fucked her hard, in long, slow strokes. She rode him with a fiery, wild passion he'd never experienced before.

With pure, deep, sensual pleasure she gave and took. Her mouth consumed his, her tongue warring and tangling with his own, undulating and driving hard to claim him. Their rhythm became more frantic.

He absorbed her, feeling all of her deep inside him, and there was nothing beyond the need to possess all of her. He had to have her.

He felt it building and he couldn't hold back any longer. He felt the orgasm overtake him, and pushed her back against the tree as he came and came and came. He couldn't hold back a shout of primal male triumph, a claiming of her body as she pulsed around him in her own shattering release.

Until there was nothing left, nothing but the shattering echoes of a consummation like nothing he'd ever experienced before. He slid from inside her body and sank to the ground with her in his arms.

She pulled away and leaned against the tree next to him, panting heavily. He turned his head to look at her. Her slick thighs were splayed wide, knees raised, her pussy exposed, pink and engorged, her breasts wet and glistening, the nipples still tightly beaded. Her wet hair was plastered to her head. Her eyes were closed and there was a satisfied smile on her parted lips.

And he wanted her again. He leaned back and closed his eyes. He'd not only fucked her, but himself as well. Damn, he needed a cigarette right now. But he knew the pack sitting in his coat pocket were pretty much sodden and worthless. Just like he felt.

But damn it had been good. No, it had been fucking great.

"That was very…satisfying, Detective. You're not like the others."

"What the hell is that supposed to mean?"

"You like it hot and hard. You demand. Each of my lovers is different, but you, you were magnificent."

Suddenly, he rose to his feet. "It shouldn't have happened." He straightened his clothes and then turned to help her up.

She slid against his body. "But it did and I'm glad it did."

He picked up her sodden robe and pulled it around her shoulders. Then he reached down to pick up his coat. "I have to go."

"So soon? I thought we were just getting started." She thrust against his body. "The others know they owe me for their livelihood. They give me what I demand because they owe me. You—you're different. I can't buy you, but I want you anyway. Again and again."

"I'm afraid not, Mrs. Willmington. It's not going to happen again. It shouldn't have happened this time. You're a prime murder suspect and I'm one of the detectives investigating the case."

"Do you think I murdered him? Why?"

He shrugged. "Blackmail maybe? Could be he was about to air all your dirty little secrets in a lucrative deal to the tabloids."

"Do you really think I have many secrets that aren't well known? Do I seem like a woman who is afraid to have others know about her sexual needs?" As he watched, she pulled the front of the robe closed.

"Mrs. Willmington, Pandora, you've got two men in your life dead—a husband and a lover. It doesn't look good. You have to understand my perspective."

He saw a flicker of what looked like hurt vulnerability cross her face as she looked up at him. Then it changed; it was masked by more jaded knowledge and wisdom in her eyes than he would have expected. He caught his breath. For one second he saw a spark of something even deeper. Instinct said there was more to this woman than she allowed anyone to see.

"My husband was a very demanding man. He was the one who

taught me how to use my body to get what I wanted in life. He was not adverse to using it to gain what he wanted as well. I learned early to accept, to become what he needed from me. I am what he made me. But I didn't kill him. His work killed him. His demand for perfection killed him. I didn't."

She lifted her head proudly, her emotions shuttered, and swung away from Alex, striding back toward the house. The rain had let up and was now a soft sprinkling of drops as he followed her back along the path and toward the mansion. He reached her side as she was about to mount the steps. She stiffened when he touched her shoulder. He couldn't help himself.

"I'm sorry if I've hurt your feelings."

She whipped around, a glacial look on her face. "Hurt my feelings? Hardly, Detective. Have I answered your questions? Probably not, but do you think we could save it for another day? I'm rather tired right now." She walked through the open glass doors and was met by another man who held open a thick, terrycloth robe. She dropped the ruined silk one she was wearing and allowed him to enfold her in the dry one.

Alex watched as the attendant's muscular arms wrapped around her and felt envious as the possessive need to have her rose inside him again.

He picked up another towel and dried her wet hair. This woman obviously had more attention than he could ever have imagined. All male.

She turned to look at him. "Erik is my personal trainer and masseuse. He'll take care of me from here. Another time, Detective." Alex followed as Erik trailed behind her when she left the room and mounted the steps he'd first seen her on. She never looked back.

"I think it's time for you to leave." Alex turned around to find Arturo hovering behind him. "I'll show you out."

Alex left the house, no wiser about the young widow than when he'd entered. Except he now knew all the stories about her need for sex were true. And he did have at least three other suspects to add to his list, along with an aching erection that should have been appeased.

Did he think Pandora Willmington had killed her paramour? His own body still felt the lingering aftershocks of his fall from grace at her feet. He was probably more confused than when he'd started. Like being caught in a tidal wave, he had the urge to race back up those steps and claim her for himself again.

With a shaking hand, he pulled out the keys to the old, rusted Chevy and quickly started the engine. He had to get out of here before he made a bigger fool of himself than he already was. Hank was going to rip up one side of him and down the other. It would be a miracle if he hadn't totally destroyed his career by his actions today.

He still wasn't any closer to finding Marco Korvanti's killer than he had been before. And he was more confused than ever.

*   *   *

After stopping at home to change his clothes to something dry, he drove to his favorite hangout on Twenty-Seventh Street. He sat staring at the glass in front of him that contained the shot of whiskey he'd asked for. The liquid reminded him of Pandora Willmington's eyes. He picked it up and downed it fast, praying it would numb his memory. It seared his throat and heated his belly.

He pulled out his cell phone and found there was one voicemail message. It probably had come while he was otherwise engaged at the Mulberry Estate. He listened, only to discover they'd picked up a suspect who they were charging with the murder of Marco Korvanti. Turns out it was his on-again off-again girlfriend. Her fingerprints where found at the scene and a witness had heard a loud argument coming from the room where he'd been killed and saw her leave the scene of the crime. He closed the phone and shoved it back in his pocket. So much for his instincts.

It had still been a mistake allowing himself to lose control with Pandora. Big one. He never should have let his libido consume him the way it had, but she'd woven such a silky web around him he'd been unable to resist her. She sure knew a man's weakness and struck fast to the heart of it. He took a long drag on his cigarette and exhaled.

"I'll have one of those," a familiar voice next to him informed the bartender.

He stiffened and turned his head. "What are you doing here?" he ground out as the vixen, dressed in tight, white, expensive silk perched herself on the stool next to him. He noticed she wore short white silk and lace gloves that emphasized the delicacy of her creamy, bronzed limbs. His cock tightened at the memory of those sexy, sheathed hands stroking him.

She looked far different from the sodden, wild siren he'd left just hours ago.

"I have a proposition for you."

"A proposition? What kind of proposition?"

113

She lifted the glass from the bar, swiveled toward him, and spread her thighs as far as the flimsy material would allow. The skirt of her suit was short and tight, barely covering the feminine assets it was supposed to hide from view. And when she spread those creamy legs, he saw the glimmer of her shaved, pink pussy. His cock hardened against his thigh, remembered the hot, murky afternoon with himself buried inside her slick depths.

She sipped at the whiskey, the liquid reflecting the color of her eyes—a vision seared into his memory. He felt like he was slogging through a Georgia swamp, unable to break free of the muggy heat and sucking earth.

"You're not happy, Alex, I can sense that. And you're lonely. But I made you feel good. I made you forget." Her hand slid along the length of his inside thigh, making his balls tighten. "I made you come, and I know you wanted to do it again. We can have more of that. I need a bodyguard. And I want you to take the job."

A bodyguard. She had to be kidding. "I'm not for sale, Pandora. I thought we established that this afternoon. I'd have thought you'd have someone lined up for that position—looks like you've got every other position covered."

Again, for just a moment, that look of hurt vulnerability passed through her eyes. Then it was gone and she shook her head. "I'm not trying to buy you. I'm offering you a job because I know you can handle it. Not every position on my staff is filled. Almost every position. There are just a few, more intimate ones, I require just the right person for. No one has appealed to me that I'd want to fill this particular position. No one strong enough to do the job right. No one that I felt safe with." She took another sip from the glass and looked up over the rim at him. "Until now. I want you, Alex."

"I don't think so, Pandora."

She lifted her leg onto his thigh and twirled her foot. "Do you like my new shoes?" She was wearing white stilettos with sparkling rhinestones. "They're new. I had them made to go with this outfit."

He glanced down. "They're snazzy all right. But how the hell do you wear those things all the time?"

As he watched her, she looked down to admire her display "When I married Al, I'd never owned a pair. Certainly nothing that had been made especially for me. He's the one who insisted I wear them—all the time. He said I had beautiful legs and he loved to see me show them off. Even in the bedroom, especially when we were making love. After five years, one becomes accustomed to wearing them." Her gaze slid to his. "You liked them this afternoon."

Yes, he had. By the time he'd ripped off her camisole, those black stilettos were the only thing she'd been left wearing. She'd looked damned sexy wearing only pink skin and the black heels.

"I don't know what we have to talk about. I'm not looking for a new job."

She lowered her leg and shrugged from the stool. "Come with me, Alex," she coaxed. "Let's go someplace private to talk about it." She reached out for his hand.

Someplace private. How the hell did her husband handle her with such a high sexual libido? She was insatiable. At last count there were three men who worked for her, obviously all her lovers. She had a dead lover, making that at the very least four. And now she wanted Alex. To take the place of her dead lover?

He looked at her, trying to disassociate from the need to give her exactly what she was looking for and keep the uninvolved, unemotional detective at the forefront. Unfortunately, the detective mantel had melted beneath the blaze of an afternoon of hot sex—a lot easier than he would have liked. One session and he was addicted. The afternoon had ripped away the protection of his role as investigator and fitted him with something else—a role he didn't want to get too comfortable with. It was damned dangerous. *She* was dangerous.

He hopped down from the barstool and swallowed the last of the whiskey.

"Someplace private. I could do that."

She smiled. "Good." Reaching for his hand, the cool satin of her glove slid erotically against his skin as they exited the bar. A sleek, silver Rolls was standing at the curb. "Come with me. You can pick your car up later. Harry will drive you back."

Harry. A man exited from the driver's side of the car and came around to open the back door. Unlike the others, he was older, with silvered hair. And Alex had to wonder. This guy made five. How many others did she have at her beck and call? This was obviously a woman with varied taste in men. He climbed into the back of the car after her.

As the Rolls slid away from the curb, Pandora climbed onto his lap, long legs splayed wide to either side. Damn, Eric must be a real fine trainer because this woman was certainly limber. Her skirt climbed up to bunch around her hips. He couldn't help himself, and his hands came to rest on her bare, rounded curves. Such warm, silky flesh. Expensive skin.

She reached down to unleash his thick, hard penis. It sprang free, more than ready for some hot attention.

She smiled. "That's what I like about you, Alex. Always ready to do your duty, aren't you?"

She clasped him with both gloved hands and began to stroke up and down. Damn, what a feeling. New sensations raced through him at the feel of satin stroking over his heated, throbbing sex.

"Is this what you call private?" he managed to mumble.

"This is just a little pre-negotiation foreplay, darling. A little taste to—ummm—harden you up for the more difficult negotiations later."

Oh, yeah, she knew how to harden him up all right. He leaned his head back against the seat, enjoying her expert foreplay, his fingers kneading at her warm, rounded buttocks. A groan escaped his throat as she rubbed her slick pussy against his burgeoning cock.

Long moments later, the car came to a stop and he slitted his eyes open. With some difficulty, she replaced his now steel-hard cock back into his pants, and zipped him up. Then she moved from his lap and straightened her skirt.

"We're here. Now for the real negotiations to begin. I handpick all of my employees. And the negotiations are always quite...rigorous." She looked at him. "Think you're up to the challenge, Alex? I really hope you are."

Harry came around and opened the door. Pandora slid out effortlessly with his assistance. Alex couldn't peel his eyes away from her as the driver helped her to smooth her skirt down over her perfectly rounded ass. She smiled up at him and stepped away from the car. It took Alex a little more work to climb out as he was hot and hurting. He glanced up at the sign above the building—The Dark Temptations Inn.

He looked back at Pandora, who stood waiting, with a challenging look in her eyes. His glance fell to her glove-covered hands and the hairs on the back of his neck stood on end. He remembered that her fingerprints had never tied her to that room in The Dark Temptations Inn. And now he began to wonder. His gaze moved back to her face. She looked at him steadily.

"The man I hire to be my bodyguard would understand why I brought him here. The man I hire as my bodyguard would be eager for the danger in discovering what's beneath the black veil." She turned and looked up at the sign. "My husband introduced me to the Inn a long time ago. Did you know I own part of it now? Do you know what goes on behind the doors of this place? Are you willing to find out?"

She challenged him like no one he'd ever known before. Was she guilty of the murder of her lover in this place after all? Right now, he fucking didn't care. He'd tasted her, sampled what she had to offer, and he wanted more—a lot more. Maybe he did need a change of professions. He liked the danger—thrived on it. And he damn well wanted this woman. He knew he sure as hell would never be bored.

She was a smart woman and she knew what she wanted. It wasn't money she used to bribe him into becoming a member of her exclusive staff. It was sex, and her whole attitude. And the damn vulnerability he'd caught a glimpse of. It was the freedom she exuded, and the touch of taboo. He could be dead tomorrow, a body sitting on the slab right next to Marco Korvanti.

His heart pumped faster and the hot blood rushed through his veins. His cock throbbed in anticipation of exposing the layers of this complicated vixen. Doing it slowly, inch by inch.

"Lead on," he finally said, giving in to his baser instincts, following her up the steps.

She turned to reach for his hand and smiled up at him, the seductress lurking in her eyes. "By the way," she asked. "Do you by any chance have a set of handcuffs with you?"

Lead on, said the hard, eager fly to the sensual, dangerous spider.

CARNAL CARNIVAL

MARIPOSA SOUL

CHAPTER 1

Andre looked down at the woman as she slept, a satisfied smile on her gently parted, soft lips. One arm was thrown upward curved around her head, the silky exposed flesh would have been enough to draw any other man back to her bed to stroke her drowsily awake.

Any other man would be eager to suckle her breasts as he parted her legs to burrow inside the welcoming satin heat of her vagina. She had been wet and ready for him immediately and his cock had slid effortlessly inside her silky passage.

She was a beautiful woman by anyone's standard. She was responsive and sensual and he'd given her pleasure, brought her to orgasm more than once, hence the contented, peaceful look on her face right now. And stroking her heat had brought his own orgasm spurting forth with ease. If only it had been thoughts of the woman lying beneath him that had fueled his explosive climax.

He smoothed the wrinkles from his shirt and reached for his jacket that was resting on a chair near the bed. He sat down and slipped into his shoes, tied the laces, then leaned back and watched her for long moments.

Why did he feel so removed from his emotions? He should be feeling satisfied and happy. He'd met her in a bar earlier that evening. It was one he frequented often, meeting up with other journalists like himself, chatting for long hours over several beers, debating current issues. More times than not, leaving with a female colleague to end the night in her bed or his. They were casual encounters, scratching an itch, and then they'd go their separate ways, on to the next story. No commitments, no ties, no part of his inner self shared with another human being. That had occurred only once, and he shied away from remembering the ecstasy of that particular memory. No, he wouldn't think of that.

Recently, he'd returned from an assignment in South America, and had spent the night swapping stories as he often did. She'd walked up to him, having recognized him from a picture she'd seen in a current article of his and introduced herself, offering to buy him a drink.

She'd told him her name, but for the life of him, he couldn't remember it right now. Maybe he didn't want to remember it. Once he walked out of her apartment, she'd be no more than a fleeting snip of a memory, hardly more than a quick byline in a newspaper. A blur among other nameless female faces, and, like inexpensive wine, he'd used them to numb his thoughts and make him forget—just a quick, cheap fix of forgetfulness. Only it didn't work the way it was supposed to. All it did was emphasize the deep well of loneliness he was always on the verge of tumbling into head first.

Sometimes he felt like Prince Charming looking for the owner of the glass slipper. Finding that one person who fit him like no other in the kingdom would or could. And sometimes he felt like the girl in the story, where he was the one quickly slipping away, fearful of discovery, yet holding fast to the dream her prince would find her. And knowing that for one brief moment, he really did exist.

He now had to wonder whose discovery he was more afraid of—his own or his friends and colleagues?

He rose from the chair, gave one last look toward the bed, then turned away to walk out of the bedroom, quietly letting himself out of her apartment. Sometimes the painful loneliness he felt inside yawned like a chasm of darkness waiting to consume him entirely.

He felt it more deeply now than he had six months ago. He didn't want to acknowledge the reason for the deep, gnawing pain that seemed to be ever present. If he attempted to pry open his soul and look inside, he was afraid of what he'd discover. It would be a negation of all he thought he was.

It was one of the reasons he'd fled on assignment to South America, putting some distance between himself and temptation.

He stepped out of the elevator, strode across the floor, and out onto the sidewalk. He breathed in the scent of nighttime and it seemed to cleanse him somewhat or at least helped to clear his head.

Pulling out a pack of cigarettes and the lighter from his inner pocket, he quickly put one in his mouth, lit it, and inhaled, feeling the bite of the nicotine as it attacked his lungs. He looked down at the lighter, studying the elongated silver outline and the deeply etched multicolored butterfly on its face. It caused a deep ache inside him, a longing for something ethereal and delicate he couldn't touch, couldn't hold onto. Was afraid to capture.

Being in South America had only exacerbated the need and the feeling of solitude. There were lots of butterflies in the jungles of South America. He should have known better than to take that particular assignment to try to forget. His fingers tightened around the lighter, the metal beginning to warm in his hard clasp.

His footsteps carried him along the wet, silent street, shoulders hunched forward against the damp night air, his mind focused on internal thoughts. And memories.

The encounter with the woman upstairs had meant nothing. It was a sad fact, but true nonetheless. He'd wanted it to mean something—he'd wanted to feel, to embrace her fragrance and femininity. He wanted her to offer him forgetfulness. He willed her to make his soul come alive, to be able to answer her mating call.

But like all the many meaningless times before, it hadn't happened.

He turned a corner, heard the echo of a lonely siren in the distance, felt the moisture of late night rain cling to his face.

He should take that assignment his editor had offered him today. It would send him far away from the temptation for a good year. Then maybe the aching need would finally dissipate and he would remember how good it felt to ease his body inside a woman's soft caress.

Who was he trying to kid? Those days had been destroyed forever. He shoved a hand into the pocket of his coat. His fingers encountered the sharp edges of a business card and a wave of longing sliced through him. He didn't have to pull it out to know whose card it was. He had it memorized, the name seared into his brain.

You have a butterfly's soul, Andre, beautiful and fragile. I await the day you set it free to live the way it is meant to live. Come to me when you are ready.

He'd fought it for so long, trying to lose himself within other warm bodies, in other arms, through other lips. He'd tried so damned hard to surround himself with the scent of women, to make him forget.

But they had all paled, and were all forgotten because he could only remember one set of arms, one mouth that consumed and pulled at his soul, eyes that stroked him to life and filled the loneliness of his soul, like nothing had ever done before.

His response had scared him, yet excited him. He'd wanted to give in to the feelings, and although they'd felt right at the time, he'd shied from acknowledging what they meant about him.

He stopped walking and looked up at the street sign and sighed. Pulling deeply on the cigarette, he tossed it down and ground it with the heel of his shoe. It was as though it was inevitable his footsteps should have carried him to this particular street corner. He'd fought the feelings for so long and was tired of the struggle. The confusion inside him swirled around him, ever present no matter where he went or whom he was with.

But suddenly, as he looked up at the street sign, his hand closed over the card in his pocket. Mariposa Street. Was it a sign that he should accept the message of the soul he'd tried to forget? In Spanish, mariposa meant butterfly.

Was he finally ready to accept the nature of his needs to feel complete? He turned toward the street, saw a taxi, and hailed it. He felt the flutter of trapped wings beating inside his soul. Was he ready to fly? He knew he feared leaving the safe, familiar boundaries of his cocoon.

The taxi pulled up, he opened the door, and stepped inside.

"Where to?" the older gentleman asked him.

Again, his fingers encountered the card in his pocket, like a talisman. He didn't need to take it out to provide the driver with the address.

"Twenty-one Morgan Street—to the Morgantown Apartments."

The driver nodded, pulled away from the curb, and Andre settled back in the seat, his heart pounding—was it excitement or fear?

How could he have known that signing up for that investigative journalism conference would change his life? That it would alter everything he'd thought true about himself. It had been the moment when he'd known why every relationship he'd attempted to have over the years had ended up transitory and fleeting. Unfulfilling. Somehow his unconscious mind had refused to accept picking a long-term partner simply to assuage his superficial requirement for intimate contact with another human being. It wasn't just a body he needed to fill the solitude, he knew that now. He wanted a heart and a mind that understood who and what he was inside.

Those encounters had paled when he'd been confronted with the one person who connected with him on more than a surface level. They had touched at so many levels and in such a short space of time. And, yet, he'd run from the knowledge. Was it too late?

The taxi pulled up to the curb in front of a brownstone apartment building. He pulled out his wallet and paid the driver, offering a generous tip. Then he stepped from the taxi. He stood there, staring up at the building.

Once he walked up those steps, there would be no turning back. Not this time. The person waiting there would expect more than just a fleeting one-night stand. Was he ready to look deeper into what was in his soul? To accept who he was?

He ascended the steps, pulled open the outer door and stepped inside. He surveyed the apartment numbers, stared at the one he wanted for long, tense moments. His body had begun a low humming of anticipation. He wanted to feel, wanted to acknowledge what was in his soul, and only one person could help him find himself—help him break free of the rigid cocoon that forced him to traditional boundaries.

He reached out and pressed the bell, waiting for a response. He wanted to be inside, out of the cold darkness. He wanted warmth, understanding. He wanted to feel true passion, not just sexual release. He had experienced both for just one moment—a delirious, wonderful afternoon of love that he'd never experienced before.

He was finally ready to accept the lessons Simon Doran was willing to teach him. If he still wanted that as well.

CHAPTER 2

That morning of the conference his alarm had failed to sound off. He was late for the panel he was supposed to sit in on. As quietly as possible he slid into a seat near the front. He'd signed up for this conference particularly for this session and he couldn't believe he'd almost overslept and missed it.

Simon Doran was scheduled to be a participant and Doran was one of Andre's heroes, so to speak, an active investigative journalist himself at one time, he now spent his time teaching at the local university and writing about his adventures as a journalist who had ventured into some of the most explosive moments in history. South Africa. Kuwait. China. Just to name a few.

Andre had first watched an interview with him on television when he was sixteen. Simon Doran must have been around his own age at the time—maybe thirty-five or so. Almost twenty years had passed since that moment when he connected with the passion and excitement of the image on the television screen. Since that time, he'd practically inhaled every ounce of information on the man, studied his techniques, read his autobiography, and consumed the events surrounding the stories he'd covered.

But this was the first opportunity he'd had actually to hear him speak. Usually, when he was in town, Andre was away at college, or in recent years, gone on assignment. But this time everything had worked out where he could be present at the same time his unknowing mentor was giving a presentation.

Andre looked at all the panelists, studied them, but his attention was drawn to only one man. With a head of gleaming white hair, a warm, golden tan to his skin, and the riveting turquoise depth of his eyes, he stood out far and away from the rest of the panelists, who dimmed well into the background.

One would have thought that after all these years, Andre's fascination with the adventures of a journalist who was now, for all intents and purposes, in retirement, would have paled. It was no longer the hero worship of an adolescent sixteen-year-old, but had developed into more of an appreciation and recognition of a talented colleague.

For two hours he sat and listened attentively to the well-modulated voice, the passion and excitement still evident in every fiber. Other than the white hair, he didn't have the look of a man pushing toward sixty; he radiated energy. There didn't appear to be one ounce of extra flesh, and the suit he wore fit cleanly over his solid, muscular frame.

He was a man comfortable with himself and his environment. Andre knew, from watching his many interviews in various parts of the world, that was true no matter where he was—he always seemed to fit within his environment. Adaptable, like a chameleon. It was one of the things he'd always admired about him and had tried to emulate. To become one with the culture offered him a better opportunity to get the story beneath the surface—and had worked for him in a number of situations.

When the discussion ended, he was surprised to look at his watch and realize two hours had passed since he'd walked into the room. And he regretted the conclusion. He left the room in a daze as his thoughts continued to digest the discussion, remembering the vibrant speech. His attention had never wavered, not for an instant.

He pulled out his program schedule and noted the next session he planned to attend, and he walked down the hall toward the appropriate room. The day moved by swiftly, and the last session of the day ended. It was five o'clock and he had a couple of hours to kill before the awards dinner that would begin at seven. Instead of heading back to his apartment, he made for the bar.

Grabbing a vacant stool at the bar, he ordered a neat Scotch. As he downed his first swallow, someone sat on the stool beside him. He glanced up and swallowed hard. It wasn't possible.

The man who'd sat down next to him turned and smiled. Small lines of maturity crinkled near his eyes and Andre was held fascinated by the depth of those deep blue mirrors.

"Simon Doran," he said as he held out a hand.

Andre nodded and extended his own hand, noting the firm, callused grip. "Andre Cordaire. Yes, I know who you are. I sat in on your discussion this morning. Great job."

"Thanks. I don't do as many as I used to, but this one sounded challenging, and I liked the combination of panelists they had lined up. Glad you got something out of it."

Andre took another swallow of his Scotch. This was more than he could have hoped for—to actually hold a conversation with Simon Doran. Once Simon's drink arrived, he took a long swallow and leaned back with a sigh.

"Yeah, I needed that. Conferences are thirsty work."

Andre chuckled. "Yeah, I guess they are."

"Are you staying here at the hotel?" Simon's gaze studied Andre. Andre recognized that look—it probed for a way to get inside his head, to find out what made him tick. He met the look, guessing it would challenge Simon to dig past it.

Simon leaned back against the stool, visibly relaxing, and grinned. Andre felt an unfamiliar heat dig inside him at that look of acceptance. What surprised him was that Simon looked as magnetic and attractive in person as he did on television or in photographs he'd seen of him.

"I know your name. You've done some great investigative pieces recently, if I remember correctly."

Andre nodded. "Thanks. Yes. I have to say, I've followed your career pretty closely and it's an honor to finally meet you in person."

Simon chuckled. "Don't tell me you became a journalist because of me. You'll make me feel a whole lot older than I want to."

It was Andre's turn to grin. "Wouldn't think of it. I will say you inspired me in the right direction. I've always written, but you got me on the road to investigative reporting—and I have to thank you for that."

Simon nodded. "I'll accept the compliment as graciously as I can. You've obviously got the talent for what you do, at least as far as I've seen, so if I helped you find the path, that's great." He turned his head and surveyed the nearly empty bar. "Let's find a table, get more comfortable, and compare war stories. I've got an urge to kick back a little. Do you have the time, or maybe you've got someplace you need to be?"

Andre shook his head. "No, sounds like a plan to me. I've got some free time and I'd enjoy a chance to talk with you."

They left the stools, drinks in hand and sauntered over to a vacant table.

Andre never made it to the dinner, and instead they shared a plate of chicken wings and potato skins, and another round of drinks. They had more in common than Andre ever could have expected, and their conversation went on well into the night. It was the wee hours of morning before they looked up and realized how much time had passed.

"Wow," Andre remarked as he rose from the table. "I can't believe how the time has flown. I'm sorry I kept you so long."

Simon shook his head. "Hey, I enjoyed it. But it is getting late and I need to get some sleep. I'm planning to hike up the mountain tomorrow and need at least a few hours of rest."

They walked through the glass front doors of the hotel. Andre turned to Simon and held out his hand. "I enjoyed the conversation and the panel discussion. I hope we'll have a chance to meet again."

Simon reached out and engulfed his hand in a firm grip, held it for long moments, staring into Andre's eyes.

Andre felt a warmth pervade his bones and dig deep inside. He felt regret at the parting, feeling there was something more to be shared with this man. There was something about him that he didn't want to let go. For a few short hours, the loneliness that had always been a part of him had faded away.

"You live in town?" Simon finally asked as he released his grip.

"Yes, not too far from here as a matter of fact."

The doorman waved a taxi forward.

"Care to share a cab? I have an apartment in town as well."

Andre nodded and followed Simon into the taxi, and gave his directions to the cabbie, then settled back.

Andre felt the hard heat of Simon's firm thigh almost touching him, hips close, his warmth and vibrancy reaching toward him. In a sense it made him uncomfortable that he was responding to him in much the same way he would to an attractive woman. Except it was more—something deeper inside him, something far stronger.

He looked at Simon's hand lying at rest on his thigh. He wore a gold ring with a black onyx stone. He remembered the firm grip when they shook hands. He found himself wondering how he used them to make love to a woman. Was he as smooth and in his element in bed as he obviously was when reporting? And for some reason his balls tightened at the thought of discovering how the hard touch of a man was different from the softness of a woman.

He shook his head, trying to dispel the foreign erotic thoughts running through his mind, and turned to look out the window at the passing buildings, noting the streets were beginning to fill as people rose to begin a new day. He'd never thought of himself in those terms before, not ever. So why now?

He must be tired, and then there were all those Scotches he hadn't noticed himself downing as they talked through the night. That must be it.

The taxi pulled up in front of his building. He opened the door, then felt Simon's firm grip on his arm. He turned to look inquiringly.

"I mentioned I'm going hiking...well, later today. I know it's short notice, but if you don't have anything better to do, maybe you'd like to join me?"

Andre's heart seemed to stutter to a halt in his chest. It was one of the things they'd discussed in their conversation—how they both enjoyed rock climbing and hiking. Something odd was taking place inside Andre and he didn't understand it, and the excitement stirred him in strange and pleasurable ways. The idea that the loneliness he always felt was drawing farther and farther away in the company of this man, the fact that the touch on his arm felt good, and he wanted to pursue the friendship that seem to be budding between them, had him nodding his head. Anything to hold onto the magic of Simon's presence.

The warmth in Simon's eyes drew him in. His firm lips lifted upward into a smile. Andre had the overwhelming urge to lean forward and find out what those lips tasted like—how would they be different from a woman's, and instead reared back, afraid of the turbulent emotions swirling around inside him.

He saw something in Simon's eyes, a flicker of—regret maybe? About what? The moment passed.

"I'd like that, Simon." He could not turn this man down. They had touched tonight in a way he'd never been touched before and was afraid to lose the connection. He'd never felt that in a relationship before—this need for more—for everything.

Simon nodded. "I'll pick you up. You bring the coffee and beer, I'll bring food. I think you'll find it illuminating, if nothing else. Eleven work for you?"

Again, Andre nodded. "Fine with me. Five or six hours of sleep will do me fine. I'll be ready."

He swung the door of the yellow cab closed and walked into his apartment building. This whole day had been like a fantasy from a long-forgotten dream. It was the first day in his life he'd felt there was a place he belonged in the world, but the closer he got to his apartment, the feeling of separation settled back in. Panic set in and he began to wonder about the plans for the day. Did Simon mean to keep the date? Or had he offered it on a whim and would call and cancel? It hadn't seemed real somehow, and he found himself wanting, no, needing, it to be tangible.

There was some other element at work here as well, and he hid from discovering it—what it might mean. Finding someone to share his thoughts with, and who shared his own—who made him feel a bond with another human being, and a likeness of mind. He'd never had that before. Not on this level.

He tossed and turned in his bed trying to sleep, yet kept waking up. His dreams weren't filled with fucking women, making him hard for release. They were different this time. His dreams were of Simon Doran. Of Simon kissing him, touching him, of being naked in bed. He dreamed of bodies touching, as their minds had, feeling his flat nipples grinding against his own chest, cocks touching and sliding against each other, hard lips and tongues mating and slipping together in hot abandon.

He'd awoken with his hand on his cock, slick with the orgasm the dream had elicited. It felt good, but it confused him. How could he possibly find it arousing to be making love—no, wanting to *fuck*—with another man. He'd never had dreams like that before, and it was troubling, and he didn't understand it, not one bit.

He got up, padded to the bathroom, and then on toward the kitchen for a drink of water. Too much alcohol the night before—that had to be the problem. He downed the glass of water, placed the glass in the sink, and went back to bed. If he did end up going hiking, he was going to need more energy than he had right now.

The dream was troubling, yet a part of him had enjoyed the erotic fantasy encounter. He found himself wondering what Simon looked like in the buff. Would he be as hot as Andre imagined in his dreams?

He found himself stroking his cock again as he visualized in his mind the melding of their bodies. He tried to imagine a woman, but a female form wouldn't materialize. He wandered into sleep too tired to force his dream world down a path it didn't want to take. After all, it was only fantasy, right? And Simon would never know he was the subject of his erotic fantasies. Dreams were safe. He would worry about it later. Right now, he enjoyed the feeling of connecting with someone, of sharing more than his body with a person who made him feel not so alone. At least he hoped it was right and he hadn't misunderstood.

He'd never had a close friend, always too immersed in succeeding in his chosen profession and following the scent of the next story.

But this relationship was different. And something told him it was going to change everything for him.

CHAPTER 3

Andre was up, showered, and ready when Simon rang the bell announcing his arrival. He was pumped, more than ready to begin the day. Surprisingly, he felt well rested and more awake than he'd expected to be. He pulled opened his apartment door and raced down the steps rather than taking the cranky old elevator.

When he saw Simon waiting for him, he felt a rush of pleasure surge through him. He tried not to think about the erotic dreams he'd had the night before, but couldn't help himself. He'd never been sexually attracted to a man and couldn't quite figure out what was going on inside his head. Whatever it was, he'd keep it to himself. It had to be just a passing phase—the excitement of meeting the person who had previously been just a distant, untouchable icon to him. He had friends who were gay, but he'd never felt sexually attracted to any of them. He had no problem making love to women. Maybe it wasn't always the earth-shattering experience he would have liked to experience during sex, but he'd always been satisfied. He just figured he was waiting for the right one to show up.

So what was this sudden desire in fantasizing about making love to a man? True, he'd hero-worshiped this particular man for years, but this was different than that adolescent pedestal thing. This was some kind of attraction of a different sort. Something he'd better bury before it ruined a relationship he was determined to enjoy, mano to mano.

His own father hadn't been a particularly good role model, coming home drunk more often than not, and eventually ending up in prison. In those early years, Simon had been the man he'd looked up to. But this attraction he was feeling wasn't for a father figure, even though Simon was quite a bit older than him.

He was actually attracted to him in a physical way. Just looking at him aroused passions in him no one else ever had. But he refused to let it affect this new relationship, and he shoved it back deep inside. He was looking for an intellectual friendship with someone who understood his profession, his lifestyle, and not in adventuring into anything more than that—no matter what his dreams were like.

He couldn't remember a moment when he'd been happier than he was right now. Blood pumped through his veins at a surprising rate and he eagerly pushed through the door to greet the man waiting for him.

Simon smiled as he reached his side. "Morning. Ready to go?" He gazed up at the blue, cloudless sky as they walked toward Simon's vehicle, which turned out to be a beat up, old brown Jeep. "Looks like it's going to be a great day for hiking. Throw your pack in the back and we'll get going."

Eagerly, Andre did as instructed, climbed into the vehicle, and fastened his seatbelt. Simon got in and the vehicle rumbled to life. He'd never been this excited about a trip to the mountains. He watched Simon as he deftly wove through the busy Saturday traffic with a sure hand.

"Have you hiked these mountains before?" Simon asked him.

"Yes, a few times, when I was younger. Haven't had much time in recent years—I'm usually out of town on assignment someplace and when I get back it's not hiking I'm usually looking to do."

Simon chuckled. "I know what you mean. Since I stopped traveling I've been spending more time up there—communing with nature, getting grounded. There's a small, private glen near the top of the mountain I'd like to show you. I study butterflies and it's a sort of special place where they seem to gather. It's not well known, so I expect they feel pretty safe there as opposed to other places."

Andre would never have expected butterflies to be one of Simon's hobbies. "Butterflies, huh?" It didn't seem to fit his image of him somehow.

Simon turned to glance at him as they came to a halt at a stoplight. "Surprised you, did I? We're not all what we appear, now are we? I expect you have a few secrets of your own that not everyone is aware of, am I right?" As the light turned green, his gaze shifted back to the road as he accelerated and pulled away.

It felt as though Simon had seemed to tap into Andre's mind and knew about the taboo dream he'd had the night before. It made him feel uncomfortable and he turned his gaze onto the road ahead. "I expect I do. It just caught me by surprise that you have a hobby like butterflies."

"You expected guns maybe? Or something more manly, perhaps?" Simon sighed. "I don't follow the rules, Andre. I never much liked rules. Seeing too much war and bloodshed I developed an appreciation for the simple, delicate beauty of nature. It always reminds me that life goes on, no matter what. I could be in the middle of the aftermath of the bloodiest battle and suddenly a butterfly would appear. For a moment, it would draw me out of the ugliness for just a brief second, but it was enough to get me through. Made me think somebody's soul had survived and transformed, allowing it to break free and his ravaged body could no longer imprison it inside. I began to think of them as a reaffirmation of life—that the lives lost were given a chance at freedom that humanity couldn't take away, no matter how hard it tried. A sort of metamorphosis if you will."

Andre didn't know quite how to respond—he was touched by the image it presented. He'd always thought of himself as hardened to the effects of the viciousness he witnessed daily in his line of work. It was as though experiencing the ravages of humanity he'd cut himself off from feeling any sort of emotion and that was the reason he couldn't connect on an intimate basis. Simon's remarks were beginning to make him think about his own experiences. As he tossed the memories around inside his head, he suddenly realized he unconsciously did something very similar.

"Flowers."

Simon glanced at him again. "What?"

"I look for a flower when I get in a situation like that. It didn't even register until just now. Something fragrant and beautiful. Just one flower." He turned to look intently at Simon. "It yanks me out of the darkness for only a second. My focus changes." His mind fought against the memory of a recent encounter.

"You understand, don't you?" Simon's eyes blazed into him.

Andre's gaze turned to the window, unfocused on the present, rooted in the past. "There was a white flower blooming at the center of a village that had just been demolished by a rebel group. I heard a child crying. He was sitting outside this hut next to the body of a woman. I picked the flower and I went to the child and handed it to him. For one moment he stopped crying and the look he gave me—" Andre shook his head, remembering that stark moment, and shuddered.

Suddenly he felt a warm, comforting hand over his, pressing, reassuring. Andre's gaze rose to meet Simon's and an understanding melded them. It was a deeper sense of communication with another human being than he'd ever felt before. He had a strong urge to reach over and embrace Simon, to feel his strong warmth against him, filling him, knowing he understood exactly how he felt at that moment.

Again, he turned away, afraid of the feelings this man invoked inside him. Simon's grip on his hand tightened for an instant and then was gone, and Andre felt a loss.

"I think you'll like the glen. It's peaceful and renewing. Sometimes we need that."

Andre's gaze was again drawn to Simon—he couldn't seem to keep his eyes off of him. "I've never felt this kind of kinship with anyone else," he admitted to him. "Shit, I can't figure this out. What is it about you? It's an odd feeling. I've met lots of people over the years that have shared the same experiences as me, yet with you, something is different. You understand."

He saw Simon's lips curve into a smile. "You'll figure it out. Sometimes people just connect on more than one level." He turned again to pin Andre with a penetrating look. "And sometimes people don't meet until the time is right in their lives." He shrugged. "Maybe you weren't ready to meet me before this, and you are now. Who knows the plan the universe has in store for us? All we can do sometimes is relax and enjoy the ride." Simon turned his attention back to the road.

Something special was happening here, but Andre couldn't quite put his finger on it. The air inside the vehicle seemed to be charged with potent energy, his body wound tighter and tighter, waiting. And he yearned for...something. He didn't understand, wasn't sure he wanted to know the source. All he knew was that in the short space of time he'd known Simon, he felt closer to him than anyone else he'd ever known. And he liked the camaraderie, the kinship. It felt like some part of him was an exact match to the other person in this vehicle.

It frightened him...and excited him.

CHAPTER 4

They climbed the mountain pass and then Simon veered off to the left into a makeshift parking area and turned off the engine. Theirs was the only vehicle parked in this particular location. He turned to look at Andre.

"Here we are." He pointed to the left. "We'll follow that path for about three miles up, and then we'll turn off. It's one of the more advanced trails and I usually don't encounter too many hikers up here. Another mile along the other path will get us to the glen. Ready?"

Andre nodded his head. "Yep. Let's do it."

He opened his door and stepped out. Reaching into the back, he yanked out his backpack and hefted it onto his back. He found he was actually looking forward to the physical activity of the climb up the mountain; it might help to settle his churning thoughts. It was different when he was on assignment—he was more focused on the story and not on the beauty of the surrounding area. Today he could enjoy the experience, unworried about the human dangers lying in wait.

Simon locked the Jeep and turned toward the path he'd pointed out. He turned to grin at Andre—it was an expression of kinship as they embarked on an adventure—and he felt something inside his chest expand and warm, blotting out the dark solitude that always seemed to be a part of him. They both started walking.

"I could probably follow this path blindfolded." He turned to look at Andre. "It's nice having company this time. Usually I come up here alone."

They trekked up, Simon pointing out various vegetation and rock formations along the way that he found interesting. The path was steep and required concentration. They halted at about two miles and rested on a flat-faced rock.

"I'm glad you asked me along," Andre said after he gulped down some water from one of the bottles he carried with him. "You're right, it is peaceful up here." He reached inside his pocket and pulled out a cigarette and a book of matches, needing a nicotine hit to help settle him.

He felt like a bundle of nerves inside him wanted attention, to be freed and experience the allure of the primal environment. His heart raced inside his chest. There were other urges there, ones he couldn't quite acknowledge. His eyes turned to watch Simon as he took a long drag on his cigarette.

Simon nodded as he gulped from his own water bottle, then wiped his mouth with the back of his hand. He squinted and looked around. "One of my favorite places. You doing okay with the climb? I'm used to it, but let me know if you need to rest again."

Andre laughed. "I'm used to a lot worse than this. No problems here."

"Right then. Let's get going. We started out late, so I'd like to make up some time if we can."

Pinching the end of the cigarette butt that remained, he then jammed it into his pants pocket. Shifting his pack, he straightened from leaning against the rock and followed Simon upward. As they moved from the main path and veered to the right, the trail was not nearly as well marked, but Simon seemed to know where he was headed. The path became steeper and required some climbing over jutting rock.

Simon reached down to give him a hand over a particularly tricky patch and then they were over the top. He still marveled at the dexterity of the man, admiring his strength and agility in maneuvering the terrain.

Another half mile and they reached a clearing, overlooking a meadow. What looked like a glacier lake was off to the left—the water clean and mirror-like. There was little movement in the air today and the water was calm and quiet. To the right was a meadow filled with the bursting color of wildflowers.

"Man, this is great," he murmured as he pushed forward down the incline that hid the meadow from view of anyone on the path. He turned to look at Simon. "Is this it? The place you were talking about? I don't see any of your butterflies."

Simon smiled as he followed Andre down the small hill. When they reached the bottom, he shouldered off his backpack and began unbuttoning his shirt.

"What are you doing?" Andre asked, perplexed by his actions.

"I'm going to show you how to commune with the environment—how to call the butterflies." Simon didn't look at him, but continued to shed his clothes. First his shirt, then he leaned down and unlaced his boots, pulling them off. The rest of his clothes followed quickly.

"I'm getting back to nature. I have to shed a bit of civilization to get in the right frame of mind. This is a secluded area, which is why I like it." He straightened back up, now free of every stitch of clothing.

Andre felt something odd shift inside him at the attractive, masculine physique displayed before him. All sinewy muscle, Simon exhibited the body of an extremely virile, much younger man. Except for the full head of white hair, one would never guess at his real age. And even that gave him a depth of beauty in contrast to the youthful body, making Andre want something he couldn't quite identify—or maybe something he just didn't want to acknowledge.

"Wait here," Simon instructed, as he leaned over and pulled a small bag from inside his larger backpack. "Just watch. It may take a while, so try to be patient." He strode down toward the center of the meadow, then sat down in a lotus-style fashion. As Andre watched, he placed the bag next to him, unzipped it and pulled out a small bottle. He poured some of it into his hand and smoothed the liquid over his skin, giving his flesh a shimmering gleam. After returning the bottle to the small bag, he held out his hands, palms to the sky.

Andre couldn't help but admire the flow of muscles gleaming beneath the sun, of the light and shadow highlighting every hard, bronzed inch of his body. When he sat, it was a fluid movement, nothing halting or ungainly about it. What he also noticed was the hard, thick cock rising between his legs. He felt his own hard length against his leg and shifted uncomfortably with the knowledge that the sexual attraction he'd tried to suffocate was again rising to the surface. What the hell was wrong with him, anyway?

For long moments, Andre watched him. Simon's eyes were closed and his expression calm and serene. He didn't move a muscle and Andre marveled at that kind of ability to control his actions for such a long period of time.

And then he saw it—one butterfly flew to him and landed on his shoulder. Then another. And another, until he was covered with butterflies in a myriad of colors. Delicate fluttering wings, ethereal, drawn to the man who sat like a statue in the middle of the field, yet appearing to be so much a part of the land.

Finally, Simon opened his eyes and looked directly at Andre, with a look that summoned him across the field. Long moments passed and then the butterflies left him one at a time. Only then did Andre walk across the field to stand before him—drawn to him like the butterflies had been, unable to resist. His cock pressed against his pants, hard and insistent. His body wanted to be free of the clothes smothering him. He wanted to know what Simon felt. He wanted to feel the same freedom in the meadow, the same earthy energy that seemed to exude from Simon.

As he reached him, he could see a different kind of calm energy that seemed to surround him. It almost felt sensual. Simon rose to his feet in one fluid movement, his body hard and almost inviting. Again, Andre couldn't believe it. He had to have been sitting there for more than an hour and should be aching and stiff from the enforced position.

His eyes were an intense, clear turquoise, as calm and deep as the glacier lake, reflecting the surrounding meadow, calling to Andre. He couldn't look away, mesmerized by this intriguing man.

He could feel Simon drawing closer, felt he should break the moment, tried to think rationally. Something was about to happen that was going to change everything he knew about himself. But hadn't that happened already? And he'd just been afraid to admit it?

Simon's hands lifted to cup Andre's face. He felt the strong warmth, was aroused by his touch, blood boiling inside him. His attention was drawn to the firm lines of Simon's mouth as it drew inexorably closer and then finally they were touching.

An electrical surge like lightning zapped through him at the first touch of those firm lips on his own. Unable to resist, he reached out to touch the warm, solid flesh of his arms and pulled him closer, wanted to feel his body touching, like in his dream.

Simon coaxed his lips apart with teeth and tongue and then he was driving inside, Simon's mouth claiming him in ways Andre never could have imagined. His groin was pressed to Andre's, their erections sliding and gliding against each other, the friction driving Andre higher toward a summit of need, the intensity of desire like he'd never experienced before.

Simon broke the connection of their mouths and looked deep into

Andre's eyes. "I want you, Andre. I don't know if you're ready for it, but I want to fuck you. I knew we had connected in some special way last night, that you were the one to share my meadow with—my inner soul. But I want to experience all of you. Let me show you what it means to bond with another human being in all the ways that matter. Let me show you how to let go of the loneliness that I know exists inside of you, that I see in your eyes."

Andre couldn't breath, couldn't think. But he knew he wanted to feel those lips on his again. He wanted the erotic dream to be real. And although he'd never wanted a man before, he did want *this* man. Wrong or right, he had to have him.

"I want to know," was all he could manage to utter.

Simon's mouth claimed his again, as his hands reached forward to unbutton his shirt, pulling it from his pants. His own hands glided across Simon's naked sun-warmed, oil-slick flesh, hard peaks and valleys, firmly muscled ass. He ground his hips against Simon, the friction of male-to-male heat blinding him, urging his actions forward.

Simon worked slowly at helping Andre undress, taking his time, stroking his flesh, eating at his lips. Andre returned the caress, enjoying the feel of peaked, hard nipples, flat, strong chest, his hands exploring the contours of his rock-hard abs.

He sat on the ground and Simon bent to remove his boots, then began unbuckling the belt at his waist. As his hand brushed against his arousal, Andre inhaled sharply at the exquisite sensation. He wanted to be naked, to feel Simon's hot flesh against his own, grinding body to body in the cool, fresh meadow. He couldn't remember ever wanting anything as much as he wanted Simon right now.

Finally, he was naked, feeling the warmth of the sun on his body, feeling free and uncluttered. Simon's mouth was on his skin, at his nipples, drawing them erect, razing with his teeth across his body, until finally he felt his mouth at his cock, surrounding and swallowing his hard prick inside the moist, hot, demanding chasm of his mouth.

It wasn't possible, but he felt like he was being consumed not only bodily, but his spirit was being drawn from him, through his cock and melding with Simon's soul. He pumped his hips against Simon's demanding mouth, wanting to fly, drawn to Simon like the butterflies in the field, needing to be consumed by him.

CHAPTER 5

Simon raised his head, turned away to reach over to the small bag he had carried with him to the field. He pulled out a tube, different from the bottle he'd seen him use to coat his body, then he looked down at Andre spread out before him.

"Spread your legs. Have you ever been fucked, Andre? In the ass?"

"No."

Simon's slick fingers teased at his anus opening, and Andre shuddered in response to the taboo sensations. "I thought not. So you're a virgin, aren't you? To man-love?"

The tip of Simon's finger pierced his opening and Andre gasped. "Yes. I guess so, although I've had plenty of women in my life."

Simon's finger sank deeper, opening him, tunneling deeper. "They never penetrated you like this, did they? Did they fulfill you? Did fucking them give you what you wanted?"

He was now thrusting his finger in and out of Andre's passage, driving him higher with the hot, slick friction.

"I thought they did," he gasped as his hips began to move in counter to Simon's thrusts, his mind envisioning Simon's cock inside him, pummeling deep, opening him to accept him. Fiery need surged inside him to be penetrated and possessed by this man. "But I never felt like this before." Sweat began to break out across his skin.

He felt Simon add a second finger inside him, widening him farther, and his other hand began to stroke his cock, sliding downward and over his balls. Dammit to hell, he'd never felt so intensely in his life before—wanting something he couldn't begin to understand.

His passage was consuming Simon's fingers like a living thing as he pulsed around him. Simon leaned forward and consumed his cock again into his moist heat as he added yet a third finger in his foreplay preparation of Andre's colon.

The groan came from deep in his chest as the sensations overrode him, carrying him higher. He looked up at the sky, saw the butterflies fluttering over his head, felt himself soaring with them. Closer and closer he moved toward release, to bursting with freedom, flying into the sky.

Suddenly Simon's presence was gone and Andre turned to look at him. Simon was again reaching inside the bag and this time withdrew two small recognizable packets. He looked at Andre as he tore one open.

"I'm going to fuck you," he asserted as he sheathed Andre's prick, turned back, tore open the other one and sheathed his own. Then he rose over him, a god highlighted by the blue sky and ethereal butterflies above, and spread Andre's legs, lifting and bending them over his chest. Andre swallowed, knowing he'd never be able to go back to what he was before.

Simon stopped and looked down intently into Andre's eyes. "Do you want me to do this? Do you want my cock inside you?"

Andre had all he could do to find his voice to answer. He felt the tip of Simon's cock pressing against his opening, waiting for his assent. He nodded. "Yes, I want this with you."

"You're sure you want me to take you? I'm a man, Andre, that will never change. I'm not a woman, and I don't want you as a man wants a woman. I want you man to man. Do you understand that? Can you understand what I'm saying? And I want to see your eyes when I come inside you. I want to see your passion. I want to know that you know who's making love to you."

Andre wasn't sure he understood any of it, but he knew one thing—he wanted Simon—and he wanted him in all his male beauty. "I want you, Simon," he ground out. "I've never wanted to be fucked by a man before, but I want you."

Simon slowly began to tunnel inside him. Andre felt his large cock penetrate and pass the tight ring of muscle at his entrance and his heart pounded at the invasion.

"God, you're tight," Simon ground out as he eased in farther, inch by inch, retreating and sinking in deeper. "Do you feel me there,

Andre? Oh, God, you feel marvelous."

Thrust and retreat, deeper, longer, penetrating strokes, burrowing farther and farther inside him with each thrust, widening him—his colon expanding to accept him, until finally he was buried deep inside and Andre could feel Simon's heavy balls slap against his cheeks.

Then Simon released his legs and stretched out over him, chest to chest, man to man.

He leaned forward, his lips a breath from Andre's. "Say my name," he whispered, his eyes boring deep into him. "Tell me what you want."

Andre thrust his hips. "Simon," he moaned. "Fuck me. Please." He'd never needed anything so badly in his life as feeling that huge prick inside his ass, thrusting deep, making him want to come.

Simon licked at Andre's lips, sucked and bit, and Andre shuddered at all the new sensations. Simon's hand reached down between their bodies to encircle Andre's cock.

The sense of being filled by this man, the beauty of his face, his mouth, his eyes, the touch of his firm hand on his prick and the clear blue sky above, cushioned in the cool crisp grass at his back, was almost too much for him.

"I want you to become accustomed to me being inside you," Simon said against his lips. "I knew when we met at the bar, you were the one I'd been waiting for. You and I are of one mind, and the merging of our bodies was meant to be."

The presence of his cock inside him felt right so damned right. His hand laying claim to his flesh, the feel of this man was more exquisite than he could possibly relate. He wanted to absorb him inside himself, wanted this moment never to end, this melding of two minds and bodies that was right and perfect.

Simon kissed him, thrust his tongue inside and then with the most torturous slowness, he began to move. Andre saw stars, felt exquisite pleasure, grinding his hips against Simon's movements.

"Yes," he muttered against Simon's mouth. "More." He raised his hands and pulled Simon closer, pushed harder against him, grabbed his ass and kneaded. Simon raised up and thrust deep as he continued to massage Andre's cock, in long, slow strokes.

"You're going to come with me, Andre. When I come, so do you."

Andrew could only nod, too overcome with emotions surging inside him. He felt Simon stiffen, sink completely inside him, and felt his shuddering orgasm. It peaked his own response and he was consumed by his own release. Simon's grip on him milked him, even as his anus milked Simon's cock inside him, until they both collapsed, Simon rolling to the side and embracing Andre in his arms.

Andre had never experienced anything so earth shattering in his life. The world all around him was alive with new meaning. He was bonded to Simon in ways he could never have imagined. It wasn't simply sex—it was everything. Even the air was filled with their essence.

Simon slid from his body and Andre felt empty at his absence and he looked over at him, questioningly.

He leaned over and kissed Andre, a hand stroking his ass. "Was it what you expected?"

"I don't know what I expected, so I can't say. What I can say is that I've never experienced anything as intense and—I don't know—personal, I guess. And right."

Simon cupped his face and stared into his eyes for long moments. "For now, the loneliness is gone. I see the pleasure in your eyes." He reached over and picked up his small bag and rose to his feet in a fluid movement. "Come on, there's a stream not too far away and we can get cleaned up."

Andre rose to follow him, regretting the loss of the special closeness he had just felt to this man. Naked they walked across the meadow and toward the small stream.

"Sit," Simon directed, and Andre eased to a sitting position on the bank of the cool stream. Simon knelt in front of him and slowly rolled off the used condom. He looked up into Andre's eyes as he removed and discarded it. "I'd never put you in danger, you should know that."

Andre nodded. Simon cupped some water in his hands and proceeded to pour it over him, and Andre sucked in air at the feel of the cold wetness. Again and again, Simon dipped into the water and dribbled it over Andre's skin.

When he was done, he sat next to Andre to remove his own sheath, but Andre stopped him. Simon looked at him questioningly.

Andre knelt before him. "My turn," was all he said, as he proceeded to do the same for Simon, with painstaking slowness and care.

When he was done, Simon leaned forward and kissed him. They fell back onto the grass, stroking each other's bodies with urgent hands, pressing close, needing the contact.

Finally, they parted and lay back against the ground and Simon looked up at the sky. "I think we need to leave or we'll be caught after dark on the mountain and we really didn't come prepared to spend the night. We'll have just enough daylight to make it back to the Jeep."

Reluctant to end the idyll, Andre slowly pulled away. "I hate it to end. You've given me something—taught me something about myself."

Simon looked at him with a sadness in his eyes. "Once we leave the mountain, you'll begin to have second thoughts. It's going to seem to you like it shouldn't have happened no matter how beautiful it is right now. And you're going to not want to see me again."

"I don't know what to think," Andre admitted. "Right now it seems right, everything, for once in my life, seems right with the world. But I know when I get back to the city, things will change. But inside, I don't see how I can."

Simon's smile was sad, his eyes holding a wisdom of past knowledge and understanding. He reached out to stroke the side of Andre's face. "It's the way it works. You're going to need time to think about things. I want you to know I understand that. I don't want you to come to me until you're sure I'm what you want—that this is what you want. It won't be an easy decision for you to make." He again leaned forward and kissed Andre passionately, branding him with his taste. Then he pulled away. "But as far as I'm concerned you're worth waiting for. So when we leave here, take your time, and be sure you really want this. I've been in a significant number of relationships over the years, I won't lie to you about that. Just as you've had your share of women, I presume. I want you, Andre, more than you can imagine, and I think you want me—on more than just a sexual level. But whether you can live with knowing that is something only you can answer. I'm not after a one-night stand, I want more. But you have to decide if you want it as well."

CHAPTER 6

Andre remembered that perfect afternoon in the meadow with such clarity and pleasure, that hadn't changed, no matter how he tried to deny what it meant for him. But Simon had been right. When he'd returned to the city—to his apartment—he'd immediately begun to question what had occurred in the meadow—not that he hadn't enjoyed every minute of it, but what it revealed about Andre, how it could change the person he'd always thought he was.

A week after the incident, he'd received a package in the mail from Simon. It had been the lighter with the butterfly etched into the side, his business card, and a boldly written note on the back of the card. *You have a butterfly's soul, Andre, beautiful and fragile. I await the day you set it free to live the way it is meant to live. Come to me when you are ready.*

He'd immediately run as fast and far as he could to try to forget the only perfect day in his life. At night, in his dreams, his body would come to life with the memories of the meadow and his thoughts and senses would fill with the pleasure he'd felt. And then he would wake up.

Six months he'd spent in South America, fucking his way from one end to the other, trying to forget. Until one night, he'd encountered a beautiful young prostitute, and he'd known it was time to come home.

Tonight had been one last futile attempt to fight the need gnawing at him inside, until there was just no place else to run and he had to turn and face who he was and what and whom he needed in his life.

Everything was so empty without Simon, more so than it had been before that afternoon of delight.

"Who is it?" a deep, familiar voice came across the intercom of the Morgantown Apartment Complex.

What would he say when he realized who it was after so many long months of absence without a word.

"It's me, Simon. Andre Cordaire." Andre waited. Maybe he wasn't alone? After all, he'd left him waiting for more than six months without any word at all. And now he showed up on his doorstep.

"Just a moment, Andre." A short time later the buzzer sounded and the inner door opened. Andre stepped through, his heart pounding in his chest. What would Simon think of him?

The only thing he knew was that he wanted Simon. Through everything he'd done since that afternoon, it was the one clear thought in his mind. In any of the mindless relationships he'd had over the ensuing months, it had been the memory of that afternoon alone that had allowed him any sort of release. He'd felt like a man pushed out in a rowboat without a set of oars or motor, drifting aimlessly, without direction.

He rode up in the elevator to the fourth floor. Slowly he navigated the corridor to reach Simon's door. He hesitated, and then knocked, thrusting his hands in his pockets as he waited for Simon to answer.

When the door finally opened, all Andre could do was stare and drink in the image of the man he—loved. And he could no longer turn away from that knowledge because it had followed him to hell and back, never leaving him an instant of peace.

"Hello, Simon." He stood there, waiting, hoping for an invitation to enter—an opportunity to feel warm again.

Simon stepped back. "Come in. It's been a long time. I'm glad you came."

Andre stepped inside the apartment and Simon closed the door. He turned to face him, his gaze rising to meet Simon's.

"I've been to South America—I just got back."

Simon broke the contact and turned away. "Come into the living room and you can tell me all about it."

Andre followed him inside, shrugged out of his jacket and sat on the edge of the brown sofa. "I had a lot of thinking to do," he admitted.

Simon nodded as he sat down in an overstuffed side chair. "I thought you might."

Andre raised his eyes to Simon's. "I'm sorry it took so long."

"I told you to take what time you needed. Whatever your decision, I want you to be sure."

They sat and stared at each other for long moments. Andre felt the hunger grow inside him, wanted to experience again what they had in the meadow that long ago day. He found himself rising from the sofa.

"I've missed you."

Simon slowly rose from his chair. "I'm glad you're here."

Steps brought them together, lips found and clung, arms snatching across the distance of time, pulling and consuming.

Andre felt the energy engulf him, the warmth radiate through him at Simon's touch, like the earth opening up to the heat of the sun after a harsh winter frost.

"I want to fuck you," he gasped. "I need to feel you, to connect. I haven't connected with anyone for so long. All I could think of was you. All I wanted was you, no matter who I was with."

Simon broke the kiss and looked at him. "Are you sure?"

"Damn right I am."

Simon smiled. "It's not going to be easy, you know that."

Andre slowly began to unbutton his shirt. "I've been with women while I was gone. I've been inside their soft body, tasted their fragrance on my tongue—experienced everything I could with a woman and still was alone, as though someone else experienced making love to them and it wasn't me. I had to think of you in order to get hard enough to pleasure them—to gain any pleasure from the encounter."

Simon helped him remove his shirt and then reached to unbuckle his belt. "I knew it wasn't going to be easy for you. I knew early on I preferred a man's body and thoughts to that of a woman. It isn't that I hate women, I just can't bond with them in the same way I am drawn to a man. But I knew for you, it would take time. You never knew, did you? Never even thought you might need something different than was offered?"

Andre shook his head. "I'd still be in South America but for one incident." He toed off his shoes and then pushed his trousers and underwear down, stepping out of them. "I was in a cantina and there was a young man there. He was beautiful. His shirt was partly open revealing his bronzed chest and there was a butterfly tattoo right at the center. It all happened so fast." His eyes bore into Simon's. He had to tell him this, Simon had to know it all. "He was a prostitute and I paid him. I fucked him because I needed to see if it would be the same—if all we'd really had in that meadow was just good sex. He was good, I'll give you that. I'd never fucked a man. Even you fucked me, but this time, I took him. It wasn't love, it was pure and primal fucking. But it wasn't until I looked at his chest as I drove into him, looked at the butterfly and remembered. I enjoyed fucking him, Simon. I liked the feel of him beneath him, I liked the look of him, and I liked his hands on me. But I didn't love him, I didn't connect with him. And I wanted more."

His gaze shifted away from Simon, unable to look at him any longer. Simon cupped his face. "You had to find out. I understand that." He leaned forward and kissed him.

"The next day I caught a flight home. Even then, I couldn't accept it." He turned back to look at Simon. "I slept with a woman before coming here tonight. It was only then that I realized I just couldn't deny it any longer."

Simon shrugged out of his own clothes. Andre was finding it difficult to concentrate as Simon's hands were now on his body, tweaking his nipples into full, pointed erection. "Tell me what you can't deny."

Andre's breath caught in his chest. To admit it out loud—there'd be no going back. His gaze met Simon's. "I'm in love with you, Simon. I've never been in love before, so maybe that's the reason it took me longer to figure out what was going on with me."

"What else?" Simon's hands were moving lower, resting at his hips, pulling him closer. His cock brushed against Andre's and a surge of pleasure passed through Andre.

"Yes," he whispered as he ground his hip forward.

Simon's hands stilled his movements. "What else?" he demanded, his gaze firm, demanding the rest.

Andre sighed. "I'm a man who desires the love of another man, not a woman, to make me whole. And you're the man. You're who I dream about, who I fantasize about, and who I want as a partner in my life. It's about someone who understands me, who touches my heart, and frees my soul."

Simon smiled. "I love you, too, Andre, and I told you I'd wait. The most important things in life are worth waiting for. You get to be my age and you learn that."

Andre couldn't wait another minute, he had to have this man, be inside him and know they were melded as one being in all ways that mattered.

He surged forward, claiming Simon's lips with a hard, demanding kiss, thrusting his tongue deep inside—this time the aggressor, not simply accepting, but being a full participant in the loving.

He pushed Simon back onto the sofa and pressed over him, separating his legs, his hand going to his cock, stroking him to erection. He sucked on two of his fingers, making them wet, and then slid them into Simon's rectum, thrusting deep.

"I'm going to fuck you, Simon. I want to feel you come apart for me, the way you made me feel in the meadow.

He pulled away and reached down for his pants with his other hand and pulled out two condoms and set them on the table.

Simon groaned and thrust his hips against Andre's invasion. "Yes, do it," he gasped. "Harder. Deeper."

Andre reached out and grasped Simon's hot dick in his hand, stroking him, feeling the wet, pre-cum against his fingers. "Are you ready for me?"

"Yes," Simon growled.

Andre sat up and picked up one of the packets and slowly rolled it over Simon's thick cock. Quickly, he did the same with the second one. Then he moved over Simon. "Do you want me to fuck you?"

Simon's glazed eyes bore into him. Turquoise dark like the Mediterranean at midnight. He centered his cock and pushed inward. Simon separated to accept him, and Andre felt immense pleasure as he sank deeper.

"You feel damn good. So good. You've got a great ass, Simon. And it's all mine." He surged forward, settling himself deep inside, enjoying the pleasure of being surrounded by the intense heat of this man. "Oh, God, you feel too damn good."

With his other hand he stroked Simon's cock without moving inside him. "I want you to come, Simon."

Simon's hard body ground against him, urging him to move. He felt his cock harden even more, the purplish engorged head eager to orgasm, the veins visible and pulsing with life, and then he began moving in and out, his balls slapping at Simon's ass. Hot, deep rhythm as he thrust in and out and his hand worked at Simon's tool. He wanted Simon to come like he'd never come with anyone before, to give him as much pleasure and intimacy as Simon had shown him could occur between two men who loved each other.

Their bodies pumped and slammed together. Simon reached for him and Andre saw the primal lust that had him by the balls. He rammed hard, pulled out and did it again. Simon raised his legs to encircle

Andre's hips and his strength pulled Andre close as they both exploded with spasm after spasm of hot liquid, release.

"Oh, God," Andre groaned, feeling the spasming of his own cock, deep inside Simon. His grip on Simon's pulsing cock filled him with intense pleasure as he felt his powerful climax overtake him. Finally, he collapsed into Simon's arms and they both lay there gasping for air.

"Damn, Andre. That was so fucking good."

Andre smiled and slid his softening cock from Simon's anus. He stroked his ass, enjoying the feeling of his hard, smooth muscles. "I don't want to hide from it any longer. And it feels damn good. The butterfly has wrung its way free of the cocoon at last. You've been there for me all this time—all these years. It had to be there in the back of my mind. Nobody—no man, no woman—ever measured up. I didn't know what it was—probably was afraid to put a name to it. But when we finally met in person—it wasn't hero worship. You need to know that. It was something in you that my soul recognized."

Simon leaned back on the couch and Andre lay next to him, stroking his chest, teasing his nipples. "I'm glad we finally met. And I know what you mean. It wasn't time for us to be together before this, there were things we each had to discover. I think I'm too old for you, but maybe age isn't what it's about with us."

"It isn't," Andre answered. "What we have isn't going to be easy to deal with. But I want to find a way to make this work for us. I want to be with you as much as possible for as long as possible."

Simon chuckled. "Once you finally make a decision, you jump in with both feet, don't you?"

"Bet your ass. I've never been in love before, and it feels damn good to admit what I feel now." He looked at Simon, knowing his commitment was in the look he gave him. "I'm not alone anymore and I don't want to go back to what I was."

Simon leaned forward, his lips inches from Andre's. "You won't have to. I said I'd wait for you and I did. I think next weekend would be a good opportunity to go back up the mountain."

"I'd like that. You can teach me how to call to the butterflies. Every time I saw one in South America, I thought of you. You know in Spanish mariposa means butterfly."

Simon leaned closer to Andre. "Did you learn that on your trip? Yes, I know. And now your mariposa's soul is free—to love and to live the way it was meant to." His lips claimed Andre's offering the promise of soul-deep love in their future.

SEQUESTERED PASSION

CARNAL CARNIVAL

CHAPTER 1

At last conquering the intense scrutiny of the metal detector, and the close inspection of the guards, he replaced the contents from the small plastic tray back into his pockets. He'd been detained at a meeting and was running a little late so, of course, he couldn't make it through with strictly one pass—no, it had taken three before they'd eventually patted him down and finally used the wand to detect any illegal contraband.

Walking along the quiet corridor, he approached the heavy oak door to Courtroom No. 5, then opened it and slipped inside. The guard glanced at him and nodded, recognizing him from many past encounters. He was as familiar with Joseph as any of the other countless attorneys who passed through these doors, both in defense and prosecution of the many cases presented before the judge.

The room was packed to capacity with no seating available, so he stepped to the side, leaning against the back wall. It was a high profile case and the whole city would be interested in the final verdict and the resulting sentencing.

Although Joseph was as interested as any of the occupants in the room, it was the judge herself that Joseph Acosta's attention was focused on.

Judge Eliza O'Brien. *His Eliza.* No one had the least inkling of their relationship. It afforded him a great deal of pleasure to know that the luscious body hidden beneath that unobtrusive black robe belonged to him.

It was Eliza's choice to keep her two worlds separate. He was certain no one had the slightest indication of the passion that broiled beneath the smooth, calm exterior of the judge now seated on the bench.

But he knew. He knew exactly the seething waters that had taken Eliza thirty-five years to accept as her due. Joseph had been the one to open that door for her.

Although she'd finally offered her submission to him in one sense, she still held facets he'd been unable to conquer in her. Like her fear of what people would say if they knew about her lifestyle outside of the persona of all-knowing impartial judge.

He smiled as he thought of that impartiality. Looking at her now, with her honey-colored hair pulled back into an elegant, tight twist, her eyes the color of the Atlantic Ocean on a frigid day, all emotion locked away—the acceptable picture of what society expected of someone in her position—especially a woman. Impeccable reputation. Tastefully perfect. Totally sexless.

Meeting her at a small political gathering hosted by his friend Daimaen Sinclair and his lovely submissive, Sylvie Taylor, he'd known of Eliza, but had never had the occasion to meet her socially. Although they were, strictly speaking, both part of the legal profession, she didn't exactly travel in his particular circles. And he found hers boring and unimaginative.

But on that night everything changed—for a brief span of time their two worlds had entered the same sphere. He'd seen something in her twilight-blue eyes that had speared his interest. It was a needy, unfulfilled longing. As he circuited the gathering, he'd studied her closely as her gaze seemingly trailed Daimaen and Sylvie about the room. He saw her expression darken when Daimaen happened to slide a hand along the length of Sylvie's back to inch beneath the slippery material of her clinging dress.

Surmising that if Daimaen was hosting this party for her, then she must be acquainted to some extent with his lifestyle, he found himself intrigued. Knowing that, Joseph was more than curious as to how deep her knowledge went, and that caused his predatory instincts to surface.

She'd stood at the side of the room, greeting people graciously, with a perfect, cool smile on her composed face. But it was her eyes that told him a different story. They were the reason he'd eventually crossed the room to introduce himself. In the time they'd known each other since, it had been the only time they'd acknowledged each other publicly beyond courtesy.

His attention was brought back to the courtroom as she turned her elegant head and nodded to the bailiff. He opened the side door and the jury members filed into the room and took their seats in the jury box. The verdict was handed to the bailiff and he turned and handed the slip of paper to the judge.

Joseph watched as she nodded to the bailiff who stepped away. The stenographer, with hands poised, awaited the first words to be spoken, ready to memorialize the moment. The room hushed in anticipation.

Every movement so controlled. He admired her command of the courtroom. He liked it even more when he controlled his girl in private. When she lay writhing beneath him, naked and wanting, and willing to do whatever he directed her to do.

His erection grew thick and pressed against the front of his trousers at the memory of their last encounter.

Every time he saw her with her public face firmly in place, he imagined her in private, accepting everything he gave her—be it a soft loving, a hard fucking, or a sensual spanking. She warmed to every moment, eager to please him, urgent to submit to every sensual moment he wanted her to experience. The only one in control during those times was him—and she handed it to him willingly. He would have had it no other way.

As he watched her now, he marveled at her ability to separate these two very different parts of herself—that there was no hint of the fiery woman hidden beneath the black robe of justice. But he also knew that was the very reason she needed him, acquiesced to his demands, and reveled in her submission.

Like any submissive he'd possessed over the years, he gave her what she required—had known what she craved before she even understood it herself.

What he found surprising was that he continued to find her a challenge, looked forward to every encounter with excitement and anticipation. The fact that he actually agreed to these boundaries of hers surprised the hell out of him even more. Possessing all of her became an intricate part of his life, and he found he wanted all of her, not strictly the private moments.

But that was something that couldn't be forced. The world knew what he was, what his lifestyle was all about—he'd never hidden it from anyone. To some extent it had added to his mystique in the courtroom and in his dealings with adversaries. He was a man who took chances, not just in private, but in public as well—and wasn't afraid to break through boundaries of socially acceptable behavior.

So why did he put up with Eliza's need for secrecy? He asked himself that question almost daily. Why did he accept that she would not acknowledge him and their relationship publicly?

Of course, he knew the answer. He wanted her willing commitment and he was prepared to wait for that acceptance. For him, she was worth it. He was a patient man, especially when the prize was Eliza's complete submission. It was like mining for that pure vein of gold in a cold dark cave. To a miner, each discovery was worth the hard work it took to discover the prize.

He was more than confident that eventually she would accept her nature and what she needed to be happy, and both elements of her life would meld together to make her complete—completely his.

He watched as she scanned the paper, refolded it, and handed it back to the bailiff, who walked across the floor, and handed it to the foreman.

"Please read the verdict," Eliza instructed the foreman.

"We find the defendant guilty on all counts."

There was a roar from the spectators in response to the verdict.

The judge pounded the gavel. "Quiet, please, or this courtroom will be cleared." Her voice demanded attention and the excited conversation silenced immediately. Several reporters rushed out the door, others murmured in undertones between themselves.

Joseph again appreciated her full command of the courtroom. How had he warranted the gift of such a beauty acceding to his every desire? It had been a chance meeting, with fate playing its powerful hand that night.

He didn't need to wait for the poll of the jury. He would learn all that he needed to know later. From the moment she left the courtroom today, she would be his for the weekend. He'd arranged his schedule to accommodate her; now it was time to prepare. He planned to drive and Eliza would fly in and be met by a car from the hotel. She would expect him to break down her defenses that would be ingrained in her from the hours of control required in her position. That's what she needed him to do, and he didn't plan to disappoint her.

He smiled with satisfaction at the thought of the contents in the overnight bag in his car. She would get what she wanted—and much more.

*   *   *

158

Her Honor, Judge Eliza O'Brien, strode back into her private chambers, eager to release the mantle of authority. She sighed as she removed her robe and hung it back in the small closet. It had been an exhausting fourteen days of trial. The defendant's counsel had been one of the more flamboyant, aggressive types, loving center stage. It had taken all her patience to keep control, when what she'd really wanted to do was reach out and strangle the damn popinjay. She fully expected an appeal of the verdict. She'd given the maximum sentence in this case because she'd thought it well-deserved.

A shiver raced through her as she pulled her navy blue wool suit jacket from the hanger and slipped it on over her white silk blouse.

He had been in the courtroom today. The room had been too packed for her to actually visually locate him, but she'd known he was there, sensed his presence.

It had taken every ounce of control not to halt the proceeding just to discover exactly where he was. She'd felt a shift in the air, like invisible tentacles reaching out across the room. She'd attempted to ignore it as best she could.

He'd never come to her courtroom before. It sent a tingle of pleasure through her at the thought he'd been there today, so very close. It was followed by the usual zing of fear.

What would she do if he actually confronted her in public? Laid claim to her in front of everyone? How would she respond?

She knew deep in her heart she feared that happening and what everyone would say if they knew about her need for Joseph and the lifestyle they practiced in private. Yet she also wanted it. Wanted the subterfuge to be gone. There were times when she wanted to shout out loud, *I belong to Joseph Acosta and I adore him!*

God, he made her feel so alive, so real. She wasn't just a sexless figurehead whom the world demanded remain emotionless and impartial as well, like some statue of justice on the courthouse steps, completely without feeling.

With Joseph there was nothing but feeling, sensations that drove her beyond any possibility of control. And wherever he wanted her to go, she followed willingly. No, she amended. She followed willingly as long as they were in private. When she thought of that qualification, it felt like a weight settled inside her chest.

By making that distinction she knew she failed him, but to do otherwise could put everything else in her life in jeopardy. She simply had to maintain the separate identities or risk losing all she'd worked so hard to achieve.

After that first night, they'd talked. She'd been so confused by what he made her feel. And so afraid. To give in to her attraction to his dark, magnetic personality went against everything her life had been about up until that night. And she knew his reputation for engaging in erotic, alternative relationships. It would be tantamount to professional suicide to enter into a relationship with him.

Knowing Daimaen and Sylvie socially was a different matter. She'd always been surprised at Sylvie's ready acquiescence to Daimaen's control in their relationship and had never quite understood it. Not so long ago she'd had lunch with Sylvie and had been unable to stop herself from asking Sylvie about her relationship with Daimaen.

Sylvie had offered her a secretive kind of smile and told her it wasn't something she could really explain—it was just that Daimaen made her feel like no other man ever had and what he gave her was something she didn't plan to throw away. When she was with Daimaen, she experienced everything more intensely—sunlight, a rain shower...sex.

Eliza had come away from that lunch not exactly jealous, but envious. No man had ever made her...well...more than what she was. She had wondered what it would be like. If a momentary feeling of emptiness suddenly struck her, she quickly suppressed it. That type of relationship was definitely not for her.

Then she'd met Joseph. She knew his reputation, knew he shared the same lifestyle as Daimaen Sinclair. Maybe that's why she'd been so open to him that night. Underneath, she wanted to experience the type of relationship Sylvie seemed to enjoy with Daimaen.

At first she'd been fearful Joseph would confront her in public once they began their private relationship. She'd waited for it to happen. Most of the men she knew couldn't wait to claim a right to her whole existence. And she'd always severed the relationship when they'd become too possessive.

But with Joseph it was different. He did possess her. And she'd wanted it, still wanted it, couldn't get enough of him.

Fear of what it would do to her career kept her from acknowledging her bond with him publicly. She'd worked so hard to reach this point in her life. She had no way of knowing how the public would view an alternative lifestyle for a judge who must command the respect of a courtroom.

What would people say if they knew in private she reveled in being

Joseph's submissive? She didn't think she could take the chance on losing what she had gained. Not even for Joseph.

She had also learned to trust him. Although he would test her boundaries in private, he would never push her to acknowledge his dominance of her publicly—not until she was ready. He might dominate her, but he would never bully her—and that seemed to be what set him apart from the others.

By his patience and respect, he possessed her more thoroughly than any other.

"Is there anything else you need, Judge?"

Eliza turned away from the open closet door to find her assistant hovering in the doorway.

"No, Marie, nothing more. You can go to lunch. I'll be out for the rest of the day."

Marie smiled. "Taking the afternoon off? You certainly deserve it after the last two weeks."

Eliza walked over and picked up her handbag. "Yes. I need a little time to recharge. I'll see you on Monday."

"Enjoy yourself, Judge."

"I'll certainly try."

Marie exited the room and Eliza gazed around her office. She saw the law books, her diplomas hanging on the wall, the photographs of her graduating class from Harvard, and the one of the Governor presenting her with an award—images of her life's work were gathered all around her.

She was so torn between the two very different parts of her life and she wanted to merge them. She wanted it all. But so many people wouldn't understand that she was both people. And both parts of her needed to be acknowledged. She was so tired of hiding—of trying to maintain the balance between public and private. She wanted the world to acknowledge that Joseph was a part of her life. She wanted to admit her deference to him in that part of her life. He deserved it—and so did she.

Fear of being judged for her choices kept her from revealing her needs. To be judged instead of judging. She shied away from making that decision right now.

She walked back to the closet and picked up the small overnight bag resting on the floor. Her lips curved in a smile. For now, Joseph was waiting. She glanced at the clock on the wall. It wouldn't do to be late—not unless she wanted to be punished.

Although she didn't want to displease Joseph—it was so much more pleasurable if she didn't—being punished at Joseph's hand was not such a terrible thing.

She wondered what awaited her? Anticipation coursed through her and she felt a wetness at the juncture of her thighs. Definitely anticipation.

She hadn't been with him for the two weeks of the trial, needing to maintain her focus on the case at hand. Afraid she would lose the unemotional element her position demanded. But now. Well, now was an entirely different matter.

Once she reached her car and drove to the airport, her mindset would begin to alter—her mantle of judgeship would slowly slip away. Her Honor, Judge Eliza O'Brien, would remain here in the city; Eliza, Joseph's submissive, would firmly establish herself once they landed on the ground. She would no longer be the one in control and she needed to be of the right frame of mind when she met Joseph. He would be able to tell if she wasn't—and would take steps to remedy the situation.

She hurried to the elevators that would take her to the parking garage. Tossing the bag into the backseat, she got in and started the engine. The BMW purred to life.

Life was good the way it was. Why was it she always wanted more? Why couldn't she settle for what she had?

CHAPTER 2

The Corrigan was an old-world hotel catering to the privileged. Staff at the hotel knew how to keep a secret, each employee hand-picked and thoroughly investigated by management. This hotel was famous for its discretion as well as its clientele.

Eliza walked through the highly-polished oak door held open by the immaculate doorman and entered the richly appointed reception area.

Thick ocean-blue carpeting accented with intricate, swirling gold circlets muffled her footsteps as she approached the reception desk, identified herself, and requested her room key. Everything about this hotel spoke of quality, discreet attendance, luxuriousness. Thankfully, Joseph arranged for the room himself and all she needed to do was give her name and pick up the key.

"Everything seems to be in order, Ms. Thomas. Would you like someone to assist you with your bags?" the attendant asked as he handed her the dark gray, magnetic keycard.

"No, thank you." She accepted the card and turned away from the desk. She felt slightly uncomfortable at the use of the false name, but it provided just one more layer of protection in an uncertain environment.

Walking back across the carpeted reception area, she passed the wide spiral staircase leading to the second floor open restaurant and stopped before the mahogany and brass entrance to the elevators. Mirrored golden doors slid silently open and she entered.

Leaning forward, she pressed the black button for the tenth floor. Her stomach felt like rubber bands twisting tighter and tighter inside. In anticipation of who, and what, awaited, her awareness heightened, her skin tingled, and her breathing grew more rapid as the elevator ascended, carrying her closer to her destination. The scent in the air of the enclosure was lemon, tangy and fresh and she breathed deeply, trying to settle her nervousness.

Joseph had instructed her not to change her clothes, to arrive just as she was when she left her chambers. But he had told her exactly what to pack. And she had followed his instructions. Her bag was exceedingly light because she had included no more than he had indicated.

The elevator doors parted and Eliza stepped onto the plush dark maroon carpeted hallway of the tenth floor. The sconce lighting provided the illusion of an old-world gas-lit ambiance and any sound was muffled by the thick walls and carpeted padding beneath her feet.

Of course, there were other reasons for the lack of sound on this particular floor.

The Corrigan was discreet for very good reason. Much of the sense of quiet solitude was rooted in the unique aspects of the tenth floor. Like the floors that were made available for smoking or non-smoking patrons, handicapped and non-handicapped accessibility, the tenth floor catered to guests with unique requirements. And there were special employees who attended to the needs of the guests on this particular floor. And the rooms here were soundproofed.

Joseph had told her he personally was acquainted with the owners of this hotel. In fact, he'd assisted them in reviewing the contracts and in the closing for it some time ago. He apparently always received special consideration when requesting a reservation. He'd also been asked to assist in the plans for modifications of this particular floor.

It was a beautiful old building with the style and elegance of the early twentieth century, yet modernized efficiently and subtly.

She reached the door of their room and slipped the keycard into the metal slot. Slowly, she turned the glimmering brass handle and stepped inside.

It was dark, the drapes at the window drawn closed, and she reached out to turn on a light.

"Don't touch the light switch," a disembodied deep voice instructed her from the depths of the room. "Close the door and come inside."

She pushed the door shut behind her and stepped farther into the room. Inhaling, she smelled the familiar scent of Joseph's aftershave—woodsy, earthy. It eased its way inside her, burrowing deep.

"Stop. Set your bag and handbag against the wall." She leaned over, dropped both bags, then straightened. "Now take three steps forward and wait there." She did as he directed, feeling the control slip from her shoulders as she did so.

She heard a click and then a small fierce light practically blinded her. The illumination was altered, lowered, and she blinked rapidly trying to adjust her vision.

It was like being pinned in the spotlight on a stage, ready for performance to an audience. Its golden heat encased her in its aura. She felt the warmth flood through her, and her mantle of power slowly slid from her shoulders. She had entered another world—the other side of who she was. She embraced the feeling.

"Remove your clothes. Do it slowly."

She had no way of knowing if he was alone or if there was someone else with him. Nor did she know how she felt about that possibility. There was no knowledge beyond the unwavering, pointed heat of the glowing lamp.

Shrugging her shoulders, she allowed the wool jacket to slide down her shoulders and land at her feet. She kicked it away. Bending forward, she lifted one foot to remove her leather pumps.

"Stop," his sharp command halted her movements. "Leave your shoes on. Your underwear, slip, and shoes stay on—the rest goes."

She straightened back up and began unbuttoning the front of her silk blouse. The cool air in the room feathered against her overheated skin as she unbuttoned the last button and her shirt fell open. Pulling the hem of the shirt from the waistband of her skirt, she allowed the blouse to fall and join her jacket. Her sensitized skin responded to the cool air of the room and a shiver ran through her. She could feel her panties were already soaked with her desire.

She had a feeling she was going to appreciate the coolness of the room in a short while. Reaching around, she unfastened her skirt.

"Turn around," he instructed her. "I want to see that fine ass of yours move when that skirt dances to the floor. If I don't like what I see, you know what will happen."

"Yes, Sir," she replied in a meek, husky voice. It was a response filled with arousal, the need to be fucked. Already her body tingled and her attention sharpened. Inch by inch she lowered the zipper at the back of her slim skirt, then rotated her hips seductively as it slid to the floor. She was left wearing her creamy silk slip and lacy underwear.

"Step out of the skirt and lean over and grab your ankles. Spread those legs. You know better," he barked.

She hurried to meet his demands as desire quaked through her. It was a good thing she worked out regularly and was limber enough to perform some of the movements Joseph required.

She heard the creak of shifting leather, the muffled sound of movement, then firm hands cupped each of her rounded cheeks through the silk of her slip. He circled, lifted, separated and her pussy wept for attention. That touch ignited something inside, locking everything into place, and her spirit acceded to his firm grip.

"Well done, my girl. Beautiful form. His hands bit into her ass, bunched the slip up and over her hips. A hand against her hip grabbed the waist of her thong and pulled. The flimsy fabric separated and fell away as though made of air, and she was opened to him, ready to meet his any whim. Her breathing hitched and she wanted to move, but knew better.

"This is what you came for isn't it, Eliza? This is how you like it?" There was silence as he seemed to await her response.

"Yes, Sir," she whispered. Her arms and legs were beginning to ache from the forced position, but she would not give in to it.

He penetrated her pussy swiftly with two thick fingers, and she moaned as her passage opened to accept the rapid, unexpected entry.

"Don't move," he commanded. "And don't come until I say so."

It was a lesson in control. A reminder to her of his dominance in this room. It took all of her concentration not to come as he directed. But the feel of him inside after so long, thrusting in and out, drove her blood pulsing hard and fast through her body, rivers of molten lava oozed from her center. The pain of maintaining position, the pleasure of his fingers driving deep, slick with her cream, retreating and going deeper still. She whimpered with the knowledge of lost control, the need to bend to his will.

"Please, Sir," she begged, trying not to ground her hips against his fingers. One of his hands was anchored at the cheek of her ass as the other continued to drive into her.

"Please, Sir, what? Ask me."

Panting hard, a sweat breaking out, she knew she couldn't hold out much longer. The mantle of judgeship she wore outside this room was completely removed. In her place was a woman, someone who needed release, and needed to give over to the demands of this man. Who required his permission for her body to experience the exquisite surge of orgasm it now demanded. "Please let me come, Sir, please."

"How close are you, Eliza?" His fingers continued to penetrate and retreat, driving her higher and higher, sharp sensations winding her tighter and tighter as one tunes new strings on a violin for perfect pitch. And he expertly played her body.

"Very close, Sir," she cried. She was now wired to the breaking point of need.

Suddenly, he pulled from inside her, widened her stance, forcing her thighs farther apart. Swirling music inside her soul needed to be freed, yet the notes were captured and controlled, hovered, pressed tightly at her core waiting for that moment, the moment when the master musician with one touch would release the surge from the depth of her being.

She felt his hands clasp the top of her slip—and yank. Like thin rice paper the material parted beneath his grip, torn all the way down its length to separate and fall away. She remained as she was, now gaping open, her position revealing her desperate need for completion.

Again, he smoothed his hands across her ass, tracing their roundness. "Very nice, but a bit too pale for my liking. Do you agree with me?"

How else could she answer? His lightest touch now sent excruciating shards of desire zinging into every corner of her body. Trembling she was unable to control coursed through her body.

"Yes, Sir, whatever pleases you." No other answer was possible. She needed to please him, needed to offer him all that she was. She tingled, knowing what would come next. Obviously, he did not mean for her to come quickly, and her pussy throbbed with urgent demand.

"Stand up."

Unclasping her ankles and breathing a sigh of relief, she straightened. The small of her back ached, but her empty pussy ached more as it clamped down on vacant cold air, eager for a hot cock to fill the void.

"Turn around and come over here. You know what I want."

As she turned, she saw that he had returned to sit on an armless wooden chair. She walked over to him and spread herself across his black leather-clad legs. At first it felt chilled against her heated body, then warmed quickly.

"Are you comfortable?" he asked her when she was spread out before him, her legs open for his pleasure, her hands and feet flat to the floor.

A firm hand smoothed over the surface of her round bottom and, without warning, she felt a sting to one cheek, followed swiftly by a slap to the other cheek. She sucked in air as she allowed the throbbing sting to track its way through her, embracing the taste of pain inside her.

Again, he struck, again and again, warming her bottom thoroughly. He stopped and her ass felt hot and throbbed, the sweat poured along her neck in rivulets. She gasped as, unexpectedly, the pain was cut in half as his fingers swiftly entered her sensitive pussy.

"Come, now, Eliza. Come hard, I want to hear you orgasm, I want to feel it."

Three fingers drove deep and she let herself go as she spasmed, clamping down on his fingers, screaming as the pure and overwhelming bite of pleasure surrounded her, carried her, catapulted her into space.

She bucked and jolted, screamed again as he forced her higher, teasing her clit, driving thickly inside her, milking every ounce of her orgasm from her.

Long moments later, when at last she quieted, collapsing forward, he lifted her and held her close, wiping damp tendrils back from her forehead. Her ass still throbbed and her pussy spasmed in echoes of her tumultuous climax.

Joseph cupped her face, forcing her to look at him. "Are you all right? Do you want to stop?" He seemed to study her, trying to determine something.

"Is there more?" she asked on a shuddering breath. She already felt drained.

He rested her head against his shoulder. With one hand he lifted a glass pitcher from the end table next to him and poured some water into a glass. He picked it up and held it to her lips.

"Drink."

She gulped deeply, long, life-giving swallows of the clear, cool water. When she was done, he set the empty glass back down on the table.

"Better?" he asked her.

"Yes, thank you."

"Good." He rose with her in his arms and, when he was on his feet, he set her on hers. He stroked his hands along her back and over her warmed bottom, pressed her against him. His touch was possessive, appreciative.

She liked when he touched her like that. It made her feel—well—loved, cared for, safe. She looked up at him, knowing that all she felt was in her eyes for him to see.

He lifted a hand to cup her cheek, and she leaned into the embrace. "Go and bring me what you find in the top drawer of the dresser."

She wondered what it could be? What more did he have in store for her? Turning, she walked to the dresser. Turning to look back at him, she questioned him with her eyes before she pulled the drawer open.

"You trust me?" he asked.

She nodded. Yes, she trusted him.

"Then open the drawer and bring me what you find."

She opened it farther and her gaze widened at what was revealed. It was a flogger and several white silk scarves. Her hand trembled as she reached in to pick them up. He'd never used a flogger before. Oh, they'd spoken of it, but she'd never actually thought to the day when he would want to use one on her.

Her whole body trembled as she carried the items back to him. She'd been open to many of his suggestions, but this was something she'd been leery of trying. She hadn't exactly said no, but—

He took them from her when she reached his side. "You're afraid."

"Yes, Sir."

"Would you believe me if I told you that these are only to give you pleasure?"

She looked up and studied his face. She honestly didn't think he would lie to her. She saw warm determination in his dark eyes.

"I believe you."

He nodded. "Good." He held the flogger out to her. "Take it. Hold it. See what it feels like."

Hesitantly, she took it from him. It wasn't very heavy, a light tan color and the tails and handle were smooth and soft.

"It's made of deer skin. It's yours, Eliza. For the next lesson in your education. Do you think you're ready for more of what I have to teach you?"

She studied the new piece of equipment he intended to use on her. Was she ready? Her body still rippled with the effects of the warming from the spanking—and the shallow convulsing of her pussy reminded her of the intensity of her orgasm. It had been so powerful, she'd thought she would come apart right there and then.

She handed it back to him. Then she looked at the silk scarves. "And those? What are those for?" Although, she thought she already knew the answer.

He held them up and they trailed to the floor. "These? Why to bind you, of course."

CHAPTER 3

She trembled at the thought of what came next as he led her to the large four-poster bed. He leaned over and removed the pillows.

"Lie down on your stomach," he directed.

She got onto the bed and did as he instructed. He placed one of the pillows beneath her hips, elevating them. He lifted her left arm and straightened it, extending it outward. Feathering a finger along the inside sensitive forearm, she shuddered at the sensual contact, then the cool, smooth touch of silk entrapped her as he wound the scarf around her wrist.

She watched as he bent forward and kissed the tips of each finger as he bound her with the scarf to the wooden post of the bed. Again, he trailed a finger along her arm, across her shoulder and down the sloping curve of her back as he stepped around the bed to the other side.

It wasn't fear she felt, but the heat of desire and anticipation, his touch awakening and attuning every nerve in her body. When he reached the other side of the bed, his arousing caress ignited another path, along her hip, her back, and up her arm. She found herself eager to be bound by the silk, to experience more of his sensual awakening.

It wasn't what she expected. She'd anticipated trepidation, the shudders of anxiety, not this overriding pleasure. Again, her body was tightly wired, almost painful anticipation clinging to her, and her breaths turned to pants as she tried to control her mounting need to come. She could feel the slippery desire easing through her body.

A moan escaped her lips as his hands moved to her ass, cupping, tracing the crease, feathering a light caress across her engorged pussy lips.

"You're very wet, Eliza. Are you afraid?"

"No, Sir," she gasped. "It-it's not fear I'm feeling."

She felt his lips against her sensitive ass cheek that was still warm from the spanking. His teeth grazed over it, nipping and teasing with his tongue, pitching her onto a rollercoaster of sensation. She moaned and panted harder, trying to control her body's responses, attempted to fight the urge to draw her thighs together in an effort to ease the ache at their juncture.

"Do you like that, Eliza?"

"Y-yes, oh, God, yes!" she rasped, biting her lower lip, trying to fight the desires of her body.

A finger traced the curve along the sensitive back of her leg and she felt him bind her ankle to the bedpost. Then she felt him trail the end of the scarf over the sole of her foot and she shuddered with pleasure, wanting to scream in an effort to release some of the pressure building inside her. Her whole body was already tingling with minute awareness.

He repeated the process with her other leg. By the time he was done every nerve in her body was at attention awaiting his pleasure, his commands—eager to comply with whatever he wished.

He walked back toward her head, tested the restraints. "Are you comfortable?"

She nodded her head, shudders racking her body. "As comfortable as one can be who needs to come so badly it hurts."

She saw him smile. "You'll control it though, won't you?"

"I'm trying, Sir." Her whole body trembled with the attempt to accede to his demand that she not orgasm.

He reached to the back of her head and she felt him pulling the pins from her hair that held her twist in place. The locks fell around her shoulders.

"That's better," he murmured as he sifted his fingers through her hair. "Do you remember your safe word, Eliza?"

"Yes."

"Tell me what it is?"

"Federal," she responded.

"Good. Use it if it becomes too much. You won't hesitate."

"No. I'll remember."

He straightened away from her. She felt the fingers of the flogger pass over her back and she tensed, knowing he was about to start.

He trailed it along the same path his hand had traveled earlier, eliciting the same response. For long, endless moments, that's all he did was to sift it along her body until the tenseness eased away.

"That's better," he said as he continued to stroke her with it. "You have a beautiful body, Eliza. It's meant to be worshiped and enjoyed. It provides me a great deal of pleasure to have you here, like this. I enjoy your submission, teaching you. You are a joy to me, girl, you know that?"

Suddenly the flogger came down across her shoulders, so different from the easy stroking before. She inhaled sharply, tensed, as more blows followed swiftly.

But it wasn't what she expected, they were intense, yet not the fierce, flaying pain she'd expected. Instead, they were fingers of heat stroking through her, warming her, intensifying, spiraling inside—a cyclone of feeling building, clinging tentacles, like heated massage, forcing the need up and through her, burrowing it inside her, tightening the knot in her belly.

He struck her shoulders, her ass, her upper thighs. Endless sensation. Suddenly the force stopped and the sensual stroking began again.

Her mind grew fuzzy, her body sensitized to each minute touch—it wasn't pain—it was sensation that curled around the desire, through it. Again, the blows began and the curls grew denser, clouding her mind— her only thought was that she didn't want this to end, the pleasure was unbearable, tears streamed down her cheeks, falling onto the bed. It seemed her body reached for each touch of the flogger, each stroke reaching inside to claim and touch her core.

She was unaware of time, where she was, or how she got there. Fingers curled around the silky restraints, and an animalistic feline growl erupted from within.

As the rains stopped, fingers penetrated her hot, drenched vagina and a voice from above commanded her. "Come, Eliza, come for me."

She stiffened in response as her whole body throbbed with the force of an orgasm that she was certain tore her body completely apart. She no longer lay on the bed in a hotel room. She was spirit, moving up and above herself. She was emotion and sensation swirling in the air above her, yet surrounding her. Her scream as she plummeted back down was primal, unrecognizable as the voice of the sophisticated, unemotional judge in command of a courtroom.

This was her female emotion at its basest level. Feeling, only feeling as her body pulsed and responded to the voice and hands of the man who was her master—whom she belonged to body and soul and everything in between. Darkness descended as she surrendered all of herself to the passion, to the man.

*   *   *

Joseph quickly untied the restraints and set them aside. Carefully, he rolled Eliza onto her back, her breathing was steady and uninterrupted. He rose from the bed and walked into the bathroom, bringing back a wet washcloth, he proceeded to stroke it along her body.

She had responded so beautifully, without inhibition. He loved coaxing her from the shell she erected and this had been more intense than ever before. He knew she'd been fearful at first, but he had successfully calmed those fears enough for her to enjoy and experience fully the sensual journey he wanted her to travel.

Her body was silky soft and he loved touching her, loved watching her. Each time he was with her, he found himself feeling more possessive, reveling in the fact she gave herself to him so freely.

Lifting one of her curvy, well-muscled legs, he drew the washcloth along her thigh, down her calf and back up the front of her leg. He found himself marveling that she gave herself up so willingly to him.

He qualified that thought. She gave herself to him in private. He understood her fear of exposing their lifestyle to the public. Her position was important to her and she needed to maintain control and the facade of an impeccable lifestyle. Yet, he could not help wanting her to acknowledge their relationship as a part of who she was. He wanted her completely, not just as that part of her life to be hidden—sequestered from her public persona.

He pulled her into his arms, holding her close, and studied the quiet lines of her face. Such a delicate and beautiful countenance, the hint of a rosy blush, elegant arched golden brows, a full, sensuous lower lip—her mouth opened just the slightest fraction. It was a tempting sight. Her lashes fluttered as she began to rouse from her faint.

Blinking rapidly, she focused on his face. He felt a shudder pass through her, and then he saw her lips curve into a smile of lovely contentment. Right now, at this moment, she was all feeling, pliable beneath his hands, open to her deepest emotions.

"How do you feel?" he asked as he brushed a tangled lock of hair away from her face. She snuggled closer.

"Amazing."

He smiled, knowing he'd pushed a soft boundary of hers she hadn't thought she would enjoy. Her whole body now exhibited a rosy glow of discovered sensual knowledge.

As he watched her, she rose to her knees and straddled his legs. He felt her wet warmth against the fastening of his pants, and his cock throbbed in acknowledgment of her presence.

She began unbuttoning his black silk shirt and trailed her hands along his chest.

She lowered her head and her lips were a scant breath from his chest. Tilting her head at a slight angle, she looked at him, her eyes glittering darkly, and his whole body tightened with desire. "I want to make love to you, Joseph." Her moist whispered words felt warm against his chest as she dropped forward and her wet lips clutched at his hard nipple.

He felt the groan coil deep inside and erupt as her teeth nabbed the nipple and tugged, and he cupped her head, encouraging her closer.

She pushed the shirt over his shoulders, then inched down his body, unfastening the opening of his pants with her nimble fingers, frantically pushing them down along his hips.

His hard cock sprang free and when her hands encircled him, it was all he could do not to push her back onto the bed and fuck her hard, taking immediate control of the situation.

This was for her, he reminded himself. She wanted to give to him and he would not take that away from her. He harnessed his urges, allowing her to control her movements. The feel of her firm hands as they aroused his body even more fully made it very difficult.

"You give me so much, Joseph," she said as she stroked him, teasing the slit of his cock with her finger. As she bent forward, her hair lightly drifted over his body. He bucked beneath the hot caress. "You make me feel—everything. When I'm with you, it's as though the world comes alive in brilliant, vivid color. And I can't grab it tight enough."

He felt her shift her weight, saw her rise above him, a goddess of passion as she centered his cock at her opening and slowly lowered herself down.

Fiery sensations siezed him as he felt her silky, hot glove surround his heated, needy shaft. She took her time, easing inch by inch. One inch, and she stopped, lifted, then lowered, eating another inch.

"Don't move," she whispered. He clutched at the bed covers with his hands, the pleasurable anticipation swamping him, her arousal scenting the air. She wanted to give him this and he must allow it, must fight his own demands to control the penetration.

"Do you like being inside me, Joseph? Oh, God, you feel so good. Your cock is so hard, so alive, inside me, separating me, filling me." And he did. He felt the easing, yet tight clutching of her vaginal walls, as they accepted him, welcomed his presence.

"Eliza," he gasped, a warning that he was close.

She raised her hips, undulated against the tip of his cock. Shafts of desire arrowed from the tip throughout his body, wave after wave of pleasure, disintegrating his control.

He reached for her hips, intending to take control, but before he could do so, she dropped down, fully enclosing him within her wet, creamy channel, again she retreated, and came down with force, swirling, sucking at him, demanding. Again and again until he lost the control, finally grabbing her hips, slamming himself deep, holding her fast as he came hard and powerfully, filling her with his seed, bucking beneath her, as pulse after pulse of hot cum erupted, a fountain of passion for her, in her.

Through the immense sensations, he felt her own climax erupt. Opening his eyes, he watched her as she threw her head back, arched away and allowed it to engulf her. It was a moment of passionate beauty he would always remember.

When finally the tumult of orgasm subsided, he pulled her damp body down against his chest, feeling the tight bead of her nipples pressed firmly. Without easing from inside her, he turned onto his side, enclosing her in his arms.

As he stroked her back, he finally heard her breathing deepen and knew she had fallen into a natural sleep. Only then, did he ease from inside her, pull her closer and allow sleep to begin to overtake him. Later they would shower, but for now, he was replete with satisfaction, enjoyed the scent of their lovemaking surrounding them.

She did something for him none of his other submissive relationships had been able to. She gave him a peace within his body and his mind, and filled him with satisfaction in ways he'd never thought to attain.

There must be a way to bind her to him. He'd never thought in terms of forever before in regard to a relationship. It was an odd feeling to think in those terms now, at this point of his life. But when he looked at her, held her, possessed her, he wanted none other than her.

When he watched her at a party, or on the bench, he was proud of her, yet knowing the passion inside her belonged to him. He refused to give her an ultimatum, to force her to accept him in all facets of her life. She must come to those conclusions herself. Willingly. Eagerly.

The waiting didn't come easily to him. But she was worth it, if it gave him the prize in the end. That gift being her commitment to bind her life to him forever.

CHAPTER 4

Eliza stepped through the door of the reception area to her chambers. She'd flown back into town the previous day. Alone again, she'd tried to stuff the fierce emotions from her passionate weekend back into the dark corner where they usually resided. Back to where no one other than Joseph could find them.

But for some reason, today her mind and body weren't paying attention. Something subtle, yet monumental, had taken place this weekend. She was frightened by the impact of the emotions still prevalent inside her.

"Good morning, Judge," Marie greeted her with a smile.

"Good morning, Marie. Did you have a good weekend?"

"Great." She looked at Eliza with a bit of a quizzical look in her eye. "Looks like you had a very good weekend as well. Someone new in your life, Judge? Whoever it is, it looks like he agrees with you—you've got a glow this morning."

Eliza flushed beneath the scrutiny as she felt the slow heat rise to overtake her. She hadn't thought it would be so obvious. Looking away, and skirting around her assistant's desk, she hurried past.

"It was a nice weekend," she mumbled, unwilling to admit more.

"I'll say it must have been," she heard Marie murmur behind her as she fled inside the safer boundaries of her office.

Yes, something had changed and it scared her, and it apparently wasn't going to be easy to hide the effects. She wasn't ready for it. Loving Joseph—and yes, she did love him—wasn't a sane undertaking.

Her thoughts kept reverting back to her public image—the image she'd cultivated all these years, that had gotten her to where she was today. How did she just throw all that away for—what? She had no way of knowing that this was anything more than a brief affair that might not last beyond—well, today.

But when she was with him, nothing else mattered. Nothing. And yet everything was so much more alive, more real.

It was as though when she left him the world turned into an old black and white movie, all taste and texture gone from her life. And the longer she knew him, the worse it became coming back to it. And the harder it was to submerge that part of herself that demanded the color and taste of Joseph's world.

Her thoughts turned inward as she absently hung up her jacket and walked over to sit at her desk. Almost without thought, she glanced up and around her office, at all the mementos of her life.

How could anyone accept that other part of who she was and still respect her as someone to preside over a court? She felt the tears of hopelessness begin to pool. The frustration of her situation seemed so insurmountable at times.

Joseph never said anything, but she knew he wanted her to acknowledge their relationship in public. He had never pressed her, and he wouldn't. It wasn't his way.

She wanted to give him what he needed—what he silently demanded of her—but she couldn't. Was she too much of a coward? It was almost as though she wanted him to make the decision for her, yet knew he would not.

Again, she remembered the weekend, the silken bonds, the feel of the flogger against her skin, the taste of Joseph's heated flesh. And her body responded to the thought as it always did.

She raised her hands to cover her face, felt the heat of passion convulse inside her. If he were here in front of her right now, she wasn't sure she could stop herself from begging him to take her, to make her acknowledge what was between them.

But he wouldn't; in this way he was forcing her to make a decision. And there were two choices. Give him up completely or allow him into her life openly. She was unable to choose—not right now.

Smoothing back her hair, she sighed deeply. With a fierce determination she buried the emotional side that belonged to Joseph and opened the folder on her desk. She reached over and picked up her reading glasses and began to peruse the documents inside.

She had two more days to familiarize herself with the case that would be presented in her courtroom. That was what she must concentrate on. Yet a corner of her mind still tugged fiercely for acknowledgment, emotions rebelled at being cast aside.

A knock at the door interrupted her concentration on the pretrial motions and briefs of opposing counsel spread before her. She looked up and focused on Marie standing in the doorway.

"I'm going to lunch, Judge. Anything I can get you?"

Eliza pulled off her reading glasses and rubbed her itchy eyes. The morning had gone quickly. She focused on Marie.

"No, thank you. I need to get out to stretch my legs. It's been a quiet morning. That's a good thing."

"Sure has." Marie glanced out the window overlooking the park. "Looks like a nice day to get out. I'll see you after lunch."

Eliza rose from behind her desk and stretched. Yes, a walk in the park would help to clear her head. She pulled on her coat and walked out of the office.

It was a beautiful day, with the gold sun blazing high in the sky—not a white cloud in sight. The sky was a deep shade of royal blue.

Stopping at a vendor on the street corner, she purchased a hotdog and soft drink, then ambled across the park to a vacant bench near the reflecting pool. To her left were a group of children feeding small bits of bread to the pigeons. Some of the children were laughing and racing around attempting to see who could actually touch one of them before they flew away. It was always a nice place to come and sit. Peaceful.

Until she glanced away and across the concrete walkway and her heard thudded against her chest.

Joseph!

She swallowed hard, unable to take her eyes off his wonderful form. He carried a briefcase and was accompanied by a pretty young woman, who seemed intensely concentrated on what Joseph was saying to her.

Eliza felt a stab of jealousy chase through her and was shocked by the surging emotion. She trembled in response to the ache it caused. And it frightened her.

She wanted to get up from the bench and approach him, have him acknowledge her presence. He must have felt her searing scrutiny because he stopped walking and looked around, then spotted her.

He didn't stop talking to the young woman, but his iron-dark gaze clung to hers. She saw no change in emotion, no obvious recognition, no smile of acknowledgment. He just kept talking as though nothing had changed, yet imprisoned her with his eyes until he turned the corner and it was no longer feasible to maintain contact.

He did not look back at her, but continued walking toward wherever his destination would lead. It was as though the weekend had never occurred. She trembled in response to the thoughts swirling around in her head. With shaking hands she threw the remains of the hotdog and soft drink into the garbage can.

Wasn't this what she wanted? No contact publicly? Who was the woman with him? They had agreed to remain sexually exclusive while they were together, but what if he was growing tired of waiting for her to make a choice?

On shaking legs she headed back to her chambers. She hesitated entering her office, determined to hide her churning feelings. Gathering her emotions, slowly she walked through the outer office and back into her own, closing the door firmly behind her.

She could not be forced into making a decision she wasn't ready for. These feelings he aroused scared her. True, she willingly put herself into his hands when they were together and reveled in the knowledge. But the emotion she experienced now after that brief encounter scared her silly.

The knowledge that he had ingrained himself so deeply inside her washed over her, and she became tantalized by a forbidden thought. What if she did give herself over completely? The idea began to take root. She could actually taste the pleasure of that thought, felt it nestle pleasingly close to her heart.

Unfortunately, it was quickly dislodged by her fears. How could she be certain he wouldn't take advantage when he had her where he wanted her? How could she possibly merge both parts of herself and still maintain some kind of control in her life?

She sat down at her desk, hands planted flat on the top as panic swamped her. No, she couldn't do it. She would have to end the relationship for her own sanity. She could not allow emotion to overrule her, nor Joseph to continue to exert this kind of power in her life. No matter how much she cared for him, she could not allow this to go on any longer.

And it couldn't wait another minute. With shaking fingers, she punched in the number to his office and ended up getting his voicemail. Maybe that was best.

"Joseph. It's me. I've made a decision. I can't go on like this. I can't see you again. I've thought it over and I can't make the commitment you deserve. Goodbye." She hung up the phone and then just sat and stared at it.

Was she just being a coward? Giving in to the easiest route, the safest road?

Leaning back in her chair, suddenly she felt more alone than she ever had before. It was as though her whole world had collapsed around her and her heart had been ripped from her chest. An urge to pick up the phone and erase her words screamed denial of her actions.

Blinking rapidly to suppress the rising tide of tears, she consoled herself with the thought that she would recover from a bruised heart. It would heal and she would still have her career. She hadn't lost that much. Eventually, she would convince herself of that fact.

There would be someone else, someone acceptable that wouldn't require her to give so much of herself away. She had made herself into someone who was successful and well-respected and she would find someone to complement that.

If only the loneliness didn't eat at her so badly. She shuddered as a wave of coldness consumed her. In panic she scanned the room. Why did it feel so cold? So empty?

CHAPTER 5

She shifted first to the left and then to the right, studying her reflection in the mirror. The modest black silk sheath clothed her shapely curves appropriately. Her updo was elegant, sleek, and refined. She'd accessorized with low-slung black leather pumps on her feet and a single strand of pearls around her neck with matching pearl stud earrings.

Yes, everything worked. She was elegantly attired for the political fundraiser, reeking of prestige and acceptance. But inside—

Beneath all the fine window dressing was a woman who was emotionally a wreck. A month of solitude had passed by with no contact from Joseph. He had not returned her call. But then she hadn't expected him to. Why should he? She'd ended their association—what more was there to say?

Her body and emotions lay dormant without him, as though encased in a thin covering of ice. He alone seemed to hold the key to fuel her inner passion.

Had she expected him to beg her to reconsider? Joseph Acosta? That was not likely to happen in a million years. There were many more than willing to take her place.

As she stood there staring beyond the reflected image in front of her, her hand raised to finger the cold pearls at her neck, and she shivered. She would need to wear the matching short jacket. This whole last month, ever since she'd made that call, she hadn't been able to get warm enough. From the inside out she was bone-chillingly cold.

Staring back at her was a woman with empty, unemotional eyes. Numbness had slowly consumed her from the inside out. There had been a time when that's all she'd wanted to keep the facade of control so no one would see the churning emptiness inside.

Wallowing did no good. She pivoted away from the mirror and reached for the jacket and evening purse that lay on the bed. She'd made her decision and now she'd have to live with it, even if it choked her.

Carl would be here to pick her up shortly. Carl Anderson was a well-respected businessman in the community. Widowed, he had two children, and was the perfect foil for her. Undemanding, polite, considerate, connected. So why when he kissed her did her lips actually seemed to go numb?

Constantly she needed to remind herself he was what she required in a companion. He was perfect for her. And he had indicated he would like their relationship to be closer. So organized, he'd practically tried to make an appointment with her so they could make love.

Maybe that was the problem. He was too regimented. But wasn't that the whole point? With Carl she didn't have to fear that her primal needs would consume her. He was an assertive man, without being obvious. He had no problem running interference for her when they socialized, and handled it well. So why did she feel that if she acceded to his hints at a closer intimacy, he would take more than she was willing to give. That he would suck every bit of life from her, leaving nothing behind? There was something about him, beneath that suave exterior, something lurking that didn't quite ring true to her.

Unlike Joseph. He had been totally up front with her from the beginning. Just looking at him, one saw the untamed predator in his eyes. Suave and sleek maybe, but he refused to hide his nature behind a false face.

So different from Eliza, who feared what people would think. She had a feeling Carl used his facade to entrap, seeking to take people unaware before he pounced. She shuddered at the thought of greater intimacy with Carl.

Who was Joseph with tonight? Who had he turned to when she'd ended the relationship? Eliza knew he was too sexually intense to go long without companionship or release. Was he with the dark-haired young woman from the park?

Visions of Joseph touching her, commanding her emotions to the surface spiraled through her mind. The memory of that last weekend at

The Corrigan rose to the forefront and her nipples tightened with arousal, her pussy ached for his attention.

It took a great deal of effort for her to push that memory aside. To remind herself she had given up all rights to what could have been.

Stop it! Stop thinking about him. So many times over the last month she'd reached to pick up the phone, to call him, but she'd stopped herself from doing it. What would it change? She was still a coward, still unable to publicly acknowledge her relationship with him.

But she also knew this would be her last date with Carl. She had to at least like the person she ended up marrying and she wasn't quite sure she liked Carl. She admired him, even respected him, but that's as far as it went. It wouldn't do to attempt to create a future with a man who repulsed her in private. Would she ever find a balance she could live with?

She heard the doorbell ring and glanced at the clock on the nightstand. As she expected, he was right on time—to the second. Always prompt.

This was going to be another night of elegant boredom. Every day had seemed endless and shadowed, mere blurs of movement to carry her from one moment to the next. Like the taste of food without the proper amounts of seasoning—bland and lifeless.

She'd lost weight during the last month, so little tempting her appetite of late. She loved to distraction a man she couldn't have and disliked the one she could. Maybe it just was not in her future to have a fulfilling relationship. Maybe she was meant to remain alone. It was certainly a sobering thought to consider a life without love, especially after what she'd experienced with Joseph. And that was the problem—nothing could measure up to what she'd experienced with him—and had thrown away.

Before stepping through the doorway she flipped the switch on the wall and the bedroom was submerged into darkness.

*   *   *

As he watched an attractive woman make her way across the dining room of the elegant restaurant, his thoughts turned unwillingly to Eliza. It was like a thorn under his skin he was unable to remove.

Eliza was the succulent rose from whose stem the thorn had been borne. Just the thought of her brought the remembrance of exquisite pleasure coursing through him. There were times when he thought he could smell her and echoes of remembered desire would erupt inside.

He'd wanted to call her after listening to the message on his voicemail, but decided it was best to give her time. Four weeks without contact, of wondering who was fucking her and if she thought of him. Torture and anger seasoned with frustration had threaded through him. With those emotions surpassing any others, he knew facing her down was not an option.

So instead, he'd thrown himself into his work. Luckily he was in the middle of a large securities fraud case and it took a huge amount of his time and concentration to prepare for trial.

"What's troubling you, Joseph?"

The sultry voice of his companion for the evening called him back to the present and he turned to looked at her. Darkly sensuous, lusciously curved, she reeked ready-for-fucking lust. Her exotic make-up accented her desire to please.

He knew at the first word from him she'd make herself sexually available for his every demand. He needed release, needed to sink himself into oblivion.

But he was not the type of man to use a woman to forget another one. And that's what it would be if he took her back to his apartment. Because he was trying to forget the simple beauty of the woman he really wanted beneath him. The woman whose body radiated energy and sensuality, erotic submission when he looked at her, touched her, took her.

She pleased him in ways no woman before her ever had. He reveled in revealing the layers of her soul hidden from the world. Exposing the real Eliza offered delights unimaginable.

And he hated the feelings of frustration, anger, and impotence he now felt, knowing she'd slipped through his fingers, as ethereal as sunlight, as intoxicating as a moonlit night.

Picking up his wineglass he swallowed deeply, fixing his gaze on the woman who adorned his table tonight. He smiled his practiced smile, attentive to her comfort.

"Nothing is wrong. I was thinking about some intricacies to the case I'm involved in. I'm afraid I'm not the best company for you this evening."

Nor did he expect he would be for quite some time. He might refuse to acknowledge it, and fight it as hard as he could, but he still loved Eliza and it would be some time before he took another woman to his bed.

CHAPTER 6

Tonight he was doing a friend a favor by escorting her to another boring political function. It was his policy to steer clear of these assemblages as much as possible. Particularly in the last month. If he'd stayed away from Daimaen's party, he wouldn't be in this position now.

And then there was always the chance of running into Eliza at this party and he wasn't ready for that yet. He kicked himself every time he thought about that last weekend, running it over and over in his mind, trying to assess what he should have done differently. Obviously, he'd pushed her too far. He should have waited, given her more time.

He couldn't remember any certain point where she'd pulled back or seemed frightened. She had appeared to enjoy it, had never asked him to stop, had, in fact, seemed to submerge herself entirely into the experience. So what had gone wrong?

Swallowing another searing gulp of whiskey, suddenly an odd feeling washed over him and he shifted his attention to the doorway where people were entering. His gaze targeted her through the throng as though she wore a beacon that called only to him. The feeling that ran through him resembled that of a wild animal experiencing the first familiar scent of his chosen prey.

He saw her smile at their host. It was her public smile, not reaching her eyes. He recognized her escort, was acquainted with his squirrelly way of doing business. He also knew there were many women who fell for his suave exterior. Didn't Eliza see through the bastard?

But, of course, he was probably the type of man she thought she needed. So very different from Joseph, accepted by society even though he sometimes used underhanded methods to attain his goal.

He found some humor in the situation. Carl acceded to what society wanted to see and used it to his bloodthirsty advantage. Whereas, Joseph pretended nothing, refused to bend to society's strictures. Society accepted Carl at face value, curried his presence, and Anderson knew how to use that. Joseph, on the other hand, was thought to be a rogue, dangerous, unacceptable as an escort to the prestigious, but his attendance was also sought because of his dangerous veneer and powerful personality. Yet, he would be considered an unsuitable escort for a proper personage such as Judge Eliza O'Brien. Joseph bowed to a specific and unique code of ethics in both business and his personal life; Anderson had none.

He saw Carl lay a proprietary hand to Eliza's forearm and a dangerous red haze blurred Joseph's vision. He coveted what by rights belonged to Joseph. It was in Joseph's mind not to allow Carl to destroy the vibrant beauty he sought for himself. Rumors abounded about the death of his wife. It was his opinion that Eliza was jumping from the pot right into the core of the fire, and it destroyed him to think of her being irrevocably scarred by it.

They turned toward the room and Joseph instinctively stepped behind a wide marble pillar, cloaking his presence from their view.

He studied her as she made her way around the room, the picture of prominent political personage, her escort a perfect foil to her— courteous, considerate, handsome. Where was the passion he'd become acquainted with so well? He didn't see even a glimmer in the woman draped on Carl Anderson's arm.

A rage began to burn inside him. He'd thought she would call. He'd waited for it, but it had never happened. A week ago he'd attended a party with the full intention of finding a submissive for some play, assuring himself Eliza no longer mattered to him. Maybe he'd find two, he promised himself. Women who didn't have a career to consider, who gave themselves up freely to the experience. Pure sexual release without commitment of any kind beyond a night of primitive sensations.

In the end he hadn't been able to do it. He kept seeing her face, smelling her scent. There had been several who'd been more than willing to leave with him, but in the end, he'd left on his own. Without the proper mindset it would have been frustrating and useless. So he'd left.

He'd tried again just a few nights ago, and again, his memories thwarted his need to wipe her from his mind.

But watching her as she circuited the room on the arm of another man brought his baser instincts to the fore. As he watched, she turned to the man attending her, said something and then walked away. He knew exactly where she was headed and he meant to confront her.

As she threaded her way through the throng of people and walked past where he was hidden, he turned and followed her down the hallway. The one thing she couldn't seem to suppress was the sultry sway of her hips as she floated down the corridor. He'd always enjoyed watching her as she moved away from him. Her grace, like a ballerina's exit off stage, excited him, had his body throbbing to possess her.

He wanted to let her go, let her fly free if that's what she wanted. But something inside him couldn't let this moment pass without one last confrontation—one last chance for her to accept her nature and that she belonged with him.

She opened the door and stepped inside the powder room. He anticipated he was about to give her a surprise she least expected.

*   *   *

Eliza collapsed forward against the rim of the ebony sink, thankful for the subdued lighting in the small neatly-appointed room. Her head ached and she simply wanted to go home. She hadn't really needed to use the bathroom, she'd just wanted to get away from the stifling atmosphere in the overcrowded room. Too many people and she'd felt like screaming *leave me alone*. But she hadn't, instead retreating to the only room that might offer a small amount of peace for a fraction of a moment.

As she heard the door open and then close she sighed, straightening away from the sink. Well, that had definitely been a shorter fraction of time than she'd hoped for.

"Hello, Eliza," a deep, gravelly voice she remembered so well from her dreams greeted her.

She stiffened and whirled around, unable to believe he was real. Her hands gripped the edges of the vanity for dear life, afraid she would crumble to the floor.

"Joseph," she managed to choke out. "What are you doing in here?"

She heard the click of the lock on the door as he turned it. "Waiting for a chance to talk with you. I didn't think you would want me to approach you out there." He nodded to the room beyond the locked door. "It appears you were otherwise occupied."

"Wh-what more is there to say?" She couldn't take her eyes off him, so hungry for his image, yet fearing the leashed animal she saw lurking in the depths of his eyes.

He strode across the room to stand close. She could smell his dark, rich scent, and as always she felt the curls of desire reach out to engulf her.

She turned her head away, trying to gain control of the keen sensations that wanted to be freed. The unexpectedness of his presence made it difficult to harness.

She felt him stroke his knuckles along the exposed length of her throat and she wanted to—

"No, Joseph, please don't," she begged, yet knowing that for the first time in a month, feeling was returning to her body, to her mind, every pore opening like morning glories to the sun, ready to feed, to live. It was as though a light that had been switched off now surged to life and a powerful zing of desire raced through her veins.

"Don't what, Eliza?" He bent his head close to her neck, and she heard him inhale. "I don't smell his scent on you. Has he fucked you yet?"

She turned her head swiftly to meet his searing look. "No," she denied forcefully. "And what about you? Have you found someone to take my place?"

He feathered kisses along her neck as he pulled the strap of her dress down her arm. "There are a number of girls who would be eager to take your place as my submissive."

His mouth clamped onto her bared breast, sucking hard, his tongue circling and teasing. She was unable to move, unwilling to pull free of him, not wanting to break free. Instead, she moaned and arched into him, remembered bliss hovered at the fringes of her mind.

"Joseph, please—" she begged, but couldn't determine whether she begged him to let her go or to give her more.

He lifted his head. "Please what, Eliza? Please fuck you? Please let you go? What is it you want? Or are you afraid to ask?"

He knew her so well. Better than anyone else alive. And she had sent him away because that's exactly what she feared most. His knowledge of who she was beneath the hardened facade.

Swirling emotions collided inside her as he pulled down the strap along her other arm and nuzzled at her breast. A sharp, pleasurable pain arrowed through her as he bit down on her sensitized nipple, then swirled his tongue to ease the ache.

Oh, God, what he did to her, how he did it. Suddenly, the color was back, the scents in the air swirled and collided.

His hands lifted her skirt and his fingers found her pulsing vagina, empty for so long without him.

Just as quickly, he removed his hand from inside her panties and forced her to turn to face the vanity—and the mirror.

Again his hand slid inside her panties to tease her swollen labia. His other hand cupped her chin forcing her to look in the mirror.

His dark gaze burned her as he watched her in the mirror. "Can he give you this? Does he make you come the way I do?" Two of his fingers sank swiftly into her pussy and his thumb teased around her clit, stroking, but not touching. "Do you like my touch, Eliza? Do you crave more?"

She tried to catch her breath, but the sensations of desire buzzed around her, through her, and she needed him to fuck her.

"Joseph, please," she begged as her hips bucked against his questing fingers. She needed him to touch her clit, to let her climax.

"Please what, Eliza?"

"Please let me come—make me come. Fuck me." She couldn't believe it was her voice—that husky rasp, filled with lust and passion.

"Here, Eliza? Where everyone would know? You want me to take you? What would Carl say?" His fingers thrust inside her again, surging deep, curled to catch a sensitive spot deep inside, driving her toward the brink of uncontrolled need. Then his fingers left her as swiftly as he had taken her.

"No, girl, not here, not now. Not ever. You had your chance. You're the one who walked away. I only wanted to give you something to remember me by."

The counter was the only thing holding her up as his support disappeared. Her vision blurred, but she heard the door open and shut with finality. That quickly he was gone, leaving her in a quake of unfulfilled sensations and terrible regret.

She looked at the woman in the mirror, a wanton woman, her breasts exposed, milky white in the shadows, her nipples deeply blushed, hard and needy. Unsatisfied lust permeated the room.

With shaking hands she righted her dress and smoothed it along her hips. She couldn't go back inside that room. Not like this. Joseph had taken every vestige of composure away from her, even the semblance of civilized control was gone, and inside was a quivering mass of regret and unfulfilled longing.

He was gone and would never come back. This had been his farewell, his final exertion of control. And she would always yearn for his brand of dominance. And never again be fulfilled.

Hastily she pulled a scrap of paper and a small pen from her purse and scribbled a message. She could not face Carl again tonight. Once last glance in the mirror, and she decided she at least looked presentable enough to leave the powder room.

Would Joseph still be out there? She was unable to face him as well or she knew she would throw herself at him, begging for his forgiveness and for him to take her back.

She recognized her vulnerability—the weakest point she had ever reached in her life. And it terrified her. Pain as she'd never felt before shafted through her. She handed the note to a server and pointed out the gentleman to give it to. Whirling away, she hurried out the back door. When she reached the ground floor without incident, she hailed a taxi to take her home, back to safety and away from temptation.

Time. All she needed was time, she assured herself, and she would recover from tonight.

Unobtrusively, she closed her thighs together trying to contain the savage need for a powerful release that would never again be hers. She would be fine. She suppressed the deep-rooted sobs that choked her throat. She would not give in to the abyss of pain and hopelessness waiting to destroy her.

CHAPTER 7

Approval.
By her parents.
By her peers.
By the community.
And what had it provided her with? The need to maintain a public facade that ended up bringing her nothing but loneliness.

True, there was satisfaction in serving the people and justice in her capacity as a judge. She'd been elected to the position.

And therein lay the problem. The people had elected her and she had a responsibility to serve them. But how deep did that responsibility go? Did it mean she was required to forsake any personal satisfaction in her life?

It felt like she was back in high school and unable to date certain boys because her parents wouldn't approve. Because of how it would look. But even back then nothing lay quite so heavily on her shoulders as her decisions now, as a responsible adult.

Did she really owe the sacrifice of her personal life to the public, as well as the dedication of her public life?

She felt she'd reached a crucial turning point in her life. A decision she was about to make was going to change the path for the balance of her future. Either way it would mark how she proceeded.

Did she allow the public to dictate who she did and did not love? How she loved them?

Would thirty or fifty years pass and the only thing she'd have left be bitterness and regret? Was this job worth that? She wasn't a robot, she was human, and admitting she was a woman with all of a woman's strengths and weaknesses was not a surrender to defeat of any kind.

Choosing the right partner should be a choice about love and compatibility. She had given her soul to the right man, and then, because she feared public recriminations, she'd run from the one person who made her feel complete. He held the key to the other part of who she was. In denying him, she'd denied an essential facet of herself.

But then she had spent her life denying a part of who she was. It was only with him that those facets of her personality had been finally allowed into the light of life.

To others it was a dark side of personality, one to be feared and maintained in shadow. But for her, it had been like the sun had come out to shed light on all the varying facets of her soul.

It was like the time when she'd been a little girl and she told her mother she wanted a set of watercolors for her birthday. She'd told her she wanted to be an artist one day. Her mother had called it nonsense and berated her for even mentioning it. She'd informed her that her path lay in solid concentration to become a professional. That's where respect lay for a woman—and money to support a person. There were other times she realized now that had led Eliza to this moment. It had been a lifetime of suppressing any scrap of femininity inside her.

Everything became rooted in how other people perceived her, and nothing about what fulfilled her.

Joseph had tapped into the woman inside screaming out for attention. He had touched the woman who wanted to be allowed to be a woman, to be soft and alluring and attractive.

She realized now she'd admired him long before she'd been introduced to him. His reputation had preceded him. Why? Because he wasn't afraid to be exactly who he was. And yet he had still risen in his profession, uncaring of what others thought about his private life. Unafraid to be known as a dominant male. Yet he didn't flaunt it, he just was.

So why was it so different for her? Because she was a woman? Was the road to acceptance in her profession really found by suppressing all of her feminine instinct? And beyond that, denying her desire to submit within a lifestyle different from others? By suppressing half of who she was? There had to be another way.

From the moment she'd met Joseph Acosta she'd recognized something she'd been seeking but had been afraid to find. And out of all the men who had passed through her life, Joseph had been the one to tap into the part of her she no longer wanted to hide. She found she no longer cared about public approval or her mother's approval.

She wanted Joseph's approval. She wanted his love, and she wanted to give him hers. Freely. Openly. Completely.

He'd been patient with her and she'd failed him. He was not a man who offered second chances. His last words and actions told her that more eloquently than she could have ever wanted.

So where did that leave her? Alone, if she didn't do something about it soon.

The thought of taking this chance scared her more than anything before. Because it was so important. And she wanted it so badly. She wanted *him* so badly.

She turned away from the window and looked around the room. It was a sad thing to realize that this had been the core of her life for so long. Inanimate objects and impersonal relationships. Four walls that represented everything she'd set out to achieve in her life. But she had no one to celebrate her victories with. Nor to commiserate with her in her defeats. And the realization of the emptiness contained in this room started to close in on her.

She shuddered when a knock sounded at her door bringing her out of her soul searching, and her assistant entered.

"I have the file for this afternoon's pretrial conference."

Eliza whirled away from the window and walked back toward her desk. No more time for self-confrontation. "Remind me. What time will they be here?"

"Two o'clock, Judge." Marie seemed to hesitate. "Are you all right? You look—I don't know—sad, I guess."

Eliza smiled at her. She figured Marie was about ten years younger than she was, and exceptional at her job. She'd first met her at the law firm they'd both worked at before Eliza had been elected. She'd asked Marie if she wanted to work for her when she left the firm, and Marie had been eager to make the change.

"I'm fine." She reached for the file. "Just some memories coming back to haunt me, I guess."

"Well, they didn't look like good ones. You need another one of those weekends away, I think. You positively glowed when you came back from the last one."

Eliza felt herself stiffen and she shifted her attention to the file on her desk. Yes, that was the weekend when the crack in the wall separating her two lives began to appear—and when she'd turned tail like a coward to avoid a complete crumbling of the barricade. She now knew that in the end she should have let it disintegrate naturally and given in to the merging of her two separate existences.

She glanced up at Marie. "You're right. I do need another one of those weekends. Maybe soon."

Marie turned away to leave her office, but she pivoted back around. "Did you happen to hear the latest flurry of gossip about a very attractive attorney in town?"

Eliza had a premonition that she wasn't going to like what Marie would tell her. "No, I don't believe I have."

"There was a woman found murdered. It was discovered she'd attended one of those BDSM parties the night before it happened and left with someone. Well, you know what they say about Joseph Acosta—"

Eliza's blood chilled. "What do you mean?"

"They apparently brought him in for questioning. Gossip has always tied him into that lifestyle, you know. Do you think he did it? Murdered that girl? Wouldn't that be something if it got assigned to you? Now that would be a juicy case to hear."

"No," Eliza said more forcefully than she should have. She tried to slow her speeding pulse. "When do they say it happened?" There was no way Joseph could be involved in such a thing.

"About five weeks ago. They've apparently been investigating it and are down to several suspects who don't appear to have alibis for that weekend."

Five weeks ago she had been with Joseph at The Corrigan. He had an alibi, so why didn't he use it? He had someone to vouch for where he was. Someone whose reputation was impeccable and would end any more questions.

Damn him! She had a feeling she knew exactly why he didn't speak up. "Thanks, Marie," she said absently, her mind on what her next course of action needed to be. It seemed fate was going to rip her options out of her hands.

"No problem. I'll let you know if I hear anything else." She closed the door as she left Eliza's office.

Eliza sat staring into space, not seeing the room around her. So this was how it was going to be. The fates had decided she'd waited long enough to make a decision. She had no other choice but to present herself to the police and confirm that he had an alibi for that weekend.

Even after everything that had passed between them, he was trying to protect her at the risk to his own career—his own life. She loved him for doing it, but wanted to ring his neck at the same time.

The moment had arrived for her to destroy the walls between her worlds, to show not only Joseph, but the rest of the world who she was and whom she loved.

She got up from behind her desk and hurried to the closet to grab her coat. Shrugging into it as she left her office, Marie gaped at her in surprise as she hurried past.

"Where are you going?"

"I have some urgent business to take care of. Please cancel my appointments this afternoon," and she raced out the door.

The police station was not far from the courthouse—technically just across the street. She hurried to the corner, waited impatiently for the light to change, and raced across to the four-story granite building setting on the corner.

She walked up the steps and into the building. There was a steady hum and flurry of activity as she approached the desk. The uniformed desk sergeant looked up at her in surprise, recognizing her.

"What can I do for you, Judge?"

This was the moment she'd feared for so long, yet now embraced willingly. This must be how someone felt when they admitted to their family that they were gay. She felt a weight begin to slide from her shoulders. Whatever the outcome, she would be free from subterfuge and it was a heady moment.

"I need to speak to the detectives in charge of the investigation about that girl who was murdered. I have some information about a possible suspect they're questioning."

The desk sergeant hesitated for a fraction of a second. "Have a seat, please. I think they're in the middle of an interrogation right now, but I'll get a message to one of the detectives."

Eliza turned away and sat on the hard wooden bench. She wanted this over—wanted this first confrontation behind her. She closed her eyes and leaned her head back against the institutional green wall and waited.

*   *   *

Joseph thrummed his fingers against the scarred wooden table he sat at awaiting the return of the detectives questioning him about the murder. Just because he knew the hosts of the party the murdered girl had attended, and he wasn't able to supply them with an acceptable alibi, they were intent on grilling him until they got the confession they were sure was coming.

Their only goal was to close their files on a sticky case as quickly as possible. The party she'd been at had been attended by some very well-known individuals and this was apparently considered a very delicate case. Someone wanted it closed and closed quickly.

The fact that Joseph had no one to corroborate his stay at The Corrigan did not help him. Oh, they knew he'd been there, but there was nothing to show that he'd stayed there. He could very well have used his registration at the hotel as a smoke screen. At least that was their opinion. But there was no way he was giving them Eliza's name.

He would wait it out. Eventually they would have to let him go. They had no evidence he even knew the girl. He was sorry for her because apparently she'd gotten caught up in a very bad scene. He was sure the hosts of that particular party were torn up over the fact that whoever did it had met her at their home. Usually the guests were very well vetted out, but obviously some glitch must have occurred somewhere.

He looked up as the door to the interrogation room squeaked open. The detective looked over the rim of his glasses at Joseph.

"It looks like we're going to have to let you go."

Joseph was surprised. "Why?"

"You should have told us who you were with that weekend."

Joseph tensed. "What do you mean?"

"Apparently, she found out we were questioning you and she just walked into the station to let us know *who* you were with. You're free to leave."

He slowly rose from his chair, grabbed his gray suit jacket, slung it over his arm, and strode past the detective without speaking. What was he supposed to do—thank him for wasting five hours of his day questioning him about something he didn't do?

He was more intent on finding Eliza and discovering exactly what she'd told the detective. Inside, he felt a spark of anger that she'd exposed herself in this way, and he was going to have a few words with her.

As he exited into the main room, he stopped short. She was sitting there waiting. When she looked up and saw him, she rose slowly to her feet and waited for him to approach her. He saw the hesitancy in her eyes.

"Eliza," he greeted her. "Do you know what you've done?" He wanted to take her over his knee right there and then.

She met his gaze steadily. "Yes, Joseph. For once, I know exactly what I've done."

He shook his head. Something had changed, but he didn't know what. He gripped her arm and turned her toward the exit. This was not the place to sort this out. Not in front of all these people.

Unfortunately, when they exited the station, there were reporters waiting, and flash after flash as they were barraged with questions.

There would be no answers for them, and he forced a way through them, guiding Eliza to his car. In his opinion, they couldn't get away fast enough. She had a lot of explaining to do.

CHAPTER 8

He hadn't said a word to her. When she'd seen him walking toward her, a fierce nervous tension gripped her. What had he thought when he found out she had stepped forward with his alibi?

His tightly wound power didn't bode well as he strode toward her, a fiery aura of dark energy surrounding him, his eyes blazing with suppressed anger.

He gripped her arm, spun her around, and literally marched her out of the station.

She was shocked to find so many news reporters outside, eager for information about a break in the case. They were surrounded like a swarm of bees to a bed of succulent flowers.

She jerked back as a microphone was thrust toward her.

"Judge O'Brien what's your part in this investigation? Why are you here?"

Before Eliza could take a breath to say "no comment" Joseph thrust the hand holding the microphone aside and urged her onward. Fielding bodies quickly, he directed her to his vehicle and pushed her into the passenger's seat.

He didn't look at her when he got in behind the wheel. The tires on the Mercedes spun and squealed as he pulled out of the parking lot. She felt his displeasure fill the small enclosed space of the car.

"Joseph—"

"Not now, Eliza," he bit back.

He sped through the streets of the city. She wasn't exactly afraid with him behind the wheel. He was an expert driver, and she knew that, but the anger evidenced by his clenched jaw and rigid posture confused her.

Wasn't this what he had wanted all along? For her to admit publicly they had a relationship? So where was all this anger coming from?

She noticed they were driving out of the city. "Where are we going?" she asked, a bit hesitant to break into his mood.

"You saw all those reporters. I can't take you home just yet, and my place isn't going to be any better."

Of course, he was right. They were involved in a very high profile story right now and there wouldn't be any chance they'd be left alone for quite some time.

But she needed to be back in the office—she had commitments—she couldn't just drive away like this. People would worry if she just disappeared without a word.

She had passed the time where she wouldn't face the consequences of her actions.

"I can handle it."

He glanced at her and his eyes seared a path through her. "Can you?"

He was apparently not in a mood for conversation. Eliza leaned back in her seat and tried to relax. Everyone would have to wait for explanations. She trusted him to understand her position and have her back in time for work tomorrow.

She would have her chance soon to explain and try to get him to listen. Until then, she would simply have to wait, hoping she hadn't left it too late.

They entered the anonymous motel room, and she watched as he threw his jacket onto the bed. He strode over to the window and yanked open the curtains, staring out at the far-ranging cornfield beyond. It was a small, clean hotel, in a sleepy town, miles outside of the city.

Stiffly, she sat on the edge of the bed, watching him. What was he thinking?

He ran a hand through his hair, ruffling it. She waited. It wouldn't help anything if she pushed him. Instead, she shrugged off her coat and set it to the side.

"Do you know what you've done?" His hard statement dropped like a lead weight to shatter the tense silence filling the room.

He hadn't moved from his position at the window—didn't even turn around to look at her.

"Yes," she answered him quietly. "I know exactly what I did." She leaned down to tug off her shoes and rub her feet. How they ached. Usually her shoes were the first things to come off at the end of a day. It was unfortunate that today of all days she'd chosen to wear a particularly uncomfortable pair.

He whirled around and pinned her with a hard look. "The media is going to rip you apart, do you realize that?"

"What about you?" she countered.

"I can handle whatever they dish out. You, on the other hand, are in a more sensitive position. But you know that, you've always known that. This is a hell of a time for you to decide to announce a relationship with me."

She had to smile, because she was more aware of what she'd done than anyone. "Oh, and I don't know that?" She lifted her chin. "I can take care of myself."

"Oh, really. You hadn't thought you could in the past, what makes now so different? Why now, when we no longer have a relationship?"

She winced at the painful reminder. Taking her new determination in hand, she rose to her feet and began unbuttoning the front of her silk dress. "I've had a lot of time to think—to do a lot of soul searching."

When she peeked at him from beneath her veil of lashes, she noted his attention was on her hands, following her slow movements.

"And exactly what conclusion have you come to?"

The last button was undone, and her dress fell open, revealing the silky white slip beneath, but she didn't remove it completely. Not yet. "I've been a coward. You have every right to be angry with me. I've let my mother's ideals drive me all of my life to the point where I've allowed what I wanted, *who I needed*, to slip through my fingers because I was so intent on needing her approval. Everyone's approval and acceptance. Except my own."

Slowly, she walked to him. He stood like a statue, waiting, watching, giving no indication of his thoughts.

As she reached him, she looked up, praying she could mend what she had destroyed. She was so close she could feel the warmth of his body, wanted to feel it inside her.

"I'm sorry, Joseph. Please forgive me. I want another chance."

She couldn't tell what he was thinking. The look on his face had turned expressionless, his eyes dark and fathomless. She trembled with the uncertainty as to how he would react to her declaration. Long minutes passed.

"What is it you want, Eliza?"

She licked her lips. These next moments were so important. How she answered would color or fade her future happiness.

"I want—I want to be with you. No matter what. I love you. I was afraid at what you made me feel, but I know now without you my world is empty."

"What about Carl?"

She turned her head away, but she felt his hand cup her chin and force her to look at him.

"I panicked. I thought I knew what I should have, what was expected. But I couldn't do it. I couldn't give myself to him."

"Why not?" His steady, demanding gaze pierced her right down to her soul.

She connected with that look. "Because you already own every part of me. And I don't want to give even a small piece of that to anyone but you."

"Why?" He dropped his hand away. Just that simple gesture and she felt abandoned. She needed his touch, needed that connection. She wanted to reach out—to bring his hand back—to feel that warmth again. And again.

That question. He wanted it all, he expected it. And it was his right to have it.

"Without you every one of my senses is dead. You bring the color and life. You make me feel—everything—with such passion. I've been so cold these last weeks without you. You are the fire in my life and I don't want to be without that ever again."

He stepped around her and crossed the room. Had she lost him forever by her cowardly retreat? She turned around to look at him, blinking rapidly to hold back the tears that threatened.

"I will not change my life for you, Eliza. Do you understand that? I am active in my chosen lifestyle. I'm an advocate for it. I assist in court cases for others in my community. How are you going to handle that when it becomes a pivotal argument when election time comes around again? Are you going to retreat? How will you answer their threats?"

This was the crux. The very thing she would be required to face if she openly flaunted their relationship. It's the very reason she'd left him, the issues that had kept her awake at night.

And she'd finally reached the conclusion that this relationship was worth the price. He freed her soul, make her whole, and she could no longer separate her soul from her mind.

"With honesty. I want to be in your life. I'm willing to take the chance. If I'm asked to step down, or I fail to win the next election, so be it. I'll find another way to accomplish my goals." She walked across the room. "But I now know the rest is meaningless without you." She laid her hands against his chest, felt the rhythmic beating of his heart.

"You have to be very sure."

"I am. I'm half alive without you. But then you wanted me to see that for myself. It's why you never pushed me to make a choice, isn't it?"

"It had to be your decision. I couldn't take that from you. But this time, Eliza, there's no going back—no half measures." He gripped her wrists. "I won't accept a lukewarm commitment from you this time. What is it you want?" He enunciated carefully each word of his last sentence.

There would be no going back. He wanted her to voice her commitment. This would be the first time she'd said it out loud. In her head, in her heart, she'd known and she'd accepted. But now he wanted her to give voice to that knowledge.

She would not cower, that wasn't what she wanted, but he wanted her avowal. Straightening her shoulders, she slipped her hands free from his grasp. Slowly, she sank to her knees. He stepped away from her, watching and waiting.

She clasped her hands behind her back and lifted her head, her steady gaze connecting with his. This was the moment when she gave all of herself to him. Willingly.

"Please, Sir, I want to be your submissive. I want to serve you in all ways. I trust you to care for me and only ask that you allow me to do the same for you. Everything I am, I give to you."

There was a long silence as he seemed to contemplate the acceptance of her gift. His gaze roved over her, and she wondered what thoughts were going through his head.

"I accept your gift, Eliza."

She exhaled on a long breath. And with that breath went all her reservations. She felt a certain freedom, a lightness inside. It wasn't until that moment, that she realized how frightened she had been that he would deny her and send her away.

He walked back to her. "I should punish you, you realize that."

Their roles were chosen. "Yes, Sir."

He tilted her chin up. "Tell me why you think I should punish you."

"Should I give you a list, Sir?" She knew that response should garner her a more severe punishment and a fire began to spread inside her, so very different from the cold ice she'd been encased in for so long. The molten heat felt good.

Anticipation spread through her at what form the punishment would take and she felt the fine sheen of passion coat her thighs.

"I don't think a list will be necessary, and that response is impertinent. But, of course, you know that."

"Yes, Sir." It was her aim to goad him into touching her in the ways her spirit demanded. She didn't want polite, quiet loving, she wanted him to take, and have him make her want.

"You shouldn't have come to the police station today. There were other ways you could have gone about this."

"Yes, Sir. But I couldn't wait."

"Patience. You will learn patience tonight. And control."

"Whatever you wish, Sir. I am yours and I trust you to take care of me."

She watched him look around the room. "I see I will need to improvise." He turned back to look down at her. "Patience and control, Eliza. And trust. Do you trust me?"

"In everything, Sir. Everything."

"It's time to prepare for the spanking you deserve, girl. Stand up and prepare yourself for discipline."

As gracefully as possible she rose to her feet. Joseph was a sensualist and his form of discipline was always a pleasurable torture to the senses. She eagerly discarded her remaining clothes and awaited his pleasure.

It would be her rededication to him in accepting him as her Master. Her body thrummed with anticipation.

CHAPTER 9

Naked, Eliza knelt at the side of the bed in the motel room. And waited. Joseph had left her there to consider her digressions, with a warm and throbbing ass to remind her, and told her he needed to go out to do a short errand.

She would have protested being left behind, but knew it would not garner her the required result. She felt the cool breeze from the air conditioner swirl between the lips of her throbbing pussy. Before leaving, he'd made sure to caress and fondle her just enough to ensure she stayed at the edge of her desire. Her ass might sting from the paddling she'd received, but it was the tingle in her vagina that had her eager for his return.

Patience, he said—and control. For Eliza, who had always thought she knew what those two words meant, they now began to take on new meaning.

She maintained control of her courtroom, others acceded to her requirements. Patience, awaiting the long, drawn out proceedings, some going late into the night—times when she wanted to wring an attorney's neck.

Patience and control in rising to the judgeship. But that had been more like suppression and strangulation. Suppressing her personal needs and desires.

Joseph didn't want her to suppress her desires—he wanted her to feel every last bit.

Her lips curved into a satisfied smile as she submerged herself into the sensual echoes of her body. Wanting to climax, she wouldn't, not until Joseph gave her permission.

Her road to this moment had seemed long and hard. But this is where she wanted to be. There were many who would consider her actions as forsaking her role as a leader to women's rights. But shouldn't it be a woman's right to choose her path and not be constrained by what society decided it was?

She'd finally severed the umbilical cord that had tied her to outward approval and instead, submitted to her own need for fulfillment. It was a journey that had freed her to live.

Her attention was drawn back to the room where she knelt. Joseph entered, carrying two white plastic sacks, and another bag bearing the insignia of a carry-out restaurant.

"I thought you might be hungry," he said as he set the bags on the small circular beige Formica table near the window.

He walked over to her and placed a hand beneath her chin. "Have you had time to think about what I said?"

"Yes, Sir. I think I've learned my lesson."

The delicious smell of whatever food was in the bag had her stomach growling.

He reached down to stroke her pussy, his fingers firm and cool against her overheated lips. "You're still very wet, Eliza. Were you thinking of me while I was gone?"

"Yes."

"And what were you thinking?" He reached around to stroke her reddened ass and she sucked in sharply.

"Still sting?"

"Yes," she breathed, then caught her breath as he swiftly inserted two fingers into her channel. They retreated, then sank deeper.

"Are you angry with me for spanking your ass?"

She undulated her hips against his fingers. "N-no. I deserved the uhh-correction."

Again his fingers sank deep, his thumb rubbed over her clit and she moaned with the pleasure that coursed through her at the touch.

"You've been a good girl while I was gone." He bent closer, and she felt his breath against her lips. "Come, Eliza."

The powerful surging of her climax overwhelmed her, drove through her. She panted and gasped, bucked against his hand, arched her back as the cyclone of release overtook her.

He removed his fingers and straightened, looking down at her with dark emotion in his eyes. "I've missed watching you come like that. You are so beautiful when you let yourself go."

Her legs trembled. The aftershocks of her orgasm kept her at a slow simmer. She knew he wasn't done and she anticipated what was yet to come.

"Come over here and sit," he directed, pointing to the beige cloth-covered chair opposite him. "Remember to keep your legs apart."

She rose to her feet and walked over to the chair, wondering what he had in mind. She spread her thighs once she sat, felt the prickly fabric of the chair against her ass and shifted.

He looked at her, then leaned forward and widened her legs farther. "That's better. Your wet pussy is a delight to see. Don't ever hide your passion. Never again."

He shrugged out of his jacket and tossed it to the bed. After rolling up his shirt sleeves he reached into the first white bag and pulled out what looked to be a small whisk brush with white nylon bristles.

He turned to her and brushed his hand over the soft endings. He leveled his gaze on her. "What do you think this is for?"

"I-I don't know." She looked up at him questioningly.

He brought the brush down lightly, feathering it along her sensitive inner thighs, and she inhaled sharply at the exquisite sensation. Her body tightened and she knew he planned to torture her with the small cleaning implement.

"Do you like that?" he asked as he continued to sweep along her sensitive skin. Unexpectedly, he reached down and drew it along her calves, picked up one of her feet and feathered it along the sole. She shivered with desire, sensations swirling around her.

"Joseph—" she begged. "Please—"

"Please what, Eliza?" he asked as he continued to tease her flesh, driving her into a frenzy of feeling, of need.

Her pussy gushed with her desire, spilling onto the seat of the chair.

Joseph reached out to whisper his fingers between the swollen lips of her labia. Her hands tightened on the arms of the chair as she attempted not to scream.

"You're ready to come again, aren't you, Eliza?"

"Yessss," she moaned. "Please, let me come."

He pulled away from her and licked at his fingers covered in her juices. "Not just yet.

Laying down the bristly torturous instrument, he reached inside the carry-out back and set a foil tray down on the table. "Dinner first."

Her pussy was so hot and needy she had no idea how she was going to concentrate on food. She squirmed in her seat, watched as he pulled a container out of the other white bag. It was made of clear plastic and appeared to hold fresh, plump strawberries.

He pulled a chicken leg out of the tray and tore off a piece of the meat. He held it out to her and she took it into her mouth. The next piece he ate himself.

The next he gave her, and, as she chewed, his hand strayed to the nipple of her breast. As she attempted to eat he tweaked the hard bud.

"Swallow, Eliza," he instructed as he continued to taunt her breasts until their sensitivity drove her to distraction.

She wanted to lean forward to remove his pants, to have him fuck her. Again, she squirmed in her chair.

"You want something, don't you, love?"

"Yes," she hissed. "You know what I want."

He smiled. "You want your pussy filled, don't you?"

"Yes." This time it was a whispered moan.

She watched as he reached over to pick up a very large, succulent berry. Her eyes widened as he brought it to the entrance of her wet, needy core. She felt the seeded fruit rasp light against her lips and gasped at the sensation, then, unbelievably, it passed her outer lips and was pressed inside her.

It was an odd, erotic feeling to know what he was doing. He pulled it out and then pushed it inside her again. His gaze pulled hers. From her peripheral vision she saw him snag another. Then a third and a fourth. They penetrated and widened, she felt each one as it followed the other, until finally she was filled with succulent fruit and she no longer felt she remained in the room.

Swirling in passion, drowning in erotic decadence, she was unable to find her voice.

She was aware of Joseph's hands on her thighs, of his mouth close to hers. He pulled her close to the edge of the chair. All she could do was feel, the fullness of her pussy, the throbbing of her nipples, the sizzle of her ass.

He leaned forward and blew softly on her clit and she arched and screamed. His hard hands held her in place as he dropped his head closer.

"I want some sweet cream with my strawberries, love." His tongue swept across her clit, around and over, and she came hard, pulsing, careening over the edge.

She felt his tongue delve inside her and remove a strawberry, then another, and another, her body riding his mouth, eager for him to dig deeper and deeper as she crested the wave, unable to return to earth as he kept her flying higher, higher, and higher—

The world slowly returned as he picked her up and carried her to the bed, her body and mind still quaking from the fierce sensual journey.

He laid her down, and as she watched through blurred vision, he removed his clothing and lay down beside her. Pulling her into his arms, he brought his lips down on hers and sank his tongue deep into the recess of her mouth. She tasted strawberries marinated in her own essence. Reaching out to him, she pulled him closer, wanted to bury herself inside him.

He broke the kiss and gazed down at her. "I love you, Eliza. I would have let you go if that's what would have made you happy, but it was killing me."

"At the party," she whispered, finding her voice didn't seem to want to work properly. When he held her like this, she wanted to melt into a puddle. She cleared her throat. "At that political party, when you followed me. Why didn't you fuck me then?"

He brushed a strand of damp hair back from her face. "I was frustrated and angry. The thought of you fucking another man drove me crazy. That had never happened before. If I'd taken you it would have been in anger, to punish you. I'd never do that to you. I had to leave, and fast, before I did something we both would regret."

And she'd thought it was because he couldn't stand the sight of her any longer.

"I love you, Joseph, and it scared me how much. Knowing you changed my life and I knew I was going to have to come to terms with it. But instead, I ran like a coward so I didn't have to face that decision. It was the worst mistake I ever made."

"Don't look back. You still shouldn't have come to the police station. We could have worked it out less publicly, you know."

She smiled. "I know, but at the time all I could think of was getting you out of that police station. I couldn't just stand by and let them railroad you for something you didn't do."

His expression grew more serious. "Eventually, we have to go back and you'll have to face what they'll say about you. About us. Do you think you can handle it? What will you do if you aren't re-elected? Because of me?"

She stroked the side of his face. "It's a choice I've made. The one thing I do know is that with you I'm alive, and now I have the chance to be a whole person. I will never regret that."

"I hope not," he said, "because I don't think I can let you walk away again."

CHAPTER 10

One Month Later

He sat at the table of one of the most visible restaurants in town. Waiting. After that first public exposure, he'd insisted that they slow down and ease into the public recognition.

He smiled as he thought of how she'd tried to fight him on the issue. Once she made up her mind to pull their relationship out of the shadows it was like trying to stop an out-of-control freight train. But in the end she had acceded to his wishes. Of course, he'd had to remind her of their agreement that she would abide by his rules.

He looked at his watch and then at the entrance to the restaurant. She'd agreed to meet him here for dinner tonight. It was a test. The first public appearance since that grand presentation at the police station. He would be able to gauge how strong she would be under the close scrutiny she would receive tonight. He worried it might be too much for her to handle.

In her own right, she was a strong woman, but admitting she had a private life contrary to what was considered acceptable, and doing it so publicly when it went against everything she'd been brought up to believe might be more than she was ready for. Well this would test her commitment and he only hoped it wouldn't end up breaking her in the end.

It was her strength that drew him to her, not any weakness he'd perceived. He liked a strong, confident woman, and he loved Eliza with a passion that almost scared him with its intensity.

There she was. He watched as she handed her coat to an attendant. She turned and he caught his breath. She was radiant—not the cold beauty he'd first been introduced to, but warm and soft. He scanned the room, recognized a number of faces, noting the speculative yet appreciative glances turned her way.

The champagne beige satin dress she wore shimmered around her shapely legs as she followed the hostess to their table. The bodice cupped her breasts enticingly, narrowing to a cinched waist.

She exhibited no embarrassment in the knowledge that there were whispered conversations all around her, and that she was most likely the subject of those conjectures. Her perfect public image now had a crack in the eyes of those who felt it their job to judge others.

Through everything, she'd held her head high and had laughed at their ultimatums. She'd take her chances on election day, he'd heard her inform them on more than one occasion.

The case regarding the woman who had been murdered didn't help any, and only added fuel to the already blazing fire of animosity regarding their chosen lifestyle. There was a suspect in custody, someone totally alien to the lifestyle, yet no one cared and still chose to point their sanctimonious fingers.

He'd never forced her to make a choice and she was stronger for it. There was a time when he'd been certain he'd lost her for good. But somehow, some way, fate had deemed otherwise, and he meant to bind her to him in every way possible now that she had made her choice.

He glanced down at the gift-wrapped box setting on the chair next to him, then turned back to watch her approach. He was certain he'd never get tired of looking at her. An acquaintance caught her eye and she stopped for a moment to converse. He saw her cheeks flood with color and then she laughed and moved on.

Her scent surrounded him as she reached their table and he stood to greet her. He raised her hand to his lips, turned it over and nipped at her wrist and her fingers curled inward. After smoothing the spot with his thumb, he dropped her hand and they both sat down. The hostess handed them each a menu and then left them to decide.

"I wondered if you'd come."

She looked quizzically at him, her eyes glittering like jewels in the subdued lighting. "You knew I would. Do you really think I would have let you down? I think we've come too far for that."

"You look beautiful tonight."

She glanced downward to where his hand lay at rest on the white tablecloth. "Thank you," she whispered. "I'd hoped you would like it."

"What? The dress? It's lovely as well. But I was speaking of you. You could have walked in here as naked as I like to see you in private and you'd still outshine every other woman in here."

Her color heightened to a very deep rosy hue and he laughed. "You blush beautifully as well. I love to see that color alone covering your whole body. So tell me, how was your day?"

"A half-day of court this morning, reading briefs this afternoon, drafting an opinion—nothing out of the ordinary."

Her eyes darkened and he wondered what thoughts were going through her mind.

"What?" he asked, curious as to what that sultry look meant.

"I brought your gift with me today," she said in a hushed voice.

Ahhhh. "And did you use it?" She never ceased to surprise him. He'd dared her to do it.

She looked at him. "Would it please you to know I did?"

The waiter interrupted them at that most intriguing moment, carrying a bottle of very expensive champagne.

"Your champagne, sir?"

Joseph indicated that he should pour it. He took a sip and nodded. The young waiter left the bottle and retreated. Joseph turned back to Eliza.

"Yes, it would please me." He leaned closer to her. "Do you have it in now?"

She shook her head. "No, I took it out before I showered and prepared for tonight."

"How long did you wear it?" His body surged at the thought of her inserting the small butt plug he'd given her. He'd shown her how to use it, had carefully inserted it that first time for her. He did not plan to take her that way until she was fully prepared for him. The fact that she'd taken the initiative pleased him immensely.

"I used it for a couple of hours this afternoon. It was uncomfortable at first, but it got easier."

He leaned close and dropped a kiss on her neck. "I'm proud of you," he whispered. "I'm very turned on by you telling me about it, do you know that?"

Her intense dark eyes studied his face. "Are you? I-I wanted to please you. You really ask so little of me. If it's what you want, I want to be able to give it to you."

"Did you enjoy making love the other night. After I inserted the plug?"

She nodded her head.

"Tell me," he demanded. "I want to hear you say it."

"You know I enjoyed it. It made me feel very...full. Very naughty."

He chuckled. "I haven't asked you to use it just for me, it's for your pleasure as well."

"I know," she seemed in a hurry to assure him. "I-I just want to please you as well."

"When I take you there, you will see how it will intensify new sensations—and it will please me. You know I'd never do anything to hurt you." He stroked the side of her face with the back of his hand. Her skin was so soft to the touch, and he did love touching her.

"I know that."

He leaned back and sat up straighter in his chair. "I have another gift for you."

He saw the glimmer of surprise in her eyes. "Another one? Oh, my, what this time?"

He smiled. She probably thought it was another sex toy for her pleasure. She was going to be surprised this time. And he hoped it would be a pleasant one.

Lifting the small package from the chair he handed it to her. He saw her fingers tremble slightly as she tugged at the ribbon and then lifted the lid. Her eyes widened and she pulled out the length of ebony silk scarf. She turned to look at him questioningly.

"For later." He pointed to the box. "There's something else."

Peering closer, she reached in and pulled out the small midnight velvet jeweler's case.

He reached over before she could open it and placed a hand over hers.

"Before you open it, I have a question to ask you."

"A question? Will I like it?"

"I don't know. We'll just have to find out, won't we?"

As he watched, she bit her lower lip, and he ached to claim her lips with his own, to hear the small sound she made deep in her throat when he pleasured her.

He didn't know if she'd be ready for this or not, but it was worth taking the chance.

"Inside that case is a pledge of commitment, Eliza. I want you to marry me. I don't want you simply as my submissive, but as my wife as well. I love you and I want you with me all the time. You've taken the first step to melding both parts of yourself into a beautiful whole person. I want that person in my life full time."

She swallowed and her eyes widened. They glimmered with unshed tears and he wondered what they meant. Was she happy? Sad? Shocked? Scared?

For long moments she didn't say anything, only stared at him. Then she blinked as though waking from a long sleep.

He felt her hands tighten on the case beneath his.

"Are you sure about this, Joseph? I don't expect it. I don't want you to do this if you're just doing it for propriety's sake."

"You don't want to marry me? Is that what you're trying to say?"

"No, no, that's not it." She looked down at their clasped hands. "I don't want you to think you have to do this. I'll move in with you if you like. You don't have to marry me."

With his other hand he tilted her chin so she was looking at him. How could such a self-confident, savvy woman have no inkling what she did to him? How much he wanted her?

That was also part of what he loved about her—one moment she was a professional, skilled in handling a room full of people and maintaining order, and the next a pliant, willing passionate mate whom he wanted to spend a lifetime with.

Over the last month both parts of this woman had finally melded into one confident, sensual woman who no longer hid the deeply passionate nature he loved so well.

"I want to marry you. This is not a short-term relationship." He said it in such a way as to give her no doubt about his desire for her presence and his commitment to her in every way. She might kneel to him in the bedroom, but he wanted her to know he would stand by her side in all other aspects of her life as well.

"Yes." He saw a tear slip from the corner of her eye to slide down the curve of her cheek. She turned her head and he saw the shimmer of more to follow.

He exhaled. "Thank God." He nodded to the box beneath her hand. "Open it."

She did as he asked and lifted the lid. Inside lay a ruby ring surrounded by opals, set in gold. He had decided diamonds were not for her, too hard. For a woman with such fire in her soul, she needed something special.

What she would find out after they were married was that there was a necklace to match. A narrow, delicate collar specially designed for her that he planned to present to her on their wedding night. But that was a gift for another time.

He reached for the ring and placed it on her left hand. It fit her perfectly and the fire of the jewels flashed beneath the light. He raised her hand to his lips.

"Never doubt that I love you."

"I don't," she replied. "I'm just sorry it took me so long to recognize that what we have is so very special."

"But you did and that's what matters." He turned and grabbed the discarded wrappings and set them aside. He picked up the menu to peruse the selections. "I think it's time to order."

"I'm not sure I can eat. I think I'd rather leave. I want to be alone with you."

He turned to look at her, trying to maintain a bland expression on his face. "But I understand they offer a dessert I'm determined to try."

"What's that."

"Strawberries drizzled with sweet cream." He closed the menu and set it aside. "But maybe you're right. I think I know of a place that offers exactly the dessert I enjoy so much, prepared to perfection."

SADIE'S HOUSE OF MIRRORS, PART II

CARNAL CARNIVAL

SADIE'S HOUSE OF MIRRORS, PART II

During the ride, as Hank's mouth trailed along the column of her neck, his hand had inched beneath the hem of her skirt. His other hand had pulled her blouse free of the waistband and his hot fingers circuited around to cup her breast. She felt the heat rise inside her through the flimsy material of her bra. But trying to focus on one sensation became almost impossible.

As they passed the various sights and sounds of sensual wonder, his hands became more insistent and her body responded eagerly to his touch. The hand beneath her skirt climbed ever higher, hooking into the waist of her panties, which he inexorably drew down her legs along with her pantyhose.

She found herself unable to resist the sensual heat of his attentions and was eager for him to breach the engorged lips of her pussy. Carefully, he removed her shoes, panties, and pantyhose, leaving her naked beneath the demure paisley skirt, yet the fiery heat in her loins was so far from demure it amazed her.

Her breathing grew raspy and her heart thundered in her chest. The car halted and to her left a set of mirrored doors slid open. As she watched, a passionate story unfolded before her, holding her spellbound. Yet fueling the fire was Hank's hands on her body, driving her ever higher.

At first, Hank turned her slightly in the seat, so she was facing the open doors; his hand slid up her naked thigh, teasing at her slit. As she watched the entertainment his thick fingers entered her, sliding deep inside, teasing at her clitoris. The combination of the champagne, the story, and Hank's hands made her body hum with passion like she'd never known before.

The doors slid shut and Hank pulled her back against him as his fingers began to play her body in earnest until, like molten lava spewing from a volcano, her climax consumed her. She screamed with the intensity of her release, falling back against his hard chest.

The car pulled forward as though her climax was the signal, Hank's fingers never leaving her sopping pussy. He lifted a glass to her lips and she drank greedily of the reviving liquid. When she finished, he again tossed the glass out the window of the car.

They halted before another set of doors, which slid open to reveal another erotic story, and his fingers again began to thrust in and out of her hot, wet vagina. Throughout the telling he kept her poised at the edge of release, never letting her fall. Somehow, during the show, he had managed to remove her blouse and bra and she was now naked from the waist up. One hand slid in and out of her cunt, while the other now fondled her breasts, kneading her nipples.

She found it continually more difficult to concentrate on the passionate story being unveiled before her, but every time she would lean her head back against his chest and close her eyes, he would halt his ministration, encouraging her to watch the show.

She would blink and attempt to focus, and only then would he continue his sensual assault of her body. When the story ended and the mirrored doors closed, he again drove her to the edge, but this time he turned her so she directly faced the mirror and could see her passion reflected back to her as he sent her body pulsing with pleasure, pushing her off the edge into the swirling hot waters of her climax.

She didn't recognize the woman in the mirror; that wanton creature bore no resemblance to the businesswoman she was accustomed to seeing every day. The one who never seriously dated, and always kept to herself. That lonely spinster who attracted no one's attention other than to complete a job they knew she was skilled enough to do.

But this woman, who was she? It certainly couldn't be her.

At her scream of release the car again moved forward, to the next stop on their journey. This time, when the story was ended, she was now totally naked. Hank's hands swept over her body, which was now flushed with passion, eager to experience each sensation, and watch with eager anticipation as each story unfolded before her eyes.

Surprisingly, she felt him lift her and suddenly she was speared and penetrated by a thick cock that plunged deep, widening her to such a degree she groaned with pleasure.

Once he had completely filled her, he anchored her there and teased her clit with his fingers, her juices covering them both. She couldn't believe the intense pleasure he was giving her. To be this filled with this much passion was almost too much sensation.

Sex for her had never been like this. It had been more a duty, expected by the few men she'd dated, men who cared nothing for her satisfaction, but only their own. But now as she felt Hank filling her, offering her climax after climax, the world revolved around her in a dizzying kaleidoscope of desire, and pulse after pulse of pleasure consumed her.

Suddenly, nothing existed beyond this car, the demanding assault of her senses, the unbelievable knowledge that every touch was offered for her fulfillment. As she recovered from another powerful climax, she opened her eyes and looked at the reflection in the mirror. Her gaze moved down to where Hank was connected to her, his cock buried inside her pussy, her lips open and gaping, snugly hugging to the foot of his sex, her legs splayed across his, opening her wide. Moving upward she saw his dark hands at her breasts, playing with her nipples, watched as her body responded. Saw his dark head lower and felt his lips press against her neck, felt him licking at her flesh.

His gaze met hers in the mirror and he lifted his head and smiled. Another climax assaulted her, just that fast. The car began to move forward, then halted. No door opened, but she stared at her reflection, no longer seeing the mouse of a woman afraid to experience life, afraid of what others would think of her. On the contrary, the woman revealed in the mirror embraced her femininity, her sexuality, courageous in her heart. That was the woman she wanted to be.

Suddenly, Hank lifted her and turned her to face him, sinking into her wet channel with ease.

"Ride me, miss, ride me hard, take me deep. Show me what you've learned tonight. Show me what you want."

He lifted her effortlessly and slammed her down onto his powerful tool. She reveled with the sensations. Ride him she did, fast and hard and deep, undulating against him, taking what she wanted. She arched and circled her hips, forcing the friction against her clit. Faster and faster she powered against him, in and out, slick heat consuming them both.

She felt the car move up to a pinnacle in the track, and her climax sent her flying as the car dipped drastically, plummeting down, fast and intense as her climax washed through her, magnifying the sensations of dangerous intensity. Her body pulsed as the car moved, like a roller coaster, up and down as her orgasms surged and receded, Hank's cock solidly entrenched inside her. Until they came to a rest and she collapsed against Hank's chest, breathing fast and hard, trying to restore some sanity. Then it all receded into darkness.

She woke slowly, her entire body tingling and aware, still throbbing, yet something was different. She was different. Opening her eyes she realized she was in her car, propped behind the steering wheel, fully clothed. As she looked out the window, she realized it must be dawn because the sky was the color of morning just before the sun decided to show its bright face.

She looked to the left where she expected to see the outline of the carnival rides, but to her surprise there was nothing but open field, not a hint that there had ever been anything resting in the field.

A glint of something caught her eye. She pushed herself up and noted something resting on the dashboard. She reached out to pick it up. It was another foil coupon and a piece of folded paper. She opened the note and read.

We hope you enjoyed your ride. When you wish, here's a special coupon for your next visit.

She fingered the coupon, wondering if it had all been some kind of fantastic dream. Whatever it was, however she had been chosen to be the one to experience it, it had been wonderful. Thoughtfully, she put the coupon in her pocket and shifted upward in her seat, fastening her seatbelt. Glancing at the rearview mirror, her own eyes gazed back at her. But there was definitely something different about her. She saw a confidence that hadn't been there before.

Looking down, she noted her car key was in the ignition. She turned it and the engine flared to life. A shudder passed through her as she put the car into drive and slowly pressed the gas pedal. Some sense of a presence lingered in the atmosphere of the car as she drove away.

"Come back soon, miss."

ADRIANNA DANE

Theresa Gallup uses the pen names of Tess Maynard and Adrianna Dane. Theresa has been writing since the age of 10. A legal secretary for 30 years, she is currently working on another erotic romance, as well as a full-length romantic mystery/suspense. She has been married for 30 years and has three grown children (a daughter and twin sons), and is a new grandmother.

Writing as Tess Maynard, her first published short story appeared in the ezine, *The Whispering Forest*, in January of 2004. Writing as Adrianna Dane, where adding sensual heat to romance is her motto, *Esmerelda's Secret* was her first foray into the erotic romance genre.

Having traveled and lived from the East Coast to the West Coast, Theresa receives inspiration for her stories from a variety of sources, including music and poetry, and her tastes are eclectic.

For more information about current projects, visit Theresa's web sites at www.tessmaynard.com or www.adriannadane.com.

AMBER QUILL PRESS, LLC
THE GOLD STANDARD IN PUBLISHING

QUALITY BOOKS
IN BOTH PRINT AND ELECTRONIC FORMATS

ACTION/ADVENTURE	SUSPENSE/THRILLER
SCIENCE FICTION	PARANORMAL
MAINSTREAM	MYSTERY
FANTASY	EROTICA
ROMANCE	HORROR
HISTORICAL	WESTERN
YOUNG ADULT	NON-FICTION

AMBER QUILL PRESS, LLC
http://www.amberquill.com